Sam Hanna Bell was born in Scotland of Ulster parentage. On the death of his father, a Glasgow journalist, he was brought 'home' to Ireland at the age of seven, to be reared in a country district of Co. Down where the opening of *A Man Flourishing* and an earlier novel, *December Bride*, are both set. For twenty-five years he was senior features producer for the BBC Northern Ireland Region, where he established and compiled the archives of folklore and folk music. In 1970 Queen's University, Belfast, awarded him the honorary degree of M.A. for achievements in the arts.

M. Fraser.

From Anne Boyd

Feb 1990.

A MAN FLOURISHING

SAM HANNA BELL

THE
BLACKSTAFF
PRESS
BELFAST AND DOVER, NEW HAMPSHIRE

First published in 1973
by Victor Gollancz Ltd
This Blackstaff Press edition is a photolithographic
facsimile of the first edition printed
by Ebenezer Baylis and Son Ltd.

This edition published in 1986
by The Blackstaff Press
3 Galway Park, Dundonald, Belfast BT16 0AN, Northern Ireland
and
51 Washington Street, Dover, New Hampshire 03820 USA
with the assistance of the Arts Council of Northern Ireland

Printed in Northern Ireland by
Belfast Litho Printers Ltd

British Library Cataloguing in Publication Data
Bell, Sam Hanna
A man flourishing: a novel.
I. Title
823'.914 [F] PR6052.E447

Library of Congress Cataloging-in-Publication Data
Bell, Sam Hanna.
A man flourishing.
Originally published: London: Gollanz, 1973.
1. Ireland — History — Rebellion of 1798 — Fiction.
I. Title
[PR6052.E447M3 1986] 823'.914 86-1195

ISBN 0 85640 359 8 (hardback)
0 85640 356 3 (paperback)

The hard cold fire of the northerner
Frozen into his blood from the fire in his basalt
Glares from behind the mica of his eyes
And the salt carrion water brings him wealth.

'BELFAST'

Louis MacNeice

I

1798

IN THE PAST few days the armed men had begun to trail by in the dawns and dusks. Usually they passed on the distant hillside or over the meadows at its foot. Rarely did they come by the cart track that ran close to Sim Purdie's cottage. At times a flag with a revolutionary symbol floated above them; but always the jagged hackle of pikes, scythes, a few flintlocks, hay forks, cudgels.

When old Sim heard the trudge of the approaching feet, the voices raised in a scurrilous ditty against Authority, he hurried his family out—Hugh, and young Andrew, and their sister Kate—to hide in the turf bog behind the cottage. Their mother, poor ailing woman, couldn't be moved from her bed. God, said Sim, would fend for her.

He always arrived last to hurl himself into the peat hole. As demanded by law he had posted on the door a list of the occupants of the dwelling for inspection by any roving posse of military or yeomanry. Then, being all things to all men, he laid out oaten cakes and a crock of spring water on a stone by the roadside, to dissuade the peasant warriors from ransacking the house. The yeos, seeing the bread and water set out, might suspect his household of revolutionary sympathies and flog him and his sons and Satan only knew what they would do to his womenfolk. But the troubled times would pass, said Sim judiciously, they always did. At such times a man had to take risks to keep his property intact.

They lay on their bellies watching through the bog cotton the rebel men file past on the rough track. "I heard tell they're gathering on the hill above Ballynahinch," whispered Andrew.

Sim turned on him, "Ye heard nothing, ye whelp, and ye know nothing. Their gathering-place is Hell, for God will surely scatter vagabonds and blaggards that raise their hand against the king and them that's set over us." The old man smiled sardonically, "At the first glint o' a redcoat they'll flee like dung-flies."

They're our own kind, these rebelly men, thought Hugh. He didn't speak the words aloud. He respected as much as he detested his father's forethought and cunning. But perhaps he's right in this. Perhaps the insurgents who passed, night and day, would disperse and vanish without a cry or a blow. Perhaps all the disputation, the fierce hunger for political and religious liberty, the rage against corruption in high places, the determination to tear asunder the English connection, would fail to change these reformers into revolutionaries on the day of the refiner's fire. But as the turf crumbled in his thin grasp, he knew that this was not so. Too much suffering, too much anger and hope and long memory, had gone into preparing for this day for it to disperse like a mist.

Those who tramped the rough track beyond the thorn bushes were mostly strangers, men from other townlands. But occasionally figures passed that made the watchers shrink deeper into their peat hole, hiding their eyes and following the troop only by the rumble of marching feet. These were neighbours. It was better not to know who was passing by in the half-light. Yet the young man was powerless to resist stealing a glance between the tufted silk of the bog cotton. There were faces and figures he recognised; his cousin, Stewart Purdie, Rab McIlveen, Hans and David Echlin of Rathard. And he knew of others who had taken the rebel oath. Men like Kate's sweetheart, James Gault.

Crossing the turf bog in twilight three evenings ago he had come on the two of them standing in the gloom of an alder clump. He was surprised for he thought Gault was in Glasgow at his studies. Because of a restraint that had grown up of late between them he stopped and was about to take out over the turf banks when Gault called his name. He returned unwillingly.

"I hope I see ye well, James. I thought ye were still at the college?"

"I returned from Glasgow only this morning."

"Is there aught wrong at home?"

"No . . . no, all's well." The tall saturnine young man in the shadows paused. "I'm sorry you came up on us."

"That's easy mended. I'll bid ye goodnight."

"You misunderstand me. I wanted no one to know that I was back."

"Then you should stay in your own house."

"I had to see your sister."

The girl came forward and caught her brother by the coat. "Tell nobody you saw James. Say nothing about him to anybody."

Hugh shrugged. "What concern is it o' mine?"

"But you promise?" she pleaded. "No word to my father?"

"I'll tell nobody. Goodnight to ye, James."

He was nearing the house when Kate overtook him. In the darkness they were forced to walk the rough narrow track in Indian file but just as they were about to enter the farm close he said, "It must be something great that brought James Gault home from his books?"

His sister drew her shawl to hide her face. Then in a voice broken with tears she cried, "The fool . . . the daft fool!" and hurried past him into the house. Hugh, his heart filling with surprise and fear, followed slowly. It was evident, beyond doubt, why James Gault had come back to Ireland. Somewhere, in some townland down by Strangford Lough, the company of United Irishmen to which the young student belonged was mustering.

Hugh Purdie cursed the idle step that had taken him by the peat-bog that evening. Now that he knew of Gault's return his fear was that he might betray him by a careless word to Sim, hater of rebels. He had no evidence that his father was an informer, but he had no reason to believe that he wouldn't play the part if there was silver at the end of it. He spoke to his sister. "If my father wants an errand across the fields to the Gaults, see it's you or me that goes, nobody else."

She was as tall as her brother. Her brown hair curling in the damp air, her clear hazel eyes and the small fine nose, inherited from her father, softened the strong line of mouth and jaw. Now, as she gazed at him levelly, there was an ironic and sullen droop to her face. "It's over all that you should find James Gault any concern o' yours at this time."

"It's at your asking, sister."

Her eyes wavered. "I'll heed what ye say."

By chance Hugh had learnt the approximate strength of the government forces in the neighbourhood. On the afternoon before Gault's return his father and he had been ordered to present themselves, furnished with a side of bacon and half-a-dozen cleaned pullets, at the Big House. On a side lane to the mansion, they met, much to Sim's delight and awe, Arthur Burke, their over-landlord, and his guest, a regular officer in full regimentals. With a drunken sweep of the arm Mr Burke halted the two cottiers. "They aren't all curs, Major! Here's Sim Purdie, one honest fellow among my tenants!" Sim, laden as he was, kneaded his brow in an ecstasy of modesty and gratitude, but the officer, halting in wrathful surprise, turned and strode back the way he had come.

Yet, before the Purdies returned home, Sim, standing before them in obsequious crouch, had spoken with landlord and army officer. In the leafy lane the old man rubbed his hands in glee. "Two days fodder for fifty horse! We'll get the value o' our bacon and fowl back in siller, for the King's money's as good as that drunken fool's is bad."

*

Kate, at the dresser, spooned out a bowl of rennet for her mother. Mrs Purdie's plaintive voice from the lower room neither slowed nor hastened the girl's movements. Sim, equally unheeding, figured in a ledger laid out on a shelf beside the loom. The green eyes were hooded and intent on their task, the sallow, churlish face lowered, a face almost redeemed by the delicate, curving nose, a kestrel's beak. His elder son lounged against the doorpost, gazing over the shimmering June countryside. In the entrance of an outhouse, Andrew, white as a miller, was vigorously shaking out the last of a pile of emptied corn sacks. At the lad's feet was a soft dun heap of grain, husks and dust. Resacked, it would be traded by Andrew and his father to the cottiers, labourers and workless weavers, to make a thin gruel for human and beast.

Sim looked up from his calculations. He studied his son's back with an expression close to contempt. "Ye needna stand there brooding over what's not to be. Away and give Andra a hand." Without speaking, the young man straightened himself from the doorway, and walked across the cobbled close, past Andrew at his labour. At the stone ditch that bounded the close he stopped to look over the low rolling hills towards Ballynahinch. My father showed Kate how to load and fire the pistol hidden in the press only because she had heard the stories of what drunken yeos do to our womenfolk. But he hid the fowling-piece away from me. Two days . . . fifty troopers . . . I could get the word carried tonight to the men gathered at the lough. A stealthy drawing of the bolt, a lifting of the latch, a swift dash over the dark fields to almost any homestead in the townland of Ravara. He thought of the wary response that would greet his news, the suspicious glance quickly averted. He groaned and turned back to his brother. A man paid dear for being a son of Sim Purdie.

II

IN THE SPRING of 1755, Mr Lalor Burke, after a season of well-bred profligacy, found his pockets empty. From London he directed his agent to relet the holdings of his tenants-at-will at greatly increased rents, among them that of the Purdies. At the fall of the hammer, Sim's father, Dugal Purdie, saw himself outbid for the land he had brought to good heart, by a Belfast merchant turned land-jobber. He and his family were evicted and found shelter in a turf-cutter's shack owned by their neighbour, Samuel Gault, whose farm, lying outside Mr Burke's property, had been undisturbed.

Sim did not lightly forget what had happened to his family. To put the Purdies back on the land they had once worked became an all-pervading obsession. He saved every farthing, accepted every task, was oblivious to every insult. For the lowest of wages he worked in his neighbours' fields until the dark of evening. At dawn next day his tireless muscular figure clad in the most wretched of clothes could be seen busy in his own plot of earth.

On his twentieth birthday he applied to Mr Burke's agent, Ephraim Smart, for a rood of land. Smart rented him the patch at thirty pence more than he himself paid the land-jobber. Sim Purdie worked with a quiet ferocity. Unlike many of his fellows he never gave over to despair, never frequented the shebeens and dram shops where drunken treason was talked. When his brothers had grown sufficiently he hired them out to masters, with the parting injunction to 'whine and cry starvation when ye think fit'. Each year he took a further plot from Smart, driving himself mercilessly to subdue this extra land.

In 1780, in his fortieth year, he married Kirsty Gill of Lusky Woods. She was a weakly woman, but she brought ten guineas, a cow and a loom with her. Sim put her to the loom and in her name rented a further acre of land from Ephraim Smart.

That winter he won a grumbling consent from Smart to allow two miserable creatures, the brothers Keeran, to raise a mud and turf cot on half-a-rood of this newly-acquired land. Then, under Smart's nose, began a peopling of the land rented to Sim Purdie. A labourer or a distressed weaver would come to Sim asking for an advance of a few pence to buy potatoes or corn until the harvest was due. If the suppliant was a sturdy hardworking fellow he got it, at an interest of twenty per cent. If he was land-hungry, so much the better. He was smuggled on to a patch of the rented acres. Thus the labour that brought in turn profit to Sim, then Ephraim Smart, then the land speculator and finally Mr Burke, fell on the bowed backs of a couple of dozen or so men, women and children, who toiled through the day to fall asleep at night, huddled in their rags, around their furze and cowdung fires. By the spring and harvest of 1785, Sim had gained control over more than half the land his family had once worked.

For almost two centuries, the Purdies and the Gaults, like most of their neighbours, had clung tenaciously to the Presbyterian faith that their forefathers had brought across the narrow sea from the Mull of Kintyre. But Sim had had his second child, Kate, baptised in the Established Church. It was only a step from that to lead his family into the bosom of the Church of Ireland. The news was ill-received in the district and his neighbours weren't loath to tell him so. But it was no doctrinal nicety that had led him to his new loyalty. "If I have to pay tithes I might as well get salvation for my money," he told a kitchenful of resentful kirk elders. He said nothing of the hand laid on his head by the Rector or the secular benedictions received from Mr Burke and his fellow-magistrates. But from then on Dissenters and suchlike cattle were not welcome at the Purdie hearth, and least welcome was James Gault, Kate's follower and a student for the Presbyterian ministry.

Sim himself, in the passing years, became broader, more bowlegged, shorter in stature. What he lost in height seemed gathered up in the toiler's hump on his shoulders, as if he would not even part with that.

*

Sim, Kate and Hugh, busy in the farm close, heard the distant clatter of horses descending the hill of Ravara. The haste and urgency of the approach struck fear into their hearts. They were hurrying to finish the last tasks of the day when three horsemen galloped out of the twilight. "Raise that light!" a voice shouted. Sim lifted the lantern above his head. Hugh recognised the first man in the cavalcade as one Nugent Mullan, a leather chandler from Comber and a captain in the yeomanry. The second horseman to enter the close was the officer he had seen at Mr Burke's. Behind rode a trooper with a carbine across his saddle. Sim hurried forward. "Welcome, welcome, gentles. Ye bring guid news?"

Naked sabre in his hand, the yeoman swung himself from the saddle. He reeled as though drunk. "We don't know if you'll think it good news, ye dog. But the rebels have been soundly basted this day." He turned. "Trooper, search the kennel." His carbine at the ready, the soldier lumbered across the cobbled close and disappeared into the house.

The officer had drawn a pistol from the holster at his horse's neck. He spoke curtly from the saddle. "Have any of the men of this family been abroad of late?"

Sim spread his hands. "Why no, your honour. A wheen o' days ago, if you care to remember me, I foddered your horses up at the Big House."

"I remember. Your name's Purdie?"

"The same, your honour, sir."

"You've been told that the rebels were worsted. I have this

to add by order of General Nugent—if you know of any disaffected among your neighbours who were not ringleaders in this treason and are prepared to return to their allegiance they will be pardoned. If they do not, their families will be put out, their houses burned to the ground, and they themselves hunted down. So the wise man, Purdie, will be found at home when he's looked for."

"I've had nae dealings wi' those miscreants, your honour——"

The trooper reappeared. He spoke with a thick southern brogue. "Ne'er a thing in there but an ould wan in her bed and a brat av a gossoon."

"Very well." The officer lifted his reins. "If you're ready, captain——"

"A minute, Major Treefall." The yeo lingered over the three figures motionless in the twilight. "I'm not so readily satisfied as you, sir. They're cunning vermin, these pratie-eaters. How am I to know they haven't ridden hard ahead of us from Ballynahinch?"

"Where would our animals be, your honour, captain?" said Sim with an uneasy laugh.

"You could have driven them into that cursed bog, for aught I know. We'll judge whether your own hides are heated. Strip."

"Captain Mullan, we have to be in Belfast——"

"Respects, major, but I have my duty to do," returned Mullan sullenly. "Strip, ye curs. Trooper, keep an eye on the young 'un. Strip, damn ye!"

Slowly father and son began to remove their garments. Kate made a move towards the house. The yeo threw up his arm. "Stop! You too, missie!"

"What are you about, captain . . . we've no time for folly . . .!"

"There were rebel bitches at Ballynahinch this day, Major Treefall. This could well be one. I take no chances. Off with ye, girl, or by God I'll come and give ye a hand!"

As Hugh swayed convulsively he felt the carbine muzzle

thrust into his belly. "Ne'er a move out av ye, boy," whispered the soldier, "or I'll have to kill ye."

Slowly the girl let her few garments slip to her feet. The lantern had dropped from Sim's fingers and was extinguished. But against the dusk of the close the three naked bodies glimmered faintly in the soft light of the evening. The girl stood barely erect, crumpled over the veil of her arms. Hugh was half-hidden by the bulk of the accoutred trooper. Sim, submissive like a beast of burden, stood with bent arms and bowed head, his stained body and knotted legs darker than the flesh of his children.

Sabre drooping from his hand, Mullan strode to Hugh and sniffed his body. He struck the youth a stinging blow on the chest with the back of his hand. "Christ, bogwater!" Then almost on tiptoe he crept over the cobbles towards the naked girl. She flinched at his approach. The yeo leaned over her, sniffing gently. Hugh felt the sharp jab of the carbine in his belly. "No move from ye, now," warned the husky voice. Mullan struck down the girl's arm and cupped her breasts in his hand. They heard the moist catch in his breath. "Jasus, my lass . . ."

There was the sudden clatter of hooves as Major Treefall wheeled his horse. "Are your investigations at an end yet, captain!" he shouted.

Mullan didn't trouble to turn his head. "Ride on, major, ride on. I've business to attend to . . ."

"No, damn you, mount! I've given you an order." The major leaned forward, half-drawing his pistol. "You," he said, addressing the trooper, "assist that fellow to his horse."

Mullan laughed and drew back from the girl. "She's a plump morsel, major!" he roared. He swung on the naked, shivering peasants. "You're all too damned well-fed. Who's your landlord, old man? I'll have to tell him you're all damned fat!" He turned to the still-hesitating trooper and said coldly, "No one we want in the house?"

"Narra one there but what I reported, cap'n."

The yeo flung himself on his horse. "Remember what you've been told, Purdie. Succour a rebel and I'll be back to roast ye under your own thatch."

With an enraged spur the English officer gave his horse to the rough track that led to the town. The others followed. Their hoofbeats faded in the distance.

Silently, Kate fled into the house, her garments gathered in her arms. As Sim slowly pulled up his breeks his son rushed across the close towards him. "Those are the animals ye learned us to side with. Those are the only men, says you, that are fit to rule! I should've been at Ballynahinch this day——"

"Close your mouth . . . listen." The drumming of approaching hooves swelled in the darkness. Sim seized his son's arm in a powerful grasp and as they crouched a posse of military thundered past on the track. Painfully Sim straightened himself. "That's enough o' shouting. You'll have them back. And now to bed wi' ye. Easy minds are early abed this nicht."

"Easy minds? And shame put on our sister!"

"It's the price we have to pay. What of the poor fools stiffening in the fields beyont? You're warm and alive."

"That one. I know him. Mullan o' Comber. I'll kill the pig——"

"Peh!" The father moved away. "We came through that brush wi' little lost but pride." As he spoke a bloom of fire burst westward in Lusky Woods. "They're at their deil's work already. That's what we saved oursels from," he said shambling towards the house.

*

The tapping on the window was so faint that Hugh sat uncertain, grasping the arms of his chair. It came again, furtive and brief. Outside in the darkness was someone who was afraid. He crept across the floor and after a moment lifted the sacking. A face, pressed to the glass, stared into his.

He stumbled back, the rough curtain slipping from his fingers. Recognition came. It was his sister's sweetheart, James Gault. He sped to the door and cautiously drew back the big wooden bolt. Gault was clasping the posts of the doorway. "Is there anybody stirring? Can I come in?"

Hugh stood aside. "Come in. They're all abed. But keep your voice hushed."

"Put out the light," said Gault and the other obeyed. Silently they crept to the hearth. The tall dark-haired fugitive groaned and stretched his muddied legs to the smouldering peat. "I fell into the Langstane in my hurry, a burn that I've leapt a thousand times . . ." He looked up and saw, in the fireglow, the apprehension in young Purdie's eyes. He half rose. "I'll go . . . the yeos are still abroad."

Hugh coloured. "Sit your ground. Is there aught I can get for you?"

"A sup of buttermilk, for now. A farl of bread, if it's handy, for the road."

Seated again Hugh said, "You're going away?"

The other smiled bitterly. "Aye, you could say that. They're searching for me. I came through Burke's woods as close as I might to my own house. Thank God, they seem to be undisturbed."

"Ah, who would bother two old men and an old woman? If you gave up your arms you can ask pardon."

"My musket's at the bottom of the Langstane. Where did you hear this?"

"We had a redcoat here—a Major Treefall."

"He wasn't alone, I hold ye?"

"No, there were others—yeos."

"No one here harmed?" Gault's strongly-marked face was watchful.

"No one, no one. But how did the day go with yourself, James? You weren't hurted?"

Gault lowered his head. "I got no nearer the fighting than yourself. We were to randyvoo at Killyleagh . . ." He stood up. "That tale will keep. Every minute I stay here brings danger to this house. Kate, how is she?"

"She's well, James." Hugh saw the longing in the other man's face. "I dursn't wake her. My father would be down on us."

"To be sure." Gault moved to the door.

"Where are ye for now? Are you going back to Glasgow, to the university?"

Gault turned on him in a sort of stupefaction of anger and laughter. He pulled the youth towards him. "Go back to Glasgow? D'ye know what has happened today? Men have killed each other. I'm guilty of high treason. To the minions of King George I'm as dead as the men stiffening on the hillside at Ballynahinch. As dead as Sam Morrow and Rab McIlveen."

"Rab . . . dead?"

"Aye, dead. And many others."

Hugh was silent. He began to understand the deadly intent of the marching men, disciplined and helmeted, or singing and jostling, journeying towards their doomed assignation.

"And now you must hide?"

"Aye."

"Where?" There was a pause. "Don't you trust me?" the youth asked in an agitated voice.

"Yes, yes, I do. I'm going to find a boat bound for Ameriky. Ask me no more."

Hugh lifted a candle from the mantelshelf and lighted it. "You can at least look at her," he said. Silently he opened a door to the left of the fireplace. Her auburn hair was cast over the coarse linen of the pillow. A tear caught between nostril and eyelid threw back a needle of diamond light to the two men at the threshold.

"Why was she weeping?"

"She dreams o' nights."

Even at this moment Gault was struck by the comfort of the room hidden from the eyes of neighbours and landlord's men. The bed was of iron, there was a mat on the wooden floor, and beside the bed stood an article of dark rich wood which he guessed must be a mahogany dressing chest. The girl's garments were thrown over one of the two chairs in the room. A last lingering glance and Gault signed to her brother to draw close the door.

"What will I tell her?"

"Nothing, save that I'm alive. What more dare a man say?"

"That will serve," said the youth quietly. "My sister trusts you."

Gault looked at him steadily; then his expression softened. "If I reach safety it won't be betrayed."

"When you write, James, write to me. There's a chance my father might ha' borne with you if you'd made Kate mistress of a manse. He'll ha' little love to spare for you now you're a wanted man."

"That I can believe. Thank you, Hugh, for your offer. I'll send you word the day I land. Will you in turn get the news to my own people? Now, a further kindness, can you lend me a little money?"

With eager fingers Hugh took a purse from a drawer in the dresser and tipped two guineas into Gault's hand. "Never fear," he said, "it's my own savings."

Outside it was still dry, with a light wind rising. Low in the west they saw an inlay of crimson, but whether from the departing sun or a burning house neither could tell. "It's like blood," said Hugh.

Gault shrugged. "It's fitting there should be blood in the sky tonight. What was the distich they used to rhyme at the crossroads . . . ?

'A wet Winter, a dry Spring,
A bloody Summer and no king.'

Aye, that was it," said the young man with a sigh. He took Hugh's hand in his. "God look down on you, lad. My thanks for what you've done." The grasp tightened on

Hugh's fingers. "Tell Kate . . . I was asking after her." He took a herding stick from beside the door, stepped quickly across the cobbled close, and disappeared into the bushes that bordered the track leading to the town of Belfast.

III

THE MARKET HOUSE clock struck midnight as he came to a halt in the blackness of a doorway in the High Street. He had met few citizens abroad in his stealthy progress to the middle of the town; a drunken watchman, a drifting clamour of women and soldiers, and once he had hurled himself at the foot of a wall, lying still as death, as horsemen cantered past. A lamp above him guttered in the night air. Its light gleamed on the tilted spars of the vessels grounded in the tidal river that ran down the middle of the street. There would be shelter and hiding in one of those dark cabins. He glanced up and down the deserted cobbles then crossed swiftly to the edge of the quays. A brig, its deck canted away from him, lay in the mud a few feet from the quay. He could see neither light nor life aboard. As he stood wondering whether to board her, suddenly, from the top of the town came a musket shot, cries, the sound of running feet. Out of the far darkness came a man pursued by three or four redcoats. One of them halted to fire his musket. Gault heard the ball splinter against a gable across the street. Pursued and pursuers were heading straight for him as he crouched on the quayside. He sprang for the gunnel, missed his hold, and slithered between hull and wall to the muddy bottom of the river. Above him he heard the clatter of the pursuit fade into the distance.

The shots had roused the streets from their curfew silence. As Gault groped and stumbled downstream he saw lights appear in upper windows, heard doors opening and the cautious murmur of voices. In the distance a trumpet shrilled. He moved with great care, slowly withdrawing each step from the clinging mud. If he was to board a sea-going vessel he must reach the mouth of the river before the tide turned. Hearing the measured trample of feet above him he stopped, clinging to the wall under a low stone bridge. The trumpet sounded again, and then a voice, muffled by the stonework, cried, "... anyone who 'arbours or connives in the escape of the said William Kean will be 'anged and after that his 'ouse burned to the ground!" Gault grinned in the slimy darkness. "For I say unto thee, let all things be done decently and in order." When next he heard the peremptory blast and its warning they had moved away towards the head of the town.

A few yards below the bridge Gault heard a sound more regular than the scurrying of rats. He stopped and listened. It was the stealthy rustling and squelching steps of someone following in his wake. He backed into a crevice and flattened himself against the wall. Out of the darkness came the figure of a man, steadying himself between the wall and the curving hull of a boat. Only one pursuer. As the man let his hand drop from the vessel's side Gault caught the glint of steel. Slowly, laboriously, the other struggled forward through the sucking mud. As he drew level Gault shortened his grasp on his stick and struck down on the hand carrying the knife. Then he seized the intruder by the jacket and thrust his head violently against the ship's timbers. The attack was as successful as Gault could have hoped. His pursuer, stunned by the blow, reeled forward into his arms. Then the stranger began to struggle fiercely, searching for Gault's throat. But in that moment when they clasped each other Gault realised that his opponent was neither soldier nor yeoman, that he was young and slim, and no match for him in strength. Beating down the hands groping at his face he cried, "Are you Kean—William Kean?" The other's answer was a savage, silent attack. Gault grasped him and pinned him against the hull. "If you're Kean, hold, I tell ye!"

They faced each other in the stinking darkness, arms rigid

and locked. A rat skipped over Gault's foot. "Your name?" the young man asked.

"James Gault of Ravara."

"Are you . . . ?" the young man jerked his head towards the street above, then groaned. "Damn ye, you've cracked my skull."

"I trust not. Yes, I'm on the run."

The young man's grasp relaxed. They stumbled apart. "And I'm William Kean, the man they're after."

Warily, James groped about until he found his stick again. "And now what do we do before the tide rises and we drown in this filth?"

The young man straightened his neckcloth with muddy fingers. "You can come with me if you're willing to take the risk."

"Where would that be?"

"To visit my friend, Dr Luke Bannon of Legg's Lane."

Gault eased a foot from the sucking ooze. "I've no need of a physician. What I want is a berth in a ship leaving for Ameriky."

Kean laughed. "Such a departure would be convenient."

"If one could get aboard in the dark——"

Kean made to move away. "Come," he said, "we're wasting time. Can you swim?"

"A few strokes."

"There may be some water in the channel. Follow me."

The young man floundered through the soft mud and Gault heard him striking into the river. Following, his few strokes sufficed, and soon he was crouching beside Kean under the opposite wall. Above them the streets seemed deserted. Kean drew himself up to look around. Then his legs kicked and vanished as he tumbled over the low parapet. As he waited below Gault questioned himself. Was Belfast, the heart of a garrison, the best place in his extremity? And this Dr Bannon . . . ?

There was a low hiss from above. "All's clear. Up with ye."

They lay together on the dank cobbles barely stirring their heads to look around. In the distance a shuffling town watch, trailing his staff, passed under a lamp then disappeared. Here and there windows leaked light as if life stirred behind them, but the long quays lay silent and empty. Kean stood up. "If I run, you run. If I throw myself to the ground, do you likewise."

"A moment." Gault laid his hand on his companion's shoulder. "This Dr Bannon—is he to be trusted?"

Kean's mud-crusted face glared round at him. "Am I in a fit state to take risks? Didn't you hear that dog with his trumpet?" He put his face closer. "The question is whether your story will stand up. That's the risk I warned you of. If you're willing, follow me."

They slipped away from the waterside towards the darkness of a great warehouse that jutted over the street. Across the river a tavern door flew open emitting three drunken, reeling figures outlined in a shaft of ruddy light. "*Down!*" whispered Kean, and they dropped to the clammy cobbles. They were about to scramble up when a military patrol suddenly strode round the corner of the warehouse, headed by a young officer with a drawn sword in his hand. Oh God, prayed Gault, his face pressed to the miry ground, let us be no more than shadows in this town of shadows.

The tattoo of boots clattered past and went towards the bridge. There were sharp commands and defiant bellows from the drunkards. "*Now!*" Rising, they fled towards a black cleft in the wall. One of the soldiers turned, shouted an alarm. Plunging into the dark alley, Gault sped after his companion. As they rounded a corner they ran into a member of the Town Watch. The man gave a squawk of fear and dropped his lantern which rolled before Gault's feet. The hunted man kicked it from his path and saw it shed a trickle of sparks before it crashed, extinguished, into a wall.

Behind them they heard the uproar of the chase, now muffled by narrow walls, now uncomfortably close as their pursuers pounded across a wider thoroughfare. There was the echoing report of a musket-shot. James began to fall behind his lighter-footed companion. At a corner he lost him completely. Then, as he stood gulping painfully, the clatter of his pursuers ever nearer, he saw the young man stopped under a lantern in an adjacent courtyard. He ran to join him. Kean struck again with the heel of his hand on a door under a low arch.

A wicket swung open in the larger door. Kean sprang forward. "What's your errand?" asked a voice from the darkness.

"It's I, Kean—William Kean——"

"The Doctor's abroad, Mr Kean——"

Kean thrust himself into the narrow entrance. "For God's sake let us in! Listen, the military are after us——" At that a hand shot over the young man's shoulder and seizing James's coat dragged him inward with such vigour that he sent Kean reeling before him. The wicket was slammed on their heels and the bolt shot.

The hand that Gault shrugged angrily from his shoulder belonged to a vast fellow in a rough sleeved waistcoat and leather apron, who now stepped back and examined the interlopers morosely. At the door stood the second man, a pistol half-hidden in the crook of his folded arms. James, staring around, saw the anvil in the middle of the floor, a knot of fire still glowing under the great bellows. He drew in the pungent stench of smouldering coal slack and cooling-trough and execrated Kean. Their headlong flight away from the refuge of the sailing ships and landed them under the roof of a horse-doctor.

As he turned the man at the door raised his hand in warning. In silence they listened to the clamour of the approaching soldiers, heard them hesitate at the mouth of the court, then the word that sent them clattering on into the darkness.

Kean laughed nervously. "There were more beagles in that pack than started out after us."

"His Majesty's forces have been instructed to keep a sharp look-out for undesirables who might find their way into the town tonight," said the man at the door suavely.

James looked at him with uneasy interest. In the flickering light he saw the neatly combed wig, the clean linen, the dark, seemly clothes. An uncommon doorkeeper for a smiddy. In turn the man was examining them with even less favour than the silent blacksmith.

"The Doctor won't view your return here with any satisfaction, Mr Kean," he said at last.

"I protest, Mr Gordon, that it's none of my fault," said Kean. "Had I not been apprehended, then escaped from my escort, then been pursued, I would not have troubled you again."

"By declining to escape you could have achieved that end with less trouble to all," said Mr Gordon with a none too pleasant smile. He turned to James. "And you, sir," he said courteously enough. "Your name——?"

"James Gault."

"Were you also being pursued?"

"Yes."

"With intent or by accident, may I ask?"

"With intent," said James scowling.

"Mr Gault and I met by accident," said Kean, then added with a smile, "at the bottom of the Farset River."

Mr Gordon checked him. "Keep your tale for the Doctor. Do you still wish to see him?"

"If that is possible."

"Come with me." They followed him to the end of the smiddy. There he opened a door and motioned them to enter the brightly-lit room beyond. As they stood there blinking and confused they heard their guide say, "Master Kean and a Master Gault to speak with you, Doctor."

The chamber in which James found himself was large, so large that although the walls were heaped with what appeared to be bales and barrels and cases of merchandise, the space in the centre was greater than that of the smiddy they had left. It was illuminated by a great gilt and crystal candelabra that hung so low that a man of middle height would have had to stoop to walk under it. At a table among the bales and boxes a woman was pouring wine into glasses. A man in the waistcoat and breeches of a stablehand lounged on a bench beyond the glare of the candles. Half-hidden in a wing chair another poked indolently at the coals of a fire unseasonably large. The smith and Mr Gordon came in closing the door of the blacksmith's shop behind them. Furtively James pinched the coins in the skirt of his jacket and took a firmer grasp of his stick.

Gordon had addressed the man seated at the fire as 'Doctor'. He won no response. Nor was there any pause in the ruminative stirring of the embers. As the man in the chair leaned forward for a more vigorous thrust James saw that his head was too large, like that of a dwarf. He wore his own hair, falling to his shoulders, black and glistening, as if dressed with oil. The head sank back again into the shadow of the chair and only the clink of the poker broke the silence. Twice, as Gault watched, he caught a spark of colour from the restless hands and realised with a grimace of distaste that the fingers were laden with rings. Then, with a sudden stab of anger, he saw that the poker, building and destroying among the fiery coals, was a pike head. He thought of how, only a short day ago, his comrades had treasured such a weapon, how, at dead of night, they had watched over its shaping and tempering at some cross-road smiddy, smuggling it home, secreting it in the thatch or the couplings against the Dawning of the Day. With contempt he looked at the others waiting intently yet obediently on the pleasure of this dwarf in his finery. He thought of the day behind him, his escape, his aching, trembling limbs, his clothing soaked and fouled with mire. "Are we to be kept standing like beasts!" he shouted, and struck the floor with his stick.

Kean started in alarm, the ostler sprang to his feet, but James had eyes only for the face of the man in the chair. It was a pale, discoloured face that was turned on him, the cheeks, held apart by a great pendulous nose, were seamed as an old sheepskin. An ugly threatening face. But as he waited and watched the malevolence died in the small eyes as if a light had been extinguished. The wrinkled mouth moved in a smile. The Doctor sank back into his chair. "I'm sorry if you're fatigued, sir. Owen, fetch a seat."

The ostler brought a chair as he was bid. Still standing, James laid his hand on the back of it. "What of my companion, Mr Kean?"

"Mr Kean is not welcome in this house."

"You cannot expect me, sir, to be seated——"

A hand glittered. "I expect nothing from you. I didn't ask you to come here." The glowering face turned again. "And give me none of your damned airs, peasant, for you, too, can quickly outrun your welcome."

Kean plucked James's sleeve. "The Doctor is right," he cried hurriedly, "I am already greatly in his debt. To the tune of one hundred and fifty guineas . . ."

"More, you dog, more," said the Doctor from the depths of his chair.

"More . . . ?" echoed Kean and Gault's anger withered as he heard the falsity in his companion's voice.

The Doctor rose from his chair. He was, Gault reckoned, about four feet ten inches high, and his enormous head and the shortness of his neck gave him the appearance of a hunchback. But as he approached under the glare of the candelabra James saw that his coat lay smoothly between his heavy shoulders. The light fell unkindly on the black shiny hair, the udderlike face, the plum-coloured velvet of his coat, the cabochan garnet in his neckcloth. James could barely refrain from drawing back in repugnance at the manikin's approach, but his business was with Kean. The Doctor came to a halt before the young man, his eyes closed dreamily, his great head swaying from side to side. "More . . ." he crooned, "much more, Mr Kean." He opened his eyes wide. "I engaged for you a speedy passage on Captain Lumford's ship from Newry. I was without the services of two of my men for the three days in which they convoyed you safely to that port. Once you were out of their sight you came skulking back here. Is that not so?"

"I can't deny it."

"No, by the Wine of Cana you can't deny it. And what brought you back, you clown—a woman?"

"I can't deny that."

"And she informed on you?"

Kean paused in surprise. "Yes."

"What's her name?"

Kean threw out his hands in agitation. "No, Doctor . . . I can't tell you . . . she doesn't deserve . . ."

"I'll be the judge of that."

"No, Doctor."

The stunted creature sighed and moved away. "I'll bear with you for this night, Kean. But you well know that what I want I get in the end. A traitorous whore's name is no exception." He turned on Gault suddenly. "I understood you to be fatigued, sir. You were given a chair. Is there aught wrong with your arse?"

Outraged, James glared at him, then swung his stick above his head. The Doctor stood motionless, staring upwards into the student's eyes. James felt a sharp prodding in his side. "Down wi' that," said the ostler's voice, "or I'll gut ye like a herring."

As the tip of the stick touched the floor the Doctor spoke softly. "You will learn that I admire a man who stands by his friends, Mr Gault. But," and a venomous smile drew down the great nose, "never abuse that knowledge. Owen, put away your tickler. Our visitor has gained his point. Fetch a chair for the betrayed lover." He clapped his beringed hands together. "Poll," he cried to the silent figure at the table, "food for the travellers, wine for all!"

Dragging his chair to the hearth James fell into it wearily. He closed his eyes. Forgive my ungratefulness. If it be Thy Will deliver me also from the hands of this man and his company. He heard the slipshod steps of the woman approach, the clink of glass. He opened his eyes and looked up to see not a woman but a youth in woman's clothes, a golden down fringing his idiot's face. Dumbfounded, he fumbled at the glass then pushed it away. "I don't take liquor," he said.

The Doctor had been watching him. "It is Poll's privilege to serve his master's guests. It is fine Madeira. Overcome your scruples enough, Mr Gault, to accept it." With a shrug James took the glass and raised it as the Doctor gave the company a toast. "*May the flame of Liberty, which warms and enlightens its friends, consume its enemies!*"

The Doctor settled again into his chair. "So you are pursued by King George's government, Mr Gault?"

"Yes."

"How came that?"

Gault hesitated. The dreamy eyes of the man across the hearth were half-closed, his voice low. "If you are about to say that you are a United Irishman, do not hesitate. Such have been seen before under this roof."

"Yes, I am that."

"From where?"

"From Ravara, adjacent to Killinchy, in the County Down."

"You have travelled fast to reach here from Ballynahinch today."

"I wasn't at Ballynahinch."

"Ah," said the Doctor. The company waited.

"I'll tell what I have to tell as briefly as possible. Yesterday, when our company assembled, ready to march, our captain refused to lead us, refused, indeed, to leave his house. The rest of us could come to no firm decision and so we disbanded. Six of our fellows were caught while trying to cross the lough and hanged on the instant. I made my way across country to assure myself that my parents had not been harmed. From there I pushed on to Belfast. You've heard how I met Mr Kean."

"What if the military ask your whereabouts? They are

said to be not overgentle with the families of lusty young men who are absent when they should be at home."

"My parents will say I'm in Glasgow."

"Why Glasgow?"

"I'm enrolled at the university there as a student of Divinity."

"A college man. *Et ego in libris laboravi.* We have much in common."

James smiled politely, too politely. The Doctor's eyelids drooped. "At what time was the turnout of this puissant body of men?"

"At one o'clock yesterday morning," answered James coldly.

"And what reason did your captain give for not carrying out his duty?"

James hesitated. "Is this interrogation necessary, sir?"

"You must permit me to assess the truth of your story, Mr Gault, if I'm to help you," returned the Doctor smoothly.

Studying the plate of beef and bread on his knee, James replied, "He opened an upper window and shouted down that his mother forbade him to come out . . ." In the silence that followed he raised his head and looked around the men in the room. He saw no amusement in their faces, no surprise, no incredulity. "What I tell you is the truth."

"And the name of this citizen-soldier?"

"I took an oath——"

"Damn your oath, Mr Gault." The dwarfed man waved him away irritably. "Aeneas, bring me the East Down register. And you, Mr Gault, eat your supper," James watched apprehensively as Gordon brought a file of papers and laid them on the Doctor's knee. The ringed fingers traced the lines for a moment. "His name is Willie McIvor of Ardkeen. Is that not so?"

James chewed reflectively. "Yes."

The list of names was tilted again to the light. "I can tell you further. His lieutenants were Alexander Hanna and . . ." the thin smile appeared, ". . . one, James Gault of Ravara."

"How do you know this? It was decided only three days ago!"

"Is my information sound?"

"It is."

"Why did not Hanna or you take command?"

"I've told you. There was a dispute. McIvor's defection seemed to frighten the others. They wanted to go home. We would have led them if we had been let."

"And the sum of your miserable tale is that six honest fellows were strung up and you're on the run?"

James was silent.

"Very well. Now you want a passage out of the country?"

"Anywhere—Kentucky or Canada. I've relations there."

The Doctor smiled and nodded his misshapen head. "Anywhere but Botany Bay. We'll see, Mr Gault. You will remain hidden here for a time. Above us is a chamber where you and Kean will lodge until I've arranged a sailing for you. That will take time, weeks, possibly months. I want you to understand that once you go upstairs you bide there until you leave to board the vessel."

"If I'm to stay so long surely I can inform my friends of my safety?"

The Doctor rose from his chair. "Gault, so long as you're in this house you're dead to your friends. In that chamber upstairs you will eat, sleep, study, pray, piss, shit, and have your being. I will not risk a member of my household for any vagaries of yours." The young man, staring in sullen distaste at the ugly face so close to his, held his tongue.

Suddenly the Doctor stepped back. "Aeneas, put away the papers. Fill up the glasses, Poll, and bring me my fiddle." He turned again to Gault. "Will you stay with us for an hour or so of good cheer and good music? Those who know of these things say I play like Viotti."

James stood up. "Thank ye, Doctor. May I postpone that pleasure?"

"As you wish. But remember that from tomorrow this town will hive with search parties, spies, informers. It'll be a long day before you get the chance to spend an evening in convivial company."

"You've made that clear, sir. But I'm tired."

The dwarfish master of the house scowled and turned away. "Matt, conduct him to the upper room." James bowed to the velvet back and followed the smith. They crossed the earthen floor of the smiddy and climbed a flight of wooden steps hidden behind the forge fire. Matt raised a trap-door and James clambered after him. The candle in the smith's hand barely lit up the walls of the vast loft. The smith set down the light beside a truckle bed. "This is yours. That," he indicated another bed seen dimly at the opposite wall, "will be Willie Kean's. Is there aught I can get ye?"

"Some water, please."

"There's a ewer at your bedhead." The man lingered. "You should ha' listened to the Doctor's playing."

James turned and eyed him steadily. "I've never lived through a day that has left me less inclined to frivolity. Leave the light. That's all, my friend."

When he was alone he knelt at his bedside. From below came the pungent smells of the forge, a clamour of voices and the shrill trill of the Doctor's fiddle. Villainously played as befits the player, God forgive me, said James. He was drowned deep in sleep when Kean came stumbling up the steps, hours later.

IV

While the fugitives lay hidden in Legg's Lane, the government, with whip, pitch cap, convict ship and noose, were restoring the country to tranquillity. In Belfast the summer sun beat down on lanes and quays. Flies fed impartially on the spiked heads withering high on the Market House and on the victuals spread on the stalls below. Not once, in almost two months, had the young men been permitted to descend the wooden steps. Only when darkness came could they open the gable window and let in the cool night air.

James discovered that Kean had been no closer to the actual fighting than he had himself. "But you would have taken arms?"

"Yes, as Christ's my judge!" He smiled disarmingly. "I keep forgetting that you are almost a cleric. I'm not accustomed to such company. Why did you leave your studies?"

"Conscience, I believe. One of my instructors, John Miller, so worked on me that I could sit still no longer. Bullies and cheats were in a conspiracy to rob my fellowmen of the title which they had from the Most High, a living from the soil they laboured!" James stopped awkwardly. ". . . there may have been other reasons stirring me."

Kean smiled. "Such as boredom with your books?"

"I've given you my reasons. Do you doubt me?" He was surprised at the sharpness with which he spoke.

"By no means," said Kean leaning back on his bed and spreading his hands pacifically.

"What of you?"

"I'm what it's now fashionable to describe as one who came to the popular cause through intellectual and moral persuasion rather than a pressing lack of the necessities of life."

"I can think of nothing more pressing than the claims of morality," said James in such a way that the other burst out laughing.

"Ah well, every cobbler to his last." He sobered. "You flatter me. I was on a jaunt on the Continent when I caught Democracy, the French Plague, as they call it. It was in Paris, fittingly enough." And the young man recounted how, on his return to Ireland, his appetite for the conspiratorial and dangerous had drawn him into the Doctor's circle. "On the night he took us in he told you he was a college man. You were amused."

"I can recall no cause for amusement that evening."

"For all that he detected your disbelief. You were wrong in that. He is indeed a man of education. His name, I believe, is Luke Bannon. He claims to have studied at Padua, Salamanca and to have had a doctorate conferred upon him by the University of Paris. I've no reason to disbelieve this. Most certainly he's widely travelled. I know something of foreign cities and when I first met him I was tempted to put his claims to the test. Soon I was under such a counter-examination the company thought I was the impostor! He is fluent in French, Italian, German and Spanish, and when he requires secrecy he is likely to address his hangers-on in Irish. He is also learned in the classical tongues. In all this he takes little pride. But on the matter of playing the fiddle he is insufferable!"

"I have no music to judge," said James.

"I have, and I assure you he is the vilest performer I have ever listened to."

"And what of Mr Gordon?"

"A disbarred lawyer. He, McCoubrey the smith, and the idiot, Poll, are the Doctor's permanent lodgers and cronies."

"And what of the strange-looking creatures who seem to slip in and out at all hours?"

"They are all in the Doctor's pay or power. He is the *soi-disant* landlord of most of the courts and alleys from here to the quays. Whether he owns the rents or not, in the twinkling of an eye he can call up as frightening a regiment of ostlers, bullies, pickpockets, horse-thieves and prostitutes as you would never wish to meet. He has his spies in the Customs House, the Courts and the Town Corporation. At least three murders have been traced close to Legg's Lane——"

"Why in heaven's name hasn't he been brought to justice!"

"Who's to lay evidence against him? And who is to put it into execution? Even the military dursn't venture down here except in broad daylight."

"And we lie in his power——"

"We had an alternative on a night some time ago," said Kean dryly, "and we ran away from it."

"You did. I knew nothing of where we were going."

The days passed slowly for the two men in hiding. Kean lay on his bed, tried to read, paced about restlessly lamenting the absence of feminine company, a complaint that became more frequent as the weeks passed. James, unable to get the books he asked for, read the newsheets brought to him by Aeneas Gordon. At times he sat for hours staring out of the little window, thinking of Kate and his parents. Sometimes the Doctor clambered up to their hideout, bringing with him a bottle of wine. One evening, when Kate had been present to his mind all day, James asked if he might send her a letter. The reply of his dwarfish host was brief. "No. Don't make that request again, Mr Gault."

They came to welcome small incidents, even the annoying, as relief in the prevailing monotony. Several times, in the early hours of the morning, the two young men were almost choked by fumes floating up from the forge below. The Doctor didn't appear on those evenings and no one paid any attention to their complaints. One evening a foolhardy drunkard stumbled up the lane bawling out a new-minted ballad:

> Treachery, treachery, damnable treachery
> Put the poor Papishes all to the front;
> The Protestants nixt, that's how they were fixt,
> And the bould Presbyterians skulked to the rump——

"If I was down there," said James with a scowl, "I'd dust that sot's jacket for him."

"Ah, what are ye complaining of?" cried Kean laughing. "At least your tribe get a mention. But what of all the poor freethinkers like myself who took their place in the legions of Revolution? Nary a word, my friend!"

As the roisterer's voice died away, James said, "They're turning the Rising into a religious war——"

"Who are 'they'?"

"The Roman Catholics. It says here that in Wexford the popish Defenders have turned their arms against their protestant neighbours and burned and ravaged and slaughtered them by the hundred."

"I'm certain that's a lie," said Kean vigorously.

"Read it for yourself."

"I have. They're government papers. They're at their old game of dividing the nation."

"We don't know," said James gloomily. "Cooped up here, we don't know."

Of one thing they were certain. Kean's assurance that the military rarely ventured into Legg's Lane was sadly out. Often, sitting at the little window trying to catch a breath of air in their broiling refuge, they shrank back at the sudden tramp of feet entering the Doctor's courtyard. Then they would lie with their ears to the floor listening to the Doctor or Mr Gordon beguile the redcoats with fair words or fairer wine. One fellow, a yeo officer, was hard to budge. Kean, peering through a crack in the floor, recognised him as the captain from whom he had escaped. He was complaining to the Doctor that he had been reduced in rank and that two of his men had been flogged. It was here or hereabouts, he maintained stubbornly, that their prisoner had vanished into thin air.

The two men in the loft listened as the Doctor took up the tale. He damned Kean and his like, not, as he pointed out, for their politics, but that they ruined trade. He commiserated with the yeoman. Such a fine citizen-soldier would be unlucky if he suffered long his superior's displeasure.

"I see no end to it," responded the officer in a sullen voice. "Not until some of the not-so-loyal rogues from here who were safely indoors that night have their tongues loosened."

"My men engage in commerce, not conspiracy," said the Doctor easily. "If you wish I could speak on your behalf to your commanding officer——"

"Be damned to you for your impudence," cried the yeo truculently. "I am under the Commandant of Belfast, Major Sirr. What the hell would he have to do with the likes o' you?"

There was a silence. In the room upstairs the two men lay listening tensely. This time the Doctor had overplayed his hand. Then came the little man's silken voice. "I've heard of Major Sirr. An admirable soldier, I don't doubt. But I never deal with subordinates. The officer I have in mind is General Nugent——"

"The Commander-in-Chief . . . ?"

"I have business with him at his quarters, tomorrow morning. A matter of a score of horses, a pipe of claret, and an Irish cob to be shipped for his lady. I propose in any event to mention your name to him, Mr . . . ?"

"Ah . . . Mullan . . ."

". . . Mr Mullan . . ." There was a purr in the Doctor's voice. "But whether in restoring your captaincy is another matter."

They heard the slow drag of the yeoman's chair as he rose to his feet. "M'apologies, sir . . . I misunderstood . . . that would be damnably generous of you . . ."

From the window James and Kean watched him clatter away, like all the others, his head awhirl with the Doctor's words, a bottle of wine in his saddle-bag.

"The devil, oh, the devil!" shouted Kean, rolling on his bed. James, stretched on his, agreed silently, without laughter. From below came the snatch of a merry little reel played on the fiddle. That evening when the Doctor had clambered to their hideout, bringing with him the usual bottle of wine, Kean asked him would he have the yeoman reinstated in his rank.

"You doubt my ability?"

"But of course not."

"I shall have him reinstated."

"And then suborn him, no doubt," said James.

The Doctor examined James over his glass. "Not *suborn,*" he said in a mocking voice. "*Suborn* is too violent a word. I know something of this Mr Mullan. Strip him of his war-paint and you find underneath a modest huckster in boot leather and suchlike. When the occasion offers I'll put him in the way of some profitable business. The manner or morality of it won't concern him, for to scrabble for profit has always been a sanctified pursuit among our protestant bourgeoisie. Then, no doubt, I'll find some use for the animal in one of my concerns."

"Without wishing to be ungrateful, there seems to me to be no limit to your *concern.* It embraces both the hunted and the hunter."

"You can indeed be grateful, Gault," said the other, "that my sympathies lie where they do." He sat nursing his glass, glowering alternately at the two young men. When he spoke again the harshness had gone from his voice. "You wonder that I should concern myself with the waifs and strays of this past pitiable conspiracy? You have quizzed our friend Kean, here?"

"He appears no wiser than I."

"As you're unlikely to tarry on Irish soil once you leave here, I see no harm in telling you why you found refuge under my roof." The speaker sank his great head as if pondering how he should continue. The face that he lifted to his listeners bore a grotesque mixture of self-reproach and bashfulness. James looked away.

"The truth is that I am of a revolutionary temperament, a volatile spirit that can be shaken into a fury by injustice, historical or of today. But my mentor is the eminent Florentine rather than your Paines or Washington or Wolfe Tones. That is why, when the Volunteers were formed in this town in 1792, I took upon myself a watching brief. I sat in parlours and taverns and watched the patriotism of honest men slip into the hands of Mr Flood and my Lord Charlemont and their kind, whose interest lay not in the Irish Nation but in a protestant settlement. To them but two names for the same thing. Very well. I was not disillusioned."

The Doctor paused to refill Kean's glass and his own. "Then I considered the two-thirds of my fellow-countrymen who had never paraded to the huzzas and the fluttering handkerchiefs. Who had never shouldered arms under brave banners worked by the soft fingers of their wives and sisters. Who lacked green and blue and scarlet facings to their jackets for the simple reason that they hadn't a tatter to their backs. I refer, gentlemen, to the oppressed, the naked, those tens of thousands of our brothers who lived on the half-cooked potato and the offal of their masters' middens. Those who crawled away from their hovels at the approach of the rent collector, the title collector, the hearth tax collector. Those who watched their women and children die like sparrows in the hedges." He grinned a wide venomous smile at his listeners. "I'm sure, gentlemen, these miserable creatures were in your mind when you learned to level a pike?"

"If we had been successful," muttered James, "it followed that all men . . ."

The Doctor rode on unheeding. "These wretches must have a voice, I thought, if only to cry out in pain. And for a time I heard it in the new-formed United Irishmen, from the mouths of the men of little substance, like Jamie Hope, the Antrim weaver. But he and his like were ousted by faces wearily familiar to me, the men of interest, the Warriors of the Embroidered Banners. They couldn't get rid of me for I was privy to their secrets. Further," and the Doctor drew a finger down the velvet of his coat, "I was a man of influence and education, and therefore of use to them. So once again I sat in drawing-rooms and taverns with all those fervid linen drapers and listened to them talk about the glory of Saratogas and Yorktowns to be fought on Irish soil. Ah, how glowingly they spoke of the readiness and good faith of the English government to recognise the rights of Irish belligerents in the manner accorded to the rebelly Americans! If you were free to travel the streets of this town, my friends, I could show you one or two of those same eloquent heads blackening in the sun!"

"Some of them were my friends," said Kean angrily. "They were whole-hearted in their hatred of tyranny. If they erred in trusting their adversaries, it was a small guilt to take to the scaffold——"

"You talk like a child!" screamed the Doctor. "Revolution isn't a game of ball. 'Forward, brothers! Down with Tyranny!' . . . these are the cries of the playground. Whilst your friends cried 'Away with Tyranny,' I offered them the death of the tyrants." He leaned forward, his head casting a monstrous shadow on the wall, his eyes intent on the two young men. "I laid a plan before these parlour *fronduers*. I proposed the assassination of every high official in the state, and the simultaneous firing of government buildings in Dublin and Belfast. Camden, Castlereagh, Beresford, Clare, every bloodstained name in the administration; let them be done to death swiftly in their council chambers, their gardens, their baths, their beds, mingling their blood with that of their doxies and their wives, if need be. All that is needed is £10,000 and a few hundred dedicated men. I threw my own draft for five hundred guineas on the table before them. Do this, said I, and then by God you can cry 'Insurrection!' throughout the land!" All affectation and pretence had vanished from the sweating, malignant face. He sprang to his feet and strode through the chamber, chattering to himself and cracking his knuckle joints unmercifully. Seated again he turned a sullen questioning eye on his listeners.

"And your plan was rejected out of hand?" said James in a low voice.

There was a bitter cackle of laughter. "Yes, Gault, these emissaries of rebellion shrank chalk-faced from the argument that such a killing was no murder. They sat down to judge not its efficacy but its *morality*! These creatures who had solemnly sworn to free their country—fervently and unanimously they now agreed to betray their oath, their fellows, their country."

His listeners sat silent, turned from him. The candles guttered in the sockets. The Doctor set down his glass, rose, and crossed the room. They watched him lift the trap-door and descend clumsily, step by step, until he sank from sight. James replaced the flap. He walked thoughtfully back to his bed. "Do you think he would have carried through that bloody-minded scheme?"

"To the last iota." In the darkness James permitted himself a small smile of scepticism.

A week later he was compelled to change, once again, his opinion of his protector's nature. The Doctor came into the loft at the unusual time of mid-afternoon. "Gault," he said, "d'ye recall your erstwhile captain, McIvor?"

"Yes. What of him?"

"He's dead."

James eyed the small man. "How did that come about?"

"Yesterday morning, at Downpatrick Jail, he was given eight hundred lashes." James rose slowly. "In the end he was crying not for mercy but for death. He got his wish. Before the sentence could be fully executed his belly burst and his guts ran out on the cobbles."

"Great God, Willie McIvor took no hand in the fighting!"

"His cowardice brought six of his men to the gallows."

"He wasn't convicted because of that!"

"True, true. He was convicted of administering an unlawful oath to others."

"It was a small transgression."

The Doctor grinned. "You well know that it's punishable by death. Is there not a certain humour," he continued reflectively, "in the thought that McIvor might be alive today if he'd honoured that same treasonable oath?"

James stared in open abhorrence at the stunted figure by the trap-door. "How was he discovered?"

"Captain Mullan laid the information. His vigilance has commended him again to his superiors."

"You were the real informer!"

The Doctor's fleshy nose drooped as he smiled. "McIvor was a traitor and a coward. Such men mustn't be allowed to escape." He bowed then reached out for McCoubrey's steadying hand. As James listened to their footsteps receding on the stairs he thought of the young, vain, lighthearted fellow who had died so awfully before the jail gates. "I'll have him on my conscience till the day I die," he said.

*

"But we have been cooped up here for almost six months!" cried Kean petulantly.

"There are still spies and informers abroad," said Mr Gordon. "A careless word or move would most certainly secure you a passage to Van Diemen's Land, if not to a more intangible anchorage."

"Thank you, but I'll stick to my original choice of destination."

"No more, then," said the Doctor. "Your folly in being taken again in Belfast has made it all the more difficult to fabricate another identity for you. Gault, here, is an easier matter."

"Then why haven't I been able to get away?" said James.

"Because I don't consider it safe for you to be seen in any port as yet. For every berth out of Belfast, Derry or Newry there are three persons waiting with their papers in order. No matter how ingenious Aeneas is as a penman, there would be questions asked. They would tear an explanation from you as to where you have been lying up since June. You understand, Gault, I'm not thinking so much of your hide as my household. That must not be endangered." The Doctor sipped his wine. "And yet I think the Government's appetite is somewhat satiated. There were only three poor fools turned off in the Cornmarket last week and they were mutinous weavers at that."

The four sat in the room above the smiddy. In these dark winter evenings the Doctor and Mr Gordon often clambered there to share supper with the fugitives. Cautiously, and not without misgiving, James had taken a liking to the courteous, sombrely-dressed man, Aeneas Gordon. When he had first learned from Kean that Gordon had been struck off because of forgery and had subsequently been drawn into the Doctor's intrigues, he kept a distance. But he discovered that the ruined lawyer was a man of good sense, free from the passion and cynicism, that so bedevilled his master. It was Gordon who, one afternoon, asked him would he again take up his studies for the ministry once he had escaped his present plight.

James stared at the mild face of his questioner. "But of course, what else!" he exclaimed, and was left wondering why he had found it necessary to speak with such heat.

While he left them in no doubt as to his loyalty to the Doctor, Mr Gordon was a wise informant when the two young men wished to discover the intentions or whims of that strange creature. From him James learnt that any correspondence with his family and friends was still forbidden. He rebelled and demanded a messenger to carry his letters. The Doctor examined him through half-closed eyes. "Most certainly no man of mine will be endangered by carrying your letters through the countryside."

"Then by word of mouth."

"Who are these people you are so anxious to inform that you are in hiding?"

"My father, my mother—only to tell them that I'm still alive."

"No doubt there's a woman?"

"Well, yes. Miss Kate Purdie, a neighbour, who lives close by my home."

"Did you bid her a fond farewell after you fled the battle?"

"No," said James coldly. "I spoke with her brother."

"He was with you in the United Men?"

". . . no."

"No?" breathed the twisted little man. "Then her father?"

"No member of her family was in the turn-out."

"They were on the other side? Come, Gault, this is a grave matter."

James thrust his face close to the Doctor's. "But not a matter that requires your meddling."

The Doctor raised a hand in airy expostulation. "Ha, d'ye think I can afford the time to pursue every yellow-bellied bog-trotter in the land?"

"Let me tell you the son was with us in sympathy. If the father was against us, it was because like you, Doctor, he was too set on making money, come freedom, come tyranny!"

The Doctor's face darkened. Then the drooping nose twitched, a thin smile curved his mouth. "A most promising father-in-law to keep in pickle." The smile faded. "And you'll keep them all in pickle, Gault, until I tell you otherwise. Until then the aged can live on memories, the young on hope. Let me hear no more about it."

And yet, for all the bluster and sarcasm that he had to withstand, Gault sensed that the Doctor, for some reason, wanted to earn his good opinion. It was to him rather than to Kean that the Doctor gave his attention. When some delicacy appeared on their diet, an imported cheese, a fresh-caught trout, he clambered upstairs behind the idiot Poll, to assure himself that it was to James's taste. At the young student's request Mr Gordon had brought him a bible. His need for further volumes was referred to the Doctor.

"And what authors had you in mind, scholar?"

"For my immediate needs I would very much like to have Stapfer's *Institutiones* and Paley's *Evidences of Christianity*."

"Paley?" echoed the Doctor in mock surprise. "Surely Newton's breath must have stirred some of the dust in the divinity halls of Scotland?"

James held his tongue and got his Paley. Other books were brought to him and he began to find pleasure where, in the past, he had found only drudgery. Now when he knelt beside his bed he looked forward to another day's confinement with resignation.

One evening the trap-door lifted to reveal the Doctor and Mr Gordon. The master of the house surveyed the two young men with a benign expression.

"I have news for you, Mr Kean." He paused. "In two days' time you sail from Derry in the brig *Liberty*, bound for Philadelphia. Now, what d'ye say to that?"

James saw the apprehension on Kean's face change to bewilderment, then joy. The young man rushed forward and flung his arms around the Doctor. He thumped him on the back, crying, between tears and laughter, "God bless ye, Doctor, oh, God bless ye!" The vigour of his embrace drove some colour into the Doctor's pale cheeks. Then the small man, infuriated at the amusement he saw on the faces of the others, tore himself free. "Damn ye, Kean," he cried, straightening his coat, "try to conduct yourself like a man!" But Kean had flung himself on his bed to sob unashamedly.

James stepped forward. "What of me?"

"And what of you?"

"Am I to spend the rest of my life cooped up here?"

"Your turn will come." He waved James away then tapped the shoulder of the young man on the bed. "Listen, Kean. You will set out for Derry quite openly tomorrow, driving a waggon of kegs and barrels. Fearon will travel behind you with a similar load. You will stop the night at the inn in Ballymoney. You will not be armed. Fearon will, as will the horseman riding ahead, although you won't see him. You'll keep your mouth shut and do as Fearon bids you. Once aboard you'll go below and stay there until she's under way——"

"I promise, Doctor!"

"I don't want your promise. I'm telling you what's to happen. On the road you'll travel as," and the Doctor smiled his thin smile, "Habakkuk Poots, cooper."

"Ah, God," cried the young man, sitting up with a laugh and dashing the tears from his face, "surely you could find something more fitting to my age and station!"

"It's not of my invention. Downstairs I have the papers of one so named who set out five days ago from Fermanagh to travel to Derry. He was murdered and robbed on his journey."

The excitement died in Kean's face. He lowered his head less in horror than acquiescence. "Take the name of a dead man?"

"We all bear the names of dead men, Kean." The Doctor turned briskly. "Have Poll bring us up two bottles."

They drank much more than two bottles that night. They drank until Kean had to be lifted to his bed and Mr Gordon had fallen from his chair so often that Fearon and McCoubrey were summoned to carry him below. As their footsteps died the Doctor dragged his chair close to James's. The heavy flushed face was bland, almost kindly. He peered up at James. The young man blinked back. He too had drunk more than his modicum.

"What devilment have you in mind now, sir?" he inquired.

Amiability suffused the Doctor's face, almost reaching to his eyes. "Are you so set on going to America, Mr Gault?"

"Eh? After all this waiting . . . ?"

"Consider now the possibility of staying in your own country."

The speculations of many months faded from James's mind like mist. "It would be wonderful, nay it would be God-sent . . ." He drew back a little. "Always, of course, that it *was* God's will . . . my home, my friends . . ."

The Doctor averted his scrutiny. "Your emotion is understandable, my friend."

The shift brought James to his senses. "And why did you not make the same offer to Kean?"

The Doctor made a gesture of contempt towards the figure on the bed. "I'm addressing you, Gault. You're not a familiar figure in this town?"

"That's true."

"Good. The government's appetite is almost glutted. Trade doesn't flourish under martial law. The gallows stand empty now more often than not."

"But how will you explain my presence?"

The Doctor laid his finger along his nose. "Diligence finds answers."

"And after a time I can return to my studies?"

"Why not?" and the dwarfish man opened his arms to convey the width of his sympathy and understanding.

To his surprise James discovered that the absence of Kean made a difference in his circumscribed day that was not wholly agreeable. There was a chill in the room not explained by the dying days of winter. For the first time he became aware of the strange, scorched smells that rose in the middle of the night from the smiddy below. His books lay unopened. He lay stretched on his bed for hours, gazing into the dusty rafters. It isn't Willie Kean's departure that's unsettled me. It's the nearness of my freedom. And yet am I free to grasp this freedom, is this broad and easy road for me? He would tumble out on his knees and pray and pray. As he prayed he was aware, as of an odour stealing from below, that at that very moment the Doctor was planning his escape. And distracting him in his pleading a whisper sounded in his ear—that man is an agent of the Devil. Head buried, fingers plaited, he would pray again for guidance and a little charity.

The Doctor appeared in the loft one afternoon clutching a fistful of papers. He sat for a time studying its occupant in silence.

"Well, Doctor," said James at last, "is it prudent for you to come here in daylight?"

"I know what I'm about, Mr Gault. If you exercise the same caution it may be possible for you to enter the world again."

Recalling Kean's outburst, James answered gravely. "I'm grateful to hear that, Doctor. Whose name will I bear?"

"Your own." The Doctor waved the papers. "I have here a declaration from Captain James Rodden, master of the schooner *Glenbaan*, that you signed with him for two voyages through the Outer Isles, gathering cargoes of wool and kelp. If you're questioned, you know what kelp is?"

"Aye, rightly." James was amused. "But why should a clerical student turn deckhand?"

"Because of misgivings as to your vocation." The Doctor held up the papers to check interruption. "These are from Mr Neil Gilchrist and Mr Robert Bell, students at Glasgow University, testifying that you were in your lodgings in the Scotch town until the fifteenth of June when you left to board your vessel at Greenock——"

"These men are my friends," said James angrily. "They would never give their name to a lie!"

"They suffer from the French plague. They believe they're saving the life of a warrior in the army of Democracy. I must add that Aeneas Gordon was unable to get them to accept a trifle for their signatures."

"You sent Mr Gordon over on this errand?"

"Yes."

Abashed, James sank into his chair. "I'm in your debt, Doctor. I trust I haven't put those two good fellows in peril."

"On that you can rest assured. Now, care and discretion."

V

A MILITARY DECREE brought James into the outer world again. Pestilence had entered the town from a vessel in the port. Already a number of the beggars and outcasts who lay about the quays had sickened and died, and grave fears were expressed by the Town Sovereign and others that the scourge could move further into the town claiming victims of consequence. The active, therefore, were ordered to sweep clean the streets and alleys. When a sergeant and two troopers clattered up Legg's Lane the Doctor called down the fugitive and thrust a broom into his fumbling hands. "Out with ye," he said, "and help Fearon and McCoubrey as the sergeant commands. If one of ye leaves as much as a scitter of pigeon shit on the cobbles I'll deal with ye when this gallant officer leaves."

As he tipped tar water across the stones and scrubbed with his broom, James glanced from under his brows at the sergeant. But the soldier sat slumped in his saddle eyeing the three toiling figures with indifference. The Doctor leaned in the doorway, a benevolent but stern smile on his face, occasionally raising his voice in admonition as some particle of dirt was left unswept. The name *Gault, James Gault,* sounded more often than any other.

Pushing his broom across the cobbles, James drank in all the small noises that filled the air, the sharp rasp of the horses' hooves, the creaking of leather, a woman's laugh in the lane, the distant bustle of the streets. How often he had imagined these first moments of freedom. But they had never taken this shape. A hurried farewell, then scuttling stealthily through the darkness to a ship at the quays. Or setting out on horseback before dawn with Fearon to ride perilous roads to a distant port. And here he was brushing down cobbles like an old wife in a farm close. His mother . . . Kate . . . he would see them soon. The sergeant tipped his ale cup to the sky and set it down with a clatter on the tray held by Poll. "Thankee, Doctor. Up, men."

"Your health, gentlemen, your health." The Doctor disengaged a hand to wave to the three departing soldiers. They had barely disappeared when he cried to the three men, "Throw down those damned brooms and come in with ye!" In the big merchandise room that James remembered so clearly the Doctor poured out four glasses of wine. "To you, Mr James Gault. The law has seen you standing on your own two legs in God's daylight. How does it feel to be a solid, visible, tangible man again, eh?"

James looked at the others as they crowded round him, their glasses raised in glee. Their master, the omniscient, had again won a trick. In the service of such a man what need of God Almighty? The Doctor, caught by Gault's silence, looked up. Immediately James raised his glass and bowed. "I raise this to *you*, Doctor. You've played your part of protector admirably. And yet I feel that I might safely have trod the cobbles of your yard a month, two months ago."

The Doctor laughed. "You think so? I've planted your name and image in the skull of that sergeant. He'll report in the town barracks what he's seen and heard, for every stranger is suspect. Before nightfall some hound will be here, squinting through a glass of my wine, and reading answers therein. You, Gault, are cast as the fox."

It was the brash Mr Mullan who cantered into the court shortly after dusk, his epaulettes fresh on his shoulder, foreboding in his face that he might lose them again through some caprice of the master of Legg's Lane. He wasted no time in stating his errand. "I've to report on a stranger here, a fellow by the name of Gault."

"A stranger to you, Captain, but not to me." He waved

the student forward from the shadows. "Captain Mullan, my new under-clerk, James Gault."

A cool nod, and the two men stood measuring each other. "A clerk, you say, and you send him out to sweep your yard like a stableboy?"

The Doctor viewed the yeo in astonishment. "Since when, sir, has any citizen of this town been beyond the fiat of its military commander? Only my damned age kept me from being out with the best of them——"

"Yes, yes, yes!" cried the officer waving his arm in exasperation. He eyed James with a scowl. "Is he likely to be dangerous to us?"

"Not," said the small man softly, "if he isn't pressed too closely."

"I'll attend to that. Look'ee, Gault, move carefully, keep your face shut, and I'll see to it that you're left alone."

*

James's aversion to the yeoman might have tempted him to venture soon and widely into the town. But he was kept to the seclusion of Legg's Lane by his own prudence and the Doctor's words. "In this town a well-set-up fellow dandering aimlessly through the streets is a target for all eyes. But a man hurrying on an errand is as common as a wet wind. I'll find you an errand."

A few days later he summoned James. In the courtyard stood a fine grey horse with two or three pieces of unbleached linen thrown across it. The Doctor, his hand resting on the saddle, was waiting for him.

"Do you know anything about linen, Gault?"

"A little. At home I took my stint at the loom."

"At 14 Chichester Street lives a Mr Spifford Lamont. I want you to deliver these pieces to him. The market price today is eleven pence a yard. He will pay you, therefore, thirty shillings and sixpence for this lot. Are you willing to go?"

"Yes."

"Then fetch your hat."

When James was mounted the Doctor said, "Mr Lamont is by aspiration one of quality and by occupation a linen draper. It is a common condition nowadays and I mention it only to prepare you for the manner of individual you are likely to meet. You can find your way to Chichester Street? Very well. Off you go and speak to no one more than you can help."

As James clattered out under the narrow archway and straightened his back in the bustling High Street, the certainty that there was a spy in the throng could not restrain him from coming to a halt and gazing around in curiosity. There was the stretch of cobbles, dry under the noonday sun, where Kean and he had grovelled on that night of flight. In the channel, whose muddy bed they had forded, two or three vessels rode high on a brimming tide. The air he sucked in was laden with the odours of tar and hemp, linseed and ropes, pinewood and hides, the butcher's offal cooking on the stalls close to the archway. To James it was sweeter than a summer field.

With care he urged his horse through the noisy scattering of men, women and children who laboured, bargained or loitered on the quays. The glimmer of a smile played on his face. He felt that he could embrace everybody in this shabby, noisy crowd. He accepted their indifference to his passing with gratitude, smiled at every upturned face that moved back from his horse's nose. He was among human beings again who accorded him no more attention than he wished or deserved.

At the head of the quays he took the longer way by the castle wall. There might still be, for all he knew, grinning heads high on the Market House, and a dangling tenant in the gibbet. His face resumed its normal dour expression, he drew up the reins and composed himself as a journeyman who undertook this errand every day. As he set his mount to a sedate trot up Donegall Place, he saw, at the end of the wide thoroughfare, the merchants leaving the White

Linen Hall. They drifted in groups, blocking the pavements so that lesser citizens had to edge their way around them, pressing close to the railings or stepping out into the roadway. These, thought James, as he discreetly examined the sober, well-dressed burghers, are the real masters. Here, standing outside their elegant hall, are the men who are draining the sloblands, confining the ancient waterways, opening the port's mouth, dictating the shape of the growing town—their town. These are the men who see themselves as the real revolutionaries.

As he passed a group of merchants, one of them, a stout, nimble person in brown broadcloth, suddenly skipped into the roadway and seizing his bridle dragged his horse to a stop. Panic-stricken, James threw a fleeting glance over his burden and his mount, wondering what mark had betrayed him. "Those pieces, where are you taking them?"

"I'm on an errand for my . . . master."

"Is that cloth sold?"

"It is."

"Paid for?"

"Not as yet."

"I'll give you a shilling a yard. A penny more than the market price," said the man in the broadcloth coat.

James licked his dry lips. His panic subsided. Pointedly he stared at the restraining hand until it was withdrawn. In the silence the other merchants had moved closer and were examining him with some curiosity. He straightened up and shook his reins as one eager to be on his road. The merchant was running the cloth between finger and thumb. "A penny?" James echoed with a dry chuckle.

The hand went to the bridle again. "A penny-ha'penny, then. I need it for a pressing order. With the curst weather we've had barely a rag in the market today. A shilling and threeha'pence." The self-esteem of the clean, plump face looking up at him was somewhat impaired, James felt, by the wheedling entreaty in voice and eyes. To make money among such people as these, he conjectured, a man would need to acquire a variety of masks. "No, thank ye, sir," he said picking up his reins again. The men around him didn't stir.

"I've made you an offer tuppence-ha'penny beyond today's price."

"And I've told you the cloth's trysted."

The rosy face of the merchant darkened. "Think what you're about, m'man. Your master'll be ill-pleased if he hears you've lost him money."

"Who is he?" asked one of their audience.

James was deaf to the question. He leaned forward to the man at the horse's head. "You've done your best to persuade me to disobey my master's instructions. You've failed. And I'll thank you, sir, not to curse the weather. It was sent by the same God who made you."

The merchant's companions looked up at the horseman in mingled surprise and amusement. A lean little man in a snuff-coloured coat touched the would-be purchaser's shoulder. "Not a rebuke fitting a churchwarden of St George's, eh, William?" As the enormity of it suffused the churchwarden's face the elderly man said to James, "You seem an honest man, friend. But take my advice, don't mix piety and business. You spoil two good things." He waved his cane. "Go, finish your errand."

"I thank you for your kind word, sir," said James stiffly. "But I'm fully competent to judge on such matters." And he rode away from the surf of amusement that rose among the merchants.

Mr Spifford Lamont's house was one of the largest and most handsome in the new thoroughfare. James was to admit later that it was a sad error in propriety to make his approach by the front entrance. He tethered his horse to the elegant iron railings, then, throwing the linen over his shoulder, marched up the flagged walk between clumps of seeding gillyflowers and broad-faced pansies and knocked vigorously on the broad white gilt-lined door. It was opened by a pretty serving-maid.

"Is this Mr Spifford Lamont's residence?"

"It is," said the girl pertly, her eyes not on James's face but on the load dangling over his shoulder.

"Is he at home?"

"If you've business with the master you take it to the rear."

"Fetch him, girl," said James.

There was a quick soft step in the hall, and a tall gentleman with a peevish anxious expression appeared behind the girl, his hands held loosely before him like a begging dog. "Well, well, well, what's all this to-do? Tilda, how often have you been told, eh?" He disengaged one hand to thrust the servant back with his elbow. "Chattering with pedlars in full view of the street. What will your mistress say, eh?" He examined James from head to foot. "Well, what is it, man? What d'you want, eh?"

"Are you by chance Mr Spifford Lamont, linen draper?"

"I am, siree, and not by chance," said Mr Lamont with equal curtness.

"Then this is yours," said James, whisking the load from his shoulder. Mr Lamont's hands knotted tighter. "Where are ye from?" he demanded angrily. "D'ye think I carry on a huckster's business on my own doorstep, eh? I heard the servant ordering you round to the yard." He peered over James's shoulder, his eyes widening in horror. "Is that animal tethered to my new railings? Good gracious, heavens and earth, d'ye want to tear them out by the roots, ye pachel! What will Mrs Lamont say? Get it away, get yourself round to the yard!" And Mr Lamont teetered on his threshold while James walked back to the horse and removed the offending rein. Satisfied, he firmly closed the gold and white door.

In the spacious cobbled yard with its tree tubs, herb garden and brightly painted coach house, the linen draper was waiting. It was as if there had been no altercation on the front doorstep. "And now, my good fellow," said Mr Lamont wagging his clasped hands up and down, "you're from Legg's Lane?"

"The Doctor sends——"

Mr Lamont's hands parted in a flash. "Hush," he glanced over his shoulder as he clasped James's arm. "Legg's Lane, Legg's Lane, that's all ye need say. You're not the ordinary messenger from there."

"I'm not an ordinary messenger, sir," said James freeing himself.

"None of our friend's messengers are ordinary," said Mr Lamont with a cackle. The amusement went from his voice. "You're not before your time. I've orders hanging for this delivery." He fingered the cloth. "How much have ye here?"

James calculated rapidly. "A little over thirty-three yards——"

"Confound it, it was to be near the fifty!"

"—at thirteen pence."

Mr Lamont looked up sharply. "I'll name the price, young fellow. Eleven pence."

"Thirteen pence."

"Eleven pence, I tell ye. That was the agreed price."

A novel excitement filled James, a sharp lust to outface the linen draper. He took the horse's bridle. "I can go back to the Hall and hold out for *fourteen* pence, and get it." He pressed the head of the horse round until its hooves scraped on the cobbles.

"Your master will hear of this!" blustered Mr Lamont.

James led his horse a few paces towards the gateway. Mr Lamont stared after him sullenly. "Wait. Throw off the cloth. I'll get ye the money."

"Nothing was said about giving me money——"

"You'll take it," said Mr Lamont hurriedly. "I want no credit in Legg's Lane."

Seated at the table the Doctor listened in silence to James's narrative. When it was finished he stirred the coins with the shank of his pipe. "And this is the result? Very commendable."

His manner displeased the young man. "Well," he said, "have I done aught wrong?"

"Yes," said the Doctor, "I sent you to collect one price on the cloth and you sold it for another."

"At a profit!"

"You won a petty skirmish for yourself and made me the loser in the long run. I knew what prices were being offered in the Linen Hall. I warned you of the class of man you would meet in Mr Lamont. Now, instead of leaving him plaiting his hands over a bargain, you've won me a few measly pence and his grudge."

"Then he too, is of *use* to you!"

The small man puckered his mouth and rocked sideways in his chair. "Of use," he agreed at last.

"I knew nothing of this."

"You acted like a man of spirit. Where profit is concerned, indifference is a cardinal sin." He watched the young man through half-closed eyes. "And yet . . . and yet there are one or two things you should understand. Trading is an art insofar as one should avoid confusing the conclusion with the human imperfections of those taking part. Your distaste for Mr Lamont led you into screwing him and disrupting, for the moment, a mercantile association that has been lengthy, profitable, and on occasion, honest."

"It would pain me to think that I had put you in a bad light to Mr Lamont."

"Never!" cried the Doctor. "It's an ill-spent day for Spifford Lamont if he hasn't cheated some poor dog of a weaver. Now he's been beaten at his own game he'll mend like sour ale in summer." The Doctor waved his hand. "But I'll set about repairing matters. Meantime, urbanity, my boy, firmness when necessary, but urbanity, yes."

It was difficult not to be affected by the Doctor's ample good will. "I must admit," said James shuffling a little, "to a certain excitement . . ."

"But of course! Ah," said the Doctor shaking his head, "it's a thousand pities your future lies along another road. What you and I could do . . . Fearon and McCoubrey, honest lads, but fit only for shoving pieces of ginger up the arseholes of tired nags on a fair-day. And good Aeneas, here," the Doctor turned his malicious grin on Gordon, "couldn't drive a bargain to save his life. One whimper from that spade-faced fellow you so stoutly threw down and Aeneas would be off his horse, begging him, for the Lord's sake, to take the cloth at threepence, at tuppence, a yard. He's cursed with an angelic inability to benefit from the needs of his fellows."

Mr Gordon cocked one leg on the other and smiled gently at this honeyed scolding. The Doctor rose and pushed back his chair. He was suddenly grave and distant. "The important thing, Gault, is that you've been able to venture into the streets with safety. We must still move with care."

"Can I travel home?" asked James.

"No. I'll tell you when that's possible."

VI

IN THE NEXT few days James was to be seen more often in the lower apartments of the Doctor's establishment. He ventured frequently along Legg's Lane and made some small purchases at the stalls on the quays. But he refused to go out after nightfall, afraid of the dark, wolfish faces of the men and women who watched him from the doorways of the lane.

"You have nothing to fear from them," said the Doctor. "I know them all from here to the High Street. They are, so to say, my retainers. They have been told you belong to this household. On the darkest night you can pass among them without candle or cudgel." With as good a grace as he could muster he thanked the dwarfed man. That rabble and I have something in common, he thought wryly; we live under this man's patronage.

More often now the thought took wing in his head that there was no need to return to his studies in Glasgow. He thrust it away but never quite out of his awareness. Of course he must feel a twinge of shame when he thought of his mentor, Dr Loudan, the aged minister of Ravara, and the self-denial and hopes of his parents. As for Kate . . . well, Kate, he felt, would not care so much. The knowledge that he had been spared when so many had died or been driven out, added to the torment of his prayers. But deep within him a conviction had been shaken that he had thought immutable. This new life, he told himself sadly, with its promise of money-making, the excitements of bargaining, would not be a quarter so seductive if I were still held fast in my calling.

"I want to go to church next Sabbath," he said to the Doctor.

"And what do you hope to find there?"

"An opportunity to give thanks," said James with a note of reproof, "for I have been taught to believe, and do so believe, that the fear of God is the beginning of wisdom."

The doctor raised his fingers in ribald blessing. "And fear is the beginning of God."

"May I go?"

"I hear the Presbyterian divines are busy cleansing their republican stables. At whose feet do you propose to sit?"

"I'm going to hear Mr McCashon at Donegall Street Meeting House."

"I know of the reverend gent. Once a pillar of fire in the drawing-rooms of United Ireland, now a cloud of smoke in his own pulpit. A week ago he broke wind to say that no father need hope to receive respect or obedience from a rebel or an atheist. Words of compassion, no less, for the families of such as the late Henry Joy McCracken, wouldn't ye say?" The little man leaned forward, his yellow teeth showing in a grin. "D'ye understand? If this Javelin of the Lord spots you he'll denounce you from the pulpit."

"He has never laid eyes on me, nor has anyone in his congregation."

The church was filling rapidly. As he walked swiftly down the aisle he was conscious of handsome bonnets, fur tippets, lace discreetly scented, solid broadcloth, fine polished leather. Entering a pew half-concealed by a pillar he sat down, placed his hat under the seat, bowed his head, then composed himself to await the uprising of the minister in his pulpit. Often, as he had lain under the slates in Legg's Lane, he had dreamt of this moment when he again worshipped among his fellows. He was filled with a sudden and quiet joy. Almost from the moment he had entered the church the fear and doubt that had so distracted him had been lifted from him. He doubted the reality of his duty no longer and felt only remorse that he had ever done so. But he had stood on the edge of the tempter's snare. He scanned the crowded pews then closed his eyes: *O come, let us worship and bow down: let us kneel before the Lord our Maker . . . harden not your heart as in the day of temptation in the wilderness. And, O Lord, turn the heart of that wayward man who sheltered me when I was in danger . . .*

The Reverend Mr McCashon was a sad disappointment; a cloud of smoke with a sulphurous tang. It wasn't that he cut a poor figure in the pulpit. He was pale of face but large of body, and his voice rang and rattled in every corner of his church. But to James in his present mood, what Mr McCashon had chosen to say that morning was futile and distracting.

". . . Infidelity lifted her voice in the street, she called in the high places; she thought to dethrone the Omnipotent. Do you believe it no more than a paradox, brethren, that those who trumpeted abroad their infatuation with Catholic Emancipation learnt their notes from that country, France, where religion in any form was thrown down by an infidel phalanx?"

Was it too much to hope, cried James inwardly, that I might get one word of encouragement, of assurance, in this morning's service?

Mr McCashon leaned from his pulpit. "If there are any of you in this House of God who still hanker after the blessings of Revolutionary Democracy, have you not reason to lament that the late conspirators were not able to lay their schemes better? Then you, too, might have been emancipated; your country would have been emancipated from its wealth, your wives and daughters emancipated from everything that makes womankind revered, and you yourself, as a last blessing, would have been emancipated from daily existence . . ."

James shifted wearily, but a disturbing thought had entered his mind. The minister seemed confident of his listeners' sympathy. James glanced at the sober and attentive faces around him. Not a demonstrative people, these fellow-worshippers of his, but he could detect no flicker of disapproval with the words from the pulpit. Surely McCashon didn't lay it on them in this manner every Sunday morning? Why then this morning? Was there word again of rebellion? Had there been some singular enormity reported in last week's foreign packets? Busy with his petty transactions, talking to no one outside the Doctor's den, perhaps he had slipped complaisantly into feeling (for he had thought little on it) that with the defeat of the United Irishmen, sedition had been finally routed and silenced. The Doctor had often enough advised caution but it had taken the turncoat Mr McCashon to inadvertently thrust that warning home. It was plain that the men and women in the pews needed no such warning. The neat bonnets and wigs wagged to the closing psalm:

Now Israel
May say, and that truly,
If that the Lord
Had not our cause maintained,
If that the Lord
Had not our right sustained,
When cruel men
Who us desired to slay,
Rose up in wrath
To make of us their prey.

Outside, he picked his way among the departing worshippers, not walking too hurriedly, not lingering to be stopped in conversation. It was a fine morning and he went round by the High Street. St George's episcopal church was emptying and he saw, coming towards him, the elderly man who had spoken civilly outside the Linen Hall. With the merchant was a tall dignified woman, a schoolboy, and a girl some years older, whose grace of movement imprinted itself on James's attention. A carriage drew up beside the family. As the others paused to allow the lady to enter they considered the young man approaching. The girl's eyes passed over him, aloof, indifferent. The merchant's glance met James's, neither in greeting nor rebuff, but, as James decided later, in acknowledgment. Rather than chance being seen by them turning towards Legg's Lane he sauntered further along the quays.

An hour or so after his return from church the concern raised by Mr McCashon's sermon died somewhat in James's mind. He preferred to recall his re-affirmation as a servant of the Gospel. The next best thing to following the right path was to return to it.

"And what," said the Doctor as they sat at the dinner table, "did you learn at the feet of Reverend Reversible?"

"Much, Doctor," said James with a quiet smile.

"What of the hell fires waiting for rebels and suchlike scum?"

"I came away unscathed."

"Did ye come away unrecognised?"

"How could it be otherwise? I've only been in Belfast twice before—as a child with my father to the market. Indeed," added James, striving to keep anxiety from his voice, "there seems no reason now why I shouldn't travel to see my parents."

With a wetted forefinger the Doctor picked up a fragment of a nut from the wreckage of shells on his plate. "What d'ye think, Aeneas?"

"We need to know more about the temper of Mr Gault's neighbours," said Mr Gordon.

"You're right, as ever, Aeneas," said the Doctor approvingly.

"And what does that mean?" asked James.

"It means," said the small man, "that we want knowledge of those who took no hand in the turn-out but were aware of your presence in the neighbourhood at the time. Were there any such?"

James considered. "I spoke to a neighbour, Hugh Purdie, on the night I escaped."

"The same interesting fellow whose father . . . restrained him?"

"Yes. You have an enviable memory, sir."

The Doctor stroked the velvet of his sleeve. "Then we must avoid the Purdie household on our journey."

"Not so. I'm betrothed to Kate Purdie, the daughter of the house."

There was silence. James looked up to see malevolence and jealousy in the other's eyes. Angrily he was about to demand an explanation when the Doctor lowered his gaze.

"You have good surety for young Purdie's discretion," said the Doctor softly. "Nevertheless you must warn this youth of your possible reappearance. You will write him a letter which Fearon will deliver to your father, asking him to hand it, in turn, to Hugh Purdie. Finally, you will not skulk back as a fugitive, but ride there in broad daylight, accoutred as a man engaged in some profitable business."

"If that's so," said James smiling, "I'm also assured of old Purdie's welcome. He's warm towards such men."

An answering geniality returned to the Doctor's voice. "Then we'll descend on them like rich merchants riding from the East."

"*We* . . ." echoed James, puzzled.

"It's my intention to accompany you. Surely you won't begrudge me your parents' greetings?"

Ignoring the hint of mockery, James laid his hand on the other's shoulder. "You'll have their greetings and blessing, my dear Doctor."

*

The task of telling his sister of James Gault's imminent return was much less troublesome to Hugh Purdie than of carrying out the strict instructions of the letter and keeping the same news from his father. Not since that June dawning after the fugitive's flight had brother and sister spoken of him. To Hugh this was a relief, for as the wordless months passed he grew more certain that Gault was dead.

Now he was to learn to his surprise that such a thought had never been in Kate's head. Her silence had been that of patience. "You were sure he was safe all this time?"

"If ever I thought long, I put it down to the slow sailing of the Ameriky boat. But how did he ever get back to Ireland?"

"To learn that, we'll have to wait. But remember, ne'er a whisper to our father."

A score of times after breakfast, Robert Gault hurried down to the boretree bush at the end of his farm lane and crouched there, scanning the track. At the approach of a neighbour he retreated again to the house. About noon his patience was rewarded. In the distance he saw a solitary horseman, a stranger, on the road. The traveller was heavily cloaked and the butt of a musket protruded from his skirts. Robert recognised with joy the messenger who had brought the letter and raised his hand in salute, but the rider looked down on him in silence and rode on to disappear in the shadows of Burke's Woods. As the old man turned away in distress he saw across the turf bog and flat fields two riders pressing briskly towards him. He threw his arms in the air. This time there was no mistaking the taller of the two horsemen. Minutes later father and son were clasped in each other's arms. "And this," said James disengaging himself and indicating the observant figure on horseback, "is my friend, Doctor Bannon."

The tall, tattered old man stepped forward, hand outstretched. As he felt the Doctor's rings under his leathery fingers he faltered a little. "If I've the right way o't," he said, "you're the gentleman that saved my son's life."

Tenderly the Doctor disengaged his hand. "We seem to be of one mind, Mr Gault, that it was worth saving. Give me your reins and cloak, Gault, and go the two of you ahead."

Obediently, James handed up the reins, and stripping off his cloak, revealed that above his shining black hessians he wore a suit of fine green cloth and a waistcoat in striped tabinet. His father stopped to examine him from head to foot. They heard the laughter in the Doctor's voice. "Is he not quite the tippy, Mr Gault?"

James grasped his father's arm and hurried him forward, the Doctor coming after with the horses. At a turn of the lane James had his first glimpse of his old home. He paused. "Uncle Sam has built himself a new cobbler's shop?"

"No, no, son, you've been away over long——"

"Nonsense, father," said James laughing. "I've spent too many days in that dark wonderful hole watching him sew boots and mend harness not to know every smell and wrinkle of it."

"Aye, well, mebbe it's changed a bit——"

A streak of new thatch on the cottage caught the young man's eye. His laughter died. "What was it, father?"

"They tried to burn us out, son."

"Who, father?"

"The yeos, the Orange yeos. They came here the day after Ballynahinch."

"My mother?"

"I got a whiff o' them coming and me and your mother lay hid in the young corn till they rode off. They put a flame tae Sam's shop and tae the thatch."

"And Sam?"

"Sam was in his shop saving a neighbour's boots, when they put a match tae it. But he broke out through the wee winda and away over the bog towards Burke's Woods."

"Did the curs hunt him?"

His father laughed. "Did ye ever know a man that could catch Sam when he had his running legs on? Heth, he was in the trees before they could cock a musket at him!"

"And what of the fire?"

"Your mother and me doused it before it ate too far. Jamie, say nothing tae her. It's all over, nobody's hurted."

At the threshold of the cottage Jeannie Gault took her son in her arms. "Look up, mother," said James after a moment, "and see the man who saved my life." But over her son's shoulder she had been examining the Doctor as he rode in. "I see him," she said in a low voice. "The Lord be guid to him, but he's as ill-favoured as the Deil."

"For all that," said James smiling, "bid him welcome. Where's my Uncle Sam?"

A younger, more unkempt version of Robert appeared in the doorway, silently pressed James's hand and hurried forward to hold the horse's bridle as the Doctor climbed down. As he led the animals away, Robert ushered the travellers into the wide earth-floored kitchen and helped the Doctor off with his cloak. "Sit ye down, men." James ran his hand over the rope-bottomed chair under him, recalling every knot and roughness, and bowed his head in thankfulness that he sat again in it. Sam came in and stood in silence behind his brother's chair. The Doctor ran his eye over the Gaults. He turned to James. "You're not a demonstrative family," he said with a smile half-mocking, half-incredulous.

"We are not."

"As I waited for ye at the lane-head," said Robert, "your serving-man rode past wi' a gun under his oxter and ne'er a word. I trust he wasna feart o' trouble ahead?"

" 'Serving-man'?" repeated James. "What serving-man—Fearon?"

"Yes. I regret if he appeared uncivil, Mr Gault."

"Ah, 'twas nothing," said Robert, shifting in his chair. "Couldn't he come in wi' ye for a sup o' something warm?"

"It's a kindly thought," said the Doctor graciously, "but he's been furnished with something under his other oxter to keep him warm."

The brothers relapsed into a polite silence. But James could see the misgiving in his mother's eyes. What sort of doctor was this who rode about in broad daylight surrounded by armed men? As her gaze travelled from the elegance of the Doctor's dress to the quality of her son's clothes, her face darkened. "You're over well clad, Jamie, for a student of the ministry," she said.

Before James could speak the Doctor nipped in. "For

some time now, ma'am, your son has been far removed from the study of books. You should understand," and his look took in the three older Gaults, "that for the past half-year and more, he has lain concealed while the military and their spies searched for him. Piece by piece we have created another identity for him, another life. We think we've succeeded." He leaned forward, his ugly visage forbidding in the flickering light from the hearth. "But the bloodhounds are still about. There can be no hope of concealment again. The next time it'll be either the Ameriky ship or the noose for him." He nodded darkly at Sam and Robert as they hung on his words, then, leaning back in his chair, granted them a smile both reassuring and complacent.

But Jeannie Gault gave her attention to her son. James shrugged. "What more can I add? As for the clothes, mother, they're a disguise. I play-act as a man of business, even to the feathers. When I'll be free of that is in the hands of Providence."

"And why should the gentleman put himself about for you at all, Jamie?"

The Doctor waved his hand. "Age brings timidity, miscalled prudence, Mrs Gault, but I still admire a young man of spirit and principle——"

"In a word," said James irked at the slant of mockery in his companion's voice, "the Doctor's sympathies were with those of us who . . . you understand?"

"Aye, rightly," said Robert Gault, laying a restraining hand on that of his wife's, "and we thank him from the bottom of our hearts!"

"Say no more," said the Doctor rising. "If Mr Sam will accompany us, let's take a walk and see what's to be seen."

"Troth," cried Robert, jumping up with pleasure, "there's little enough, but you're surely welcome. Up wi' ye, Sam."

Mrs Gault watched them troop out through the low doorway and past the small window. "That man seems gey fond o' ye, Jamie."

Her son folded his arms and smiled at her. " 'Fond' is not the word I'd put on the Doctor, myself. But yes, he's been good to me."

She dragged her chair closer over the rough floor. "He wants to make ye one of his own," she whispered.

James laughed. "You think he's Satan, mother?"

"He's of the same ilk."

"They say the only thing people fear in the Devil is that he'll keep his word. I grant ye the Doctor keeps his. He saved my life."

"I'm feart 'tis for his own ends." She ran her worn fingers over the smooth material of his coat. "You're no going to return to the college, are ye, Jamie?"

"Why should you say that?" He caught the accusing hand on his breast. "Would you have been happier if I had crawled back through the ditches in rags?"

She looked at him steadily. "Yes, son, I would."

He spread his hand helplessly on the lapel of his coat. "Because of this?"

"Ah, it isnae just the fine clothes. They're but the outward sign that you're sairly changed inwardly since you left your father's house."

"In what way?"

"It's on your face and in your heart. Ye didnae lightly take it on yourself to give your life to the preaching of God's Word. Your father and me didnae lightly take it on ourselves to see you through your schooling for't." Her thin arm in its drab sleeve drew a circle round the room. "It was here you told Dr Loudan and me that ye had the call to be a minister, yourself."

"Mother, you're judging me without knowing everything. My life *was* in danger. Whatever his reasons, the Doctor sheltered me. It's only of late I could leave my hiding place and only now that I could come to see you."

"If your heart had been in God ye would have been on the next boat for Glasgow, not tripping down here in fine clothes."

How could he have forgotten the obdurate nature of this woman who had borne him? "You would rather I had done that?" he muttered.

She brushed his query aside. "I'm not going down on my knees tae ye. But I know now that I'll never see ye mount the steps of a pulpit."

He could find neither the strength nor the will to protest. All the fine resolutions that he had kept warm melted in the disappointment and bitterness of her words. She spoke the truth. "I've a life to lead, mother."

"May ye find happiness in it." Her voice was cold and flat. "And what of Kate Purdie? Are ye still for marrying her?"

"If she'll have me."

"It's unlikely that one o' that breed will find fault with ye now."

He kept silent. After a moment he heard her slow dragging footsteps as she turned away. "You'll be hungered after your journey. I'll get ye a meal." The shadow of the Doctor passed across the window. The little man stepped lightly into the room and dipping deep in the skirts of his coat, proffered a package to Mrs Gault. "Tea, ma'am. Fine bohea. You might kindly brew us a cup." She weighed the fine luxury in her hand, as if she would refuse it, then thanked him and lowered the kettle to the flames.

At the table the Doctor advanced himself further in the esteem of the Gault brothers. He told stories from his past and James was torn between apprehension and a reluctant gratitude as he watched him struggle to mute the savagery of his exploits and expressions. When the meal was ended James took his father aside and placed five guineas in his hand. The old man's thanks were interrupted by the Doctor. "Will it not be uncommon for you to take such a large gold piece to the rent-collector or into the market?"

"True," said Robert somewhat crestfallen. "We're not over throng wi' such goods."

"Change them into silver, then." He dug again into his

capacious pockets. "I can break at least three of your guineas for you."

As Robert Gault watched his son match the value of the gold with silver, he exclaimed, "How d'ye think o' these things, Doctor? I declare you've the clever head on ye!"

"The Doctor," said James piqued, "is well-versed in these things."

"To our mutual advantage, I think," said the Doctor returning the other's dry smile.

James's fingers trembled on the pillar of silver. I must free myself of this man. He can't demand my gratitude for ever. With a pricking of conscience he glanced at his mother. She's right. This man, indeed, sees me as one of his own. The counting finished, he pushed the silver towards his father. "Now," he said, "we have another errand."

"To the Purdies'?" his mother inquired.

"Yes."

"Ye may leave early then, before the light goes," said Sam Gault. "Sim's place is no that easy tae reach these days."

"I think I can find my way to the Purdies', uncle," said James laughing. "I beat a path from our house to theirs in the old days."

"Aye, well, you'll find your track's vanished under the spade. Since the fighting at Ballynahinch, landless and hungered men and their weemin and childer have been wandering the countryside. Sim, as was always his way, makes use o' such poor souls. He tosses them a rood here and half-a-rood there, and has them labouring for him like any Czar o' Roossia."

"Ha!" cried the Doctor, amused. "Tenants-at-will?"

"Aye," said Robert, "at Sim's will. They're living round his doorstep like the Children o' Israel in Egypt, as near slaves as this land has seen for many a day."

James stirred fretfully under this criticism of Kate's father. "We'll find our way there. Goodbye, mother. Now that I'm free to move again, I'll be back."

At the head of the lane the travellers parted from Robert

and Sam Gault. As they turned on to the twilit track that undulated among the alders and bracken of the peat-bog the distant drum of hooves came from Burke's Woods.

"Fearon?"

"Very likely."

James drew his cloak closer against the dank November mist. "Journeying to my own home, this surveilliance is comic." They rode for a time in silence, then James added, "I understand, of course, that this concern is on your own behalf, not mine."

"You sang a different tune before your family," said the Doctor spitefully. "But Fearon, and McCoubrey ahead of us, will be glad of your opinion."

James reined to a standstill. "D'ye mean they've been following me wherever I go?"

"To meeting-house and market."

"Let it cease!" cried the other angrily. "People must have seen these shadows and drawn their own conclusions. I'll not have this notoriety thrust on me. If I've enemies . . ." his voice trailed off in the darkness as he urged his horse forward.

The Doctor again drew alongside him. "Don't misunderstand me," said James. "I'm grateful for what you have done. But it's meaningless to win me my liberty and then so hem it in with . . . precautions that it becomes an intolerable burden and ends in loading me with suspicion."

The Doctor's hat was drawn low on his brow but James could see the glitter of his eyes. "Save your wind, honest young burgher. It shall be as you say. D'ye know where we are? Where is the house of this fellow, Purdie?"

They stopped. A luminous mist was lifting from the peat banks to meet the dusk. James was puzzled. Here, at this clump of boretree, a path should leave the road and run across the peaty meadows to Sim Purdie's house. This was his familiar journey, the track that he had jocularly claimed as his own. But it had vanished as his uncle had said. Now there was only tumbled soil, still streaked with potato haulms. He urged his horse towards it. Then, a few feet away, he saw a light where there should have been none. It glowed suddenly as if a door had been opened. It had the diffused glow of a fire rather than the sharpness of a lantern flame. "And where would you be going?" a voice demanded from the gloom.

Peering over his horse's neck, James saw that a rude shelter of turf and branches had been built to the right of the track. A man, standing at the entrance, dropped a tarpaulin behind him, cutting off the glimpse of the fire and the staring faces of two or three children gathered around it. He came close and they saw that he was a sturdy fellow, in tattered shirt and waistcoat, his breeches burst at the kneebands above his soiled and naked legs. He stared up at the two horsemen morosely.

"We're going to Mr Sim Purdie's by the moss path."

"There's no path here."

"There was."

"That's as may be—there's none now."

There was a refinement in the man's voice that went ill with his appearance and at the same time gave an edge to his stubbornness. It nettled James. He leaned forward in his saddle. "You've your crop lifted and this was a right-o'-way in the old days."

"Those days are past." As James urged his horse forward the man sprang to seize the bridle. "Before ye come champing through my patch raise yourself in your stirrups." He waved his arm into the gathering darkness. "Every spark o' light you see between here and Purdie's belongs to a man like me, maybe two or three men. You may pass me, but ye won't pass *them*, all of them. If you persist in trampling over our bits o' land we'll tumble you, men and horses, into a peat hole."

The Doctor tapped James on the shoulder. "Our friend here seems to have the best of it. Let us go by the road."

For a time James rode beside the Doctor in peevish silence. Then he said, "You were remarkably peaceable with that fellow. I'd have thought you would have ridden over him."

The Doctor laughed sharply. "Hell and all its angels preserve me from the peasant proprietor! You're a dull dog at times, Gault. I don't ride over the dispossessed. Have a look at *that*." On every perch of ground to the left of the road a crazy shelter had been raised. The voices of men, women and children came to them through the aqueous light. "Was it always like this?"

"It was not. Purdie himself laboured this ground." James looked again at the dim shapes gathering into their hovels for the night. "To me they look more like the possessors than the dispossessed."

They rode past the last of the squatters' shelters. The house they sought was before them. James reined in. "This is Purdie's house. It's imperative that we appear to him as two men of commerce who have no differences. I mean by that, Doctor, less edge to your tongue."

The Doctor turned a bland face. "But, of course, James. I wasn't aware of any differences. But if they're there, let us by all means compose them. Lead on."

As their horses' hooves rattled on the cobbled close, the door flew open, as if someone had been standing with his hand at the latch. James recognised the figure of Hugh in the doorway, and as he dismounted, the young man hurried towards him. "Welcome, James!" he cried, and then his young brother, Andrew, came running after, to lead the horses away.

Kate and her father were in the big, paved kitchen. As he approached the girl James was surprised and stung at the calmness of her expression. Even though she was under her father's eye, he had expected at least some betraying glimpse of joy or relief. She took his hand. "You're welcome, James."

Crestfallen, he turned to find quite a different expression on her father's face. Sim, with that queer lift of his shoulders, was examining him with a look half-amused, half-sly.

"You're in good health, Sim?"

"Thanks be to the Good Man," with a gesture of acknowledgment towards the rafters.

"And your wife?"

"As well as can be hoped."

Warmed again by the awareness that Kate's eyes had never left him, James turned to his fellow-traveller. "This is Doctor Bannon, an acquaintance of mine from Belfast." And you're well met, my men, he thought, as the Doctor bowed to their host. The stunted little man acknowledged the presence of the younger Purdie, and James, wary, thought that the sharp scrutiny dwelt for a moment longer on Kate than on her brothers.

"Andra," bade the father, "bring forr'ad chairs, and Kate, lower the kettle."

The Doctor accepted the chair but raised a demurring hand. "We can't stay long, so, if you please," and he addressed Kate, "no food. We've already fed well. I'm sure Mr Gault could stay longer. But for myself . . . an old man . . . the night air." He laid his hand on his breast. His rings, caught in the firelight, sparkled before the bemused eyes of the Purdies. Cautiously Sim examined his visitors. He raised his eyes from James's fine leather boots. "I never thought to see ye . . . so well-found, James. We thought for a time," he added, rubbing his brow, "that something ill had befallen ye."

"Young men of spirit, Mr Purdie," chuckled the Doctor. "Young men of spirit. Mr Gault *had* for a time the illusion that the Goddess of Liberty could be raised to a canter." His wide, creased smile oozed tolerance. "We older and wiser heads know better, eh? Fortunately circumstances saved him from putting it to the test. Just as revolutionaries do not wait for the advent of benevolent government, so Learning does not kick her heels waiting on Revolution. Mr Gault returned to his studies some time before the recent days of bloodshed and rapine."

"To the college at Glesca?" asked Sim, endeavouring to keep incredulity from his voice.

"He was busy at his books in that venerable institution from the last days of the month of May," returned the Doctor levelly. "Then he took on a bit of clerking for me."

Even in his most charitable moments James had little respect for Sim Purdie, but now he was afraid to meet the scrutiny of the man on the other side of the hearth. Above all he avoided the clear gaze of Kate and her brothers.

"Aye, so," breathed Sim assenting to a great deal. His face was hidden as he stroked his bald brow. "I think I remember hearing something o' the sort from his feyther."

"Very likely," said the Doctor briskly. "Then, some weeks ago——"

Hugh Purdie made a violent step forward. His lips quivered as he faced the Doctor. "D'ye call those animals in Westminster and Dublin a 'benevolent government'?"

Sim's head jerked up in angry alarm. "Wheesht, ye clown!" he screamed, thumping the arms of his chair. Slowly the Doctor turned his heavy, seamed face on the youth. "I but employ their own description, young man. As I was saying, Mr Gault undertook some maritime work for me before returning to this country. Since then he has been lodging with me——"

"And why couldn't he come to his own home?" demanded Kate. "Why did he stop with you?"

"For his own advantage and profit, ma'am," answered the Doctor gently. He waved his hand. "Mr Gault can answer these questions to your satisfaction at a more convenient hour. Mr Purdie, we could see little in the darkness, but your land seems to be carrying its fair load and more of working bodies?"

Sim made a gesture of one under much duress. "They came wandering on the roads after the killings at Ballynahinch. Poor homeless souls, some neighbours, most strangers. What could I do, y'honour, but give them a handsbreadth o' land to rest their bones on?" At the dresser Hugh filled a pannikin from the water crock with unnecessary noise.

"Your behaviour is to be warmly commended, Mr Purdie."

"That's close tae my own opinion, sir. But I wish ye heard the reviling thrown at me, and from those not strangers tae m'own hearth."

The Doctor shrugged. "Did you expect such an action to be understood?" Then, with genuine curiosity, he added, "But surely June wasn't the best month for a pack of vagrants to settle on a man's land?"

"Ah, we made room for some by cutting a bit o' early grass, some we put on ley, but the bulk went ontae the bog, where they had, like it or lave it, to do a bit o' draining if they werena tae founder in peat holes."

"And those who fell on good ground have done a bit of tilling for you? Admirable, admirable!" and the Doctor grinned widely. "But how are they fed?"

Sim kneaded his brow vigorously. "Some managed to bring a pickle o' money wi' them. I set up a store at the house gable—meal, potatoes, a few herring. But now their money's run out and stuff's too dear. I dunno what's to become of them and I'm loath to lose their labour on the land——"

"Are they an industrious lot?"

"They would be industrious," said Sim with a cautious glance at his questioner, "if they had aught to induster on."

"Weaving?"

"Where their huts are fit for shelter I've put in looms and supplied the yarn. But that can only tie down a dozen or so o' them——"

"The answer, Mr Purdie, is cheap food. In Lisburn, where the weavers were starving, the Quakers brought in a shipload of maize. They didn't take too kindly to it at the first, for it's gritty to the mouth. But your neighbours will live to bless you when the potatoes and fish are hard to come by."

"And where would the likes o' me get that? A shipload?" Sim chuckled mirthlessly. "Heth, that would take a mint o' money!"

The black eyes quizzed Purdie. "I could let you have a

waggonload before the week's out. Mr Gault and I have a further shipment on order from a business acquaintance of ours, who recently crossed to Philadelphia."

James barely acknowledged this remarkable piece of information. It was a chance to speak to Kate. They eyed each other and what they saw reassured them both. He took her hand, shielding the gesture with his body. "You look well, lass." She returned the warm pressure of his clasp then stepped back. "And you're out of all knowing."

"It's the plumage of disguise. Six months is a long time, Kate."

"It is," said the girl, "when you're waiting news. At first I thought you had crossed the ocean. Now I hear that you've been in the keeping of this wee knurr o' a man. Who is he, James?"

Their voices were low but Hugh must have sensed his sister's query. He left his post behind Sim's chair and came towards them. The Doctor rose alertly. "I see you have a loom, Mr Purdie. Can we have a look at what's on it?"

"For sure. But it's nothing out o' the ord'nar."

Hugh waited until his father and the Doctor were out of hearing. "This is a strange class o' man you've joined yourself to, James."

"I don't expect Kate and you to take warmly to him."

"I won't cross ye on that," said Kate with a glance over her shoulder. "The sight o' him puts a shiver down my back."

"You left here a rebel on the run, James, and come back with a man who has a good word for the government," said Hugh with a note of reproach.

Manfully James stifled his irritation. "I'm alive today, thanks to the Doctor. Believe me, he's not at all what he seems."

Sim had been watching them. "Kate," he called, "it's a hard night. We'd be the better o' a toothful o' whiskey. Get it, girl."

Hugh grunted. "Your Doctor must be out of the ordinary

when my father is moved to pour out the liquor. James, are ye free to marry my sister? I mean are ye free from being hunted?"

"Yes, unless some enemy—or a contentious friend—opens his mouth too wide." He watched Kate come from the lower room carrying the whiskey jar. "These squatters—we tried to come by the old path over the bog, but one of them, a surly fellow, blocked our way."

"Charlie Campbell, I warrant. At one time a decent tallow-chandler, now scraping a living from a potato-patch."

"But your father has given them shelter and protection."

"Protection?" Hugh smiled briefly. "Yes, his word with Mr Burke, and more important, the Orange magistrates, has kept the yeos from harassing them. But they walk about dragging sorrow at their heels."

"What do you mean by that?"

"My father's set them working like serfs. There's hardly the breadth of a man's foot between their holdings. The women and the childer are carting in dung and seaweed by the basket to put *heart* in *his* soil. At night they herd into their sties to feed on potatoes half-cooked so that they're slower to chew and blue milk that wouldn't colour a wall if you threw it against it."

"And do they all feel like this man Campbell?"

"Every sunset sees another o' his opinion."

"Well, why doesn't your father get rid of them? Sure they've no fixity of tenure?"

Hugh looked at the other with scorn. "Don't ye see, man, he'll bear with them till they've broken up his land? Then, when they've manured his fields like a herd o' swine, he'll drive them off like a herd o' swine. Or so he thinks. Men like Charlie Campbell may be ill to drive."

"What of your family?"

"Andrew backs my father in all, Kate is of the same mind, but she's only a woman."

"You fret overmuch, Hugh. Campbell and his like have to live somewhere. A passage overseas is hard to come by,

I can tell you. Which reminds me," he put his hand in his pocket and brought out a small leather bag. "The money you so kindly lent me."

Purdie took it with scarce a glance. "I can't bear this place much longer, James. Can ye get me work in the town?"

"What makes you think I've any influence in the town? Or that I'm more than a bird of passage there?"

The youth held up the purse. "You're too well-dressed to be the poor scholar any more," he said dryly. "You've the look of a man who'll prosper. You won't forget me?"

"We'll see what your opinion is in the future," said James curtly.

Kate approached him with a glass of whiskey. "Have you learnt to take this?"

James laughed. "No, I survived without it, Kate."

The girl held out the glass to her brother. "Give my mother a lip o't, Hugh. She wants to know who the strangers are. Will you light my father and that man down to her?"

Obediently, Hugh took a lamp from the dresser and led the two men away. Kate watched until they were out of hearing. "James, don't encourage him to leave home."

"I promised him nothing." He looked at her with some curiosity. "Both of you seem determined that I'm settled in Belfast."

"Are you going back to the college?"

"No, I'm not. Would it make you unhappy if I gave up the idea of the ministry and went into the buying and selling?"

"We would live in a house in the town?"

"Eh? Yes . . . yes, that would be the way of it."

There was the light of joy in her eyes as she looked at him. Yet, as he kissed her he couldn't suppress the thought that she had determined already that Hugh wasn't to follow them. Ah, well, a farseeing wife would be no disadvantage in the future . . . At the sound of a step on the threshold of the lower room they drew apart. Sim crooked a finger at the young man. "She asks would ye step down for a wheen o' minutes, James."

In his boyhood James had seen little of Kirsty Purdie. She was usually abed when he came to the house on an errand. And when she was seated in her high chair in the kitchen he would look at her in awe, as the woman over whom Death was still swithering, to take or leave. As she lay in her pillows he saw that the talk had brought a flush to her broad yellow cheeks. In the voice, usually querulous, there was a note of happiness that moved him to compassion. Timidly she advanced her plump soft hand over the quilt. It dawned on him that she expected his benediction. Aware of the Doctor standing across from him he touched the swollen fingers and murmured a few words of comfort.

"Thank ye, Jamie, thank ye," said Sim in the gratified voice of one who can call on professional services, gratis.

Returning to the kitchen the Doctor declined to be seated again. For the time being James had said all he needed to say to Kate. It was with a light heart that he took the road beside his protector and even the distant clack of horses' hooves, starting behind them, failed to dispel his mood.

He reined up. "Call Fearon to ride with us."

"No," said the Doctor. "Learn to keep your servants in their place."

"I'll never fathom you," sighed James not unpleased at the inference. "That man would give his life for you."

The cloaked figure grunted. "He owes his life to me. Tell me, Gault, are you satisfied with your excursions?"

"Aye, well satisfied. To see my parents . . ."

"Is that all?"

Kate . . . that was what he was speiring after. James kept a malicious silence as they rode through the darkness. Then, "The Purdies? I have one fear. I know the length of Sim's tongue. Tomorrow, everybody will know that I've been in the district again."

"Don't concern yourself about Sim Purdie."

"And why not?"

"He holds orders from me—from us, for his harvest of grain and potatoes—and linen, if he can do better than was on his loom tonight—at prices that will show good at the time of delivery." The dwarfed man gave a snirt of laughter. "And I've prescribed for Madam Purdie's health . . ."

James's interest was caught. "Are you fit to advise on such matters?"

"I wouldn't put up my brass as a chirurgeon. But I could have made my mark as a chiromancer. If she put those flabby fingers to a day's work she would be a healthier woman. Have no fear of her husband. It'll pay him to keep what he knows to himself. He has a nice flexibility in his principles." The Doctor tightened rein as his horse faltered. "I would be more concerned about that son of his—Hugh."

"Hugh Purdie is no informer," said James shortly.

"He has a shadow on his conscience. He took no part with the United Men, ye tell me. That's consuming him. He might well turn martyr now, and bring down the people around him. Watch him, Gault. Is he coming to Belfast?"

"It's possible."

"Don't bring him near me."

Riding in thoughtful silence, James fell behind. As the tired horse wound down the hill towards the scattered lights of the town, its rider dreamt of the day he would build a house there for his bride; of the day he would escape from Legg's Lane. In the frosty gloom he saw the Doctor jogging steadily ahead. As he studied the bowed back sudden compunction filled him and he urged his mount forward to overtake his fellow-traveller.

VII

JAMES'S DESCENT FROM the loft to a chamber behind the big ware-room was made the occasion for an 'entertainment', an evening of eating, drinking and music, all purveyed by the Doctor. The master of Legg's Lane had summoned a dozen or so of his hangers-on, among them Captain Nugent Mullan, and Peter Darragh, a hard man like his crony, Fearon. Promised a gutful of drink, they were to play appreciative audience to the Doctor's fiddling.

This they did with such good heart that soon all of them, even the morose yeo, were as full as the River Boyne. The Doctor sat cross-legged on the table, sawing away with his bow, grinning down on the suffused and glistening faces of the company. When a tankard or a glass fell empty, Poll, standing beyond the glare of the great chandelier, stepped forward to fill it. James, half-hidden between two huge casks, sipped his wine and tried to close his ears to the yowling of the fiddle and the fulsome cries of the drinkers. At times he had to close his eyes when the diabolical writhings and contortions of the man squatting above him became too sore a tax on his gravity.

The Doctor swept a last lunatic flourish and dropped to the floor. It was all over. Now the lavish host couldn't get shot of his guests quick enough. The knowing ones were already on their feet. The others, surprised with full glasses in their fists, complained that they couldn't bolt royal brandy in this fashion. But the Doctor was beyond flattery. The sight of his ill-shaped body leaning over the table, the malevolence of his glare, encouraged the laggards to gulp down their drink or thrust it away. Within three minutes Matt the smith was bolting the door on the last tottering pair of heels.

The Doctor still leaned over the table. "Well, Gault, did ye enjoy the evening?" He scowled like one expecting a rebuff.

"Moderately, Doctor, moderately," returned James in a good-humoured way as he stood up.

"*Moderately!* Damn ye, we disposed ourselves for ye!"

"That you didn't," said James with a chuckle. "I've lain above listening to many such entertainments. You'd have had your liquor and fiddling whether I'd been here or not."

"Aye, and we'll have them when you're gone," said the dwarfish man sullenly.

"You will, surely. Goodnight to you all."

James had shaken off his shoes and was about to kneel to his prayers when there was a tap on the door. The Doctor came in and sat hesitantly on the edge of the bed. "I was thinking, James, you might have taken me up wrong——"

"In what way?"

"That you were to leave us."

It was James's turn to hesitate. He had put his hand to a new way of winning his bread. But as yet he couldn't afford to cut himself adrift from Legg's Lane, for there was money to be earned and much to be learned before he could put up his own board in this growing town. "No, Doctor, I didn't understand you to say you wanted rid of me."

"Nor did I, James, nor did I."

Fearing another question, the young man hurried on. "I know you meant well tonight, and I thank you. But the truth is I've no stomach for such gatherings."

"You drank little," said the Doctor rising with a sigh. "And maybe for the best, for I'll spend the night pissing and farting. A man like me must take the lid off the seething pot. You're a creature of different clay, James. On this matter it'll be as you say."

And on all other matters if God spares me, thought James, as he knelt to finish his prayers.

For some time he had suspected that the greater part of

the Doctor's income came from smuggling. Now he discovered the origin of the odours and stinks that had vexed Kean and him as they lay in the loft. Glancing through the smiddy door late one night he saw McCoubrey and Fearon shaking riddles energetically over sheets spread on the floor. On the sheets dark cones of tea were rising. Poll stole back and forth, feeding the sieves from a couple of chests standing near the forge bellows. James recognised the chests. They had arrived at Legg's Lane three days before marked 'Spoiled No Duty to Pay'. Fearon straightened and threw the refuse from his sieve on to the fire. In the sudden flare that followed, James saw the overseer of these activities, Aeneas Gordon, seated on the breastwork of the forge. Gordon arose and approached James, closing the door of the smiddy behind him.

"Do you know what we're working at in there, Mr Gault?"

"I've smelt that reek before. The tea was adulterated on board ship, accidently or otherwise, and is now being cleaned for sale?"

Mr Gordon hesitated, then said, "Did the Doctor tell you of this?"

"No."

"Then you know nothing of it."

"And care less. I'll leave you to your labours, Mr Gordon." But the young man was ill at ease. Against his wishes he was discovering too much, becoming too well-informed, of the activities in the warehouse in Legg's Lane.

*

Marriage to Kate, he decided, would be the simplest way to bid adieu to the Doctor. On each visit to his parents he called at Sim's, and was received ever more cordially by that scheming and acquisitive individual. His courtship of Kate was acknowledged and encouraged. The two young people discussed marriage. "And where will we live?" asked the girl.

"It takes time and money to build a house. So, to begin,

we'll rent one. But a house I'm determined to own. And to earn the money I must stay a while with the Doctor."

"I don't like that creature . . . how long?"

"God willing, not too long. I attend Mr McCashon's church and have become acquainted with some respectable people in the town. A business friend of mine has offered to put in a word for me on the matter of a site for a house. But money, Kate, money, money, money."

James's new friend was Mr Pringle Hazlett, the merchant in the snuff-coloured coat. Several times he had taken the young man to the Assembly Rooms to drink tea. Hazlett's circle of acquaintances, James found, was wide, wealthy and influential. At his table he met Dr Brewster, the Town Sovereign, Mr Simmons, chief excise officer, an Englishman recently arrived, and determined, as he told the company, to stamp out smuggling through the northern ports. The well-fed faces at the table received this news with bland agreement. To be seen in Mr Hazlett's company was sufficient credential for a man's solvency and substance. Nothing is perfect, of course. There was the occasion when Mr Spifford Lamont of Chichester Street had approached Mr Hazlett's table. On seeing James he had veered away hurriedly to another part of the crowded room. James turned to find Mr Hazlett eyeing him sardonically.

"I'm afraid," said James confused and angry, "that I've deprived you of Mr Lamont's company."

"Lamont knows of your connection with Legg's Lane?"

"He's not above trading with Dr Bannon, himself."

"But he doesn't live with him. Change your abode, Mr Gault, and you're more likely to gain the confidence of most of the men in the market. That is, if you think it worth while."

"But of course I do! *You* know of my connection with the Doctor. Why are you seen with me?"

Mr Hazlett shrugged and smiled.

"Because," said the young man with some bitterness, "you have such a position in this gathering that you can indulge yourself."

"Can you afford to leave the Doctor?"

"No . . . not as yet," said James hesitantly. "There are unusual circumstances in my relationship with the parties in Legg's Lane——"

"I can believe that. In the recent unsettled times estimable men have had to lie with strange bedfellows."

"That's been so in my case."

"Let me give you some advice. If your present association is profitable and lawful, hold to it. There's more than Mr Lamont in this room has dealings with the Doctor. But they don't live under his roof."

Meantime the Doctor aware or not of his lodger's proposed defection, continued to supply him with the commodities he needed for his growing trade in the town. And James, partly in talk with Aeneas Gordon, partly by using his eyes and ears, learnt to distinguish the merchandise that came into Legg's Lane on the shady side of the law. He bought and resold grain, fruit, hides, butter and cheese, and refused to handle tea, tobacco, coffee, spices and sugar. His scrupulousness irked the Doctor.

"Why don't ye take what you're offered? You're nothing more than a common huckster as it is!"

"For all that, *I'll* decide what I buy and sell."

"Damn ye, Gault, you're supposed to work with the rest of the boys!"

"I'm no boy, Doctor. I intend to go my own road. I thought you understood that."

On an evening some weeks after the consignment of tea had been cleared from Legg's Lane, half-a-dozen 25-gallon casks of spirits were trundled into the warehouse. Their arrival stirred the Doctor's men into great activity. A still was brought from its hiding-place and assembled over the forge fire. Under the Doctor's eye Fearon fed the liquor into the contraption while Matt and Peter Darragh took turns at sentry-go in the courtyard. And James, watching cautiously, was certain that in the neighbouring hovels there were others on the alert for any prowler straying too near the smiddy.

Seated in the big room, making up his accounts with Mr Gordon, he snuffed the pungent and familiar stench. The Doctor appeared from the smiddy and stood over them. He smirked at James. "Why don't ye offer to lend a hand, Mr Gault?"

"To what?"

"To a task after your own heart. The redeeming of spirits." Chuckling at the quip the dwarfed man scuttled back into the ripe gloom of the smiddy.

For a time James considered Gordon, bent over his books. "No doubt I shouldn't ask this," he said, "but what are they brewing in there?"

Mr Gordon shook his head. "Not 'brewing', Mr Gault. They are, as the Doctor says, redeeming spirits."

"It goes without saying that whatever they're up to, at this hour and in this manner, is outside the law?"

The lean sombrely-clad man shrugged. "Then don't say it, Mr Gault."

Mr Gordon relented. He drew his chair closer to James. "The brandy in those casks is much over proof. On board ship it was adulterated with sugar candy or some such concoction. The excisemen can't tell its real strength so it comes in duty free as spoiled goods, d'ye see?"

"The impurities were deliberately introduced into the brandy?"

"What do we land-lubbers know," said Mr Gordon with a slight smile, "of the mishaps that can befall a vessel and its precious freight on the long run from the West Indies?"

There, thought James, speaks your master.

"And such an uncommon quantity of such a liquor *is* a precious freight, I assure you, Mr Gault."

"But the excise officers can't be so blind as not to know what's going on!"

Mr Gordon laid his finger along his nose. The gesture angered James. He was reminded that this quiet, pleasantly-spoken man was as inveterate a wrongdoer as any of his companions. Mr Gordon sighed and sat back dejectedly.

"No, this time it's serious . . . a new gauger, Simmons, is not to be bought off . . . we think he suspects that the consignment is here . . ."

"Well, I'll have no hand in such a business."

"The Doctor wasn't serious. Tending a still needs the skill of the Devil."

"That I can well believe."

He had meant that he would refuse to sell any of the uncustomed brandy. And he knew that Aeneas Gordon had not misunderstood him. But, two days later, the Doctor accosted him as he was about to leave for the market. "James," said the little man in a most amiable and confidential manner, "I've a surplus of spirits on hand. I want you to help me get rid of it, urgently."

"I don't know anybody who'd be interested in that class of goods."

"There's no one who isn't interested in a drop of good French brandy. What of your friends? There's Adair, or old Pringle Hazlett you see so much of——"

"Doctor, I'm not going to be agent for passing smuggled goods."

"What if I tell you that an inquisitive fool has been seen hanging round the Lane the last day or two?"

Gault laughed. "If there's an exciseman you can't bribe, more power to him! I'm not touching a drop of the stuff."

The Doctor came on another tack. "For a man of your political colour, you puzzle me at times," he said with a patient smile. "This is an English law these gaugers whip us with, not an Irish law."

"I'm not interested where the law originated—it's a law."

The smile vanished and the Doctor considered the young man from under penthouse lids. "You seem to forget that you live here, that the merchandise you sell comes from my store."

"I assure myself that there's nothing unlawful in the origin of any article I get from you."

"Do you, by Christ! You must be thought quite a pillar

of rectitude among the other hagglers who sip tea at the Assembly Rooms."

"That's as may be," said James unruffled. "I'm not dealing in that brandy."

"Even if I tell you that this cursed exciseman is getting too close and that he's neither to be scared or bought?"

"You can always rid yourself of the stuff into the drains."

"Don't be a fool, Gault. I have to pay those I bought it from and those who carried it here."

"A risk of the trade, no doubt. I can't help you."

The Doctor stared into his face then turned away abruptly. A lot of the assurance oozed from James as he watched him go. Never before had he seen him so apprehensive and ill at ease. James had an ominous feeling that if the grim little creature got himself out of this fix those to blame would pay dearly. He counts me now among his enemies. O God, help me to get away from this place in safety. He trudged despondently down Legg's Lane to his day's haggling.

But when he returned that evening he found the Doctor quietly amiable. The kegs, now empty, were piled in the courtyard. James was puzzled. It would have been impossible to distribute so quickly such a large quantity of contraband through the usual go-betweens. Then he realised, with a smirk of satisfaction, that his jibe had been acted on. In the pinch, the many gallons of valuable liquor had, somehow or other, been drained away. It was the first time he had known the Doctor thwarted.

His meal finished he turned to his accounts. Shortly after dusk the Doctor's henchmen began to drift in. James was mildly surprised, for there had been no talk of an 'entertainment'. Fearon was there and McCoubrey. A young fellow, already half-drunk, was armed in by Darragh. James recognised him as a junior gauger in the Doctor's pay. Mullan, plainly there under orders, sat glum, his legs stretched out, his chin sunk in his neckcloth. The Doctor, a flush on his seamed face, poured the liquor and drank heavily himself. His hand clapped over his mouth, the gauger staggered from his chair. "Don't vomit here, you dog!" yelled the Doctor. "Owen, lead him to the smiddy and bring him back. Because," he added with an awful grin, "we must hang together this night." A sick foreboding filled James. Indeed this was no entertainment. For the first time since he had come to Legg's Lane he really tasted fear. Time dragged on. The young exciseman had drunk himself sober and now sat, white and shivering, his hands clasped between his thighs. Just after midnight the Doctor clapped his hands. "Poll, fill the glasses again. Gentlemen, I give you absent——"

"Scald ye in hell!" cried Mullan scrambling to his feet. "No bloody toast——"

The misshapen man smiled widely. "As you please, Captain. You, after all, have been an invaluable guest this evening. A *parting* glass, then."

Violently the yeoman set down his liquor, untasted and slopping over, tore open the door and rushed into the darkness.

The Doctor stretched himself theatrically. "Darragh, return that sick whelp from whence he came, making certain that he remembers in whose company he sat tonight. Then bar up the door, Matt, bar up the door. Mr Gault, a nightcap—no? I wish ye sound and untroubled slumber."

In the Assembly Rooms next morning James was drinking coffee with Mr Pringle Hazlett.

"You look drawn, Mr Gault."

"I slept badly last night, sir."

"The night air in the vicinity of the quays is not particularly healthful," said Mr Hazlett delicately. "Perhaps a change of living might help?"

"Last night, Mr Hazlett . . ."

Spifford Lamont had entered the room. Some urgency in his manner held the young man silent. They saw the linen-draper whisper in the ear of the first person he encountered, a stout flushed gentleman who dealt in tobacco and snuffs, and watched the geniality drain from his listener's face. His words had the same effect on the second man he spoke to. And the third. He bore down on their table so gravid with news that not even the sight of James checked him. He planted his fists on the edge of the table and addressed himself to Mr Hazlett.

"D'ye remember the Excise officer I introduced here last week? Simmons was his name, new here from England."

"I do, Mr Lamont. What of him?"

"Early this morning, in Dalton's Meadow, by the river, he was found with his head beaten in."

*

Mr Gordon was figuring in his ledgers. In a corner Poll cleaned boots. The Doctor sat by the fireside, one stockinged heel perched on the hob.

"A word with you, Doctor."

For a long moment the only sounds were the scratching of Mr Gordon's pen, the scraping of Poll's knife. Then the Doctor slowly turned, his heavy face burdened with the widest of smiles. "Speak, James, speak."

"In private, if you please."

The Doctor looked at the others. "What secrets have I from my brothers?"

James turned with abhorrence from the bland slyness of the voice and the look. "Many hidden from me, thank God. I'll be in my room."

From his chamber he heard the muted murmur of the two in the ware-room, then the shuffle of feet outside his door. "Come in!" he called and tossed a parcel of books on to the bed beside his folded garments.

The Doctor examined the bundles attentively.

"I'm leaving," said James.

"I hope I'm not hearing you aright."

"Now—this hour."

"Damme, James, this is a sudden decision," said the little man sinking slowly on to the bed. His voice was laden with perplexity. "Can I ask ye why?"

The young man gave a gesture of repulsion. "You play-act too much. I wouldn't expect you to answer to anything."

"Ah, well," said the Doctor and much of the pathos had gone from his bearing, "I wouldn't ask it if I were you."

"D'ye think to frighten me?" demanded James stopping abruptly in his task. "And if you failed, would you break my skull, too, and clod me into Dalton's Meadow?"

"Me and mine were under this roof last night. You were witness."

"God will forgive me for that."

"You can prove nothing."

"— and for that."

"Your mouth's as loose as a cut purse," said the Doctor savagely. "You poor clown, if I were to admit to what you suspect, your life wouldn't be worth a tinker's turd!"

"Then, for God's sake, spare me your protection and forbearance. Let me go out of this house——"

"You can prove nothing," said the dwarfed man in a low voice. He drummed thoughtfully on the bedrail. "I can think of nothing to hinder you. Except the settlement of your debt," as the young man straightened angrily the other added, "—in money."

"I had that in mind. What do I owe?"

"Aeneas keeps the accounts. There's no hurry——"

"I'll settle now."

At the Doctor's bidding Mr Gordon got out the books and totted up the value of the goods lately drawn by James from the storehouse. The debt stood at thirty-two pounds and seven shillings.

"We'll call it the round thirty," offered the Doctor.

"I'll pay the sum that Aeneas has reckoned." He took a bag from his valise and counted out the money. "That's us clear, I think." The young man followed the glance between the Doctor and Mr Gordon. "Well," he said, "I'll thank ye for a receipt."

"Of course, of course, James," cried the Doctor. "But here's a further matter——"

"And what's that?"

"It would never have been mentioned if you hadn't been

in such a fume to leave—" began the Doctor peevishly. Mr Gordon threw open the ledger at a further page. He laid his finger on a column of entries. "Through Nugent Mullan, you owe us one hundred and twenty-seven pounds."

James's mouth fell open as he stared at the two men. "Mullan . . . what crazed nonsense is this?"

"It started a week or so after you began trading in the town," said Mr Gordon.

The young man waved him aside. "Give me the acknowledgment. I'm in a hurry."

With a shrug Mr Gordon drew forward paper and ink. The submissive gesture made James pause. He waited in silence.

Mr Gordon laid down his pen. "Mullan was suspicious." He glanced at the Doctor, "And envious of you. He threatened to have you seized in the town some night and taken up as a United Irishman, even if he had to fabricate the evidence."

"That is the truth, Gault," said the Doctor.

"We contrived to put him off your track," continued Mr Gordon, "by putting him in your debt."

James believed Gordon's words. But the uncharacteristic artlessness of the dodge puzzled and vexed him. "I'll allow that you're not trying to trick me out of what must be to you a paltry sum. But that you should do this without telling me!" He grinned angrily in the Doctor's face. "So Mullan threatened? You're not usually so canny in dealing with those who dare do that, are you? Where were your execrable crew of butchers then? Pursuing, or on a journey, or peradventure they slept——"

The Doctor darkened in fury. "Shut your face, ingrate! You value yourself too high. D'ye think I would destroy a willing animal like Mullan to save a creature that deserts me at the first whiff of danger——"

Mr Gordon, his face screwed into an expression of intense suffering, stepped between them. "Hush, hush," he whispered, seizing his master by the elbow and peering at the open door. "Sharp ears . . . sharp ears. I wouldn't be averse, James Gault, to some mishap removing Mullan," and James saw a flicker of hate on the prim clerkly face. "But he is more deadly than he knows——"

"He's loyal to his comrades," said the Doctor plucking his arm free and scowling at James.

Mr Gordon continued, addressing himself to the young man. "If he had started the whisper that was to convict you, he would have ended up by sending everyone in this house to the gallows or the hulks. How could he have avoided it? How could we have escaped? He had to be given the credit he sorely needed. By the same stroke you were made his benefactor."

"Your debtor, you mean. I haven't the money to pay you."

"You're not being pressed, Gault."

"Pay when Mullan settles. Your credit's good in Legg's Lane," said Mr Gordon.

"So it would seem," said James bitterly.

The Doctor, mutable as ever, now became the adviser, the consoler. "Dammit, what's a hundred pounds to a young rising merchant? We did what we did for the best. To hear ye one would think we'd dealt a mortal blow——"

"Not mortal, but it's vexatious to go out tied by such a debt—above all, to Nugent Mullan."

The three men were silent. James looked at the Doctor. It was monstrous, he thought, that I should be expected to show gratitude to this man on parting, a parting brought about by a callous and horrid murder. He deals in life and death. It's likely enough, in his grotesque existence, that he's saved more lives than he's taken. He saved mine. If I were asked, I'd testify that he was here, among his cronies, all last night. "I'll finish my packing," he said.

The Doctor looked at his baggage as he carried it up. Then he went to the yard door. "Darragh, ye devil's toothpick, where are ye?" The ostler came in, wiping his hands.

"Darragh will hump your bundles wherever you're bound."

James considered. He had no wish to be seen in the town accompanied by a known denizen of Legg's Lane. "Thank you. Let him go ahead and leave the valise and books at the Linen Hall with Mr Pringle Hazlett's clerk. I'll follow later."

The Doctor grinned tightly. "You're fortunate in your patrons, Gaul. You'll go far."

"I could have gone farther—to Van Diemen's Land." James brought up the witticism like a pebble.

The grin still lurking the Doctor said, "I'll understand if you prefer not to take my hand."

"No, no," muttered the young man reaching out. "Your hand. Thank you for sheltering me . . . your goodwill . . . I'll not lightly forget it."

The Doctor bowed as he relinquished the clasp. James took the hand of Aeneas Gordon the only one from whom he regretted parting. Then he was out in Legg's Lane, acknowledging the unsmiling nods, the furtive salutes, from its dark doorways. For the last time, O God, he prayed, as he kept the burdened figure of Darragh in sight.

VIII

"HOW ARE YOUR new lodgings?' asked Mr Hazlett.

"As a landlady Mrs Black is all that you said she would be. I'm enjoying the best bed and board since I left home to go to college."

Hazlett studied his companion for a moment. "Mr Gault, would you care to put your learning to use?"

"My book learning?—no," said James laughing. "My present way of living is more interesting and more profitable."

"I don't mean that you should give *that* up. But now that you're your own master, the occasional evening must hang heavy. You're not a man given to the taverns, or the gaming tables, or even the theatre."

"I read of an evening, now. You don't know what silence and solitude are until you've lodged in a warehouse for most of a year . . . What had you in mind, Mr Hazlett?"

"There are two young persons in my house, relatives of my wife, who could do with some assistance in their schooling. The girl, Sophia, is sixteen years old, and her brother Lawrence, a delicate lad, is ten."

James recalled the girl and boy in the Hazletts' company as they left St George's church. The idea of calling on one of the comfortable residences in the town attracted him.

"I'm no tutor, Mr Hazlett."

"But you would know what they need?"

James pulled at his lip. "English grammar, spelling, reading——"

"*Correct pronunciation*. Mrs Hazlett is very warm on that."

James smiled. "You would have to suffer my country tongue."

"It's not too marked," said Mr Hazlett comfortingly. "Penmanship . . . ?"

James nodded. "Mathematics? The rudiments of Latin?"

"You have it!" cried Mr Hazlett clapping his hands softly.

"It isn't sufficient," said James. "You would need much more for such an elegant young girl."

Mr Hazlett betrayed no surprise at the comment. "Mrs Hazlett sees to that. Sophie attends Mrs Ware's academy in the town. For all that you could give some help in her arithmetic and writing, eh? The boy Lawrence is taking the German flute, both are having instruction in dancing after the latest French manner."

James frowned. "For the lad at least, it doesn't seem very substantial fare."

"It is not, Mr Gault. And if you're good enough to take an interest in the matter, you'll discover that I'm under an obligement to do better for their future."

Feeling that he had shown enough reluctance, James nodded. "Very well. If you think I can be of assistance."

"You can!" said Mr Hazlett warmly. "I'm obliged to you. You could come on those evenings you found convenient——"

"No, an agreed programme of instruction and preparation would be necessary from the beginning."

"Mrs Hazlett and I would be guided by you on that. Can you come to dinner with us soon and meet your pupils?"

*

To James's eye the squatters' shelters seemed to have taken a more tenacious grip on Purdie's soil. Some had sprouted outhouses built of furze, and the pig and cow population had noticeably increased. Around each hovel usage had beaten smooth rings in the earth that merged into the web of footbreadth tracks dividing the plots of tillage. The men, women and children who watched his progress to Sim's house eyed him with an unsmiling curiosity that reminded him unpleasantly of the denizens of Legg's Lane. Kate was filling a peat creel as he rode into the yard. She came forward to hold his horse's head. "Welcome, James, how are ye?"

"Always the better o' seeing you," he answered, swinging to the ground. "Leave that," he added with a smile, taking her fingers from the bridle. "It isn't for you to play horseboy."

"Ah," said the girl laughing, "I'm not one o' your fine town ladies."

"In time, in time. I've news for you. Mr Hazlett has his eye on a wee house that might be had at a modest rent."

She took his hands between hers. "You always bring good news these days. The last time you were able to tell me that you had left that thrawn creature's house——"

Something in his sweetheart's voice and the grasp of her fingers made the young man pause. "Kate, is there aught wrong? I mean, I'm the man you should tell, you understand?"

"Yes, yes . . . nothing's changed . . . nothing's wrong."

Neither voice nor words did much to reassure James. Sim and her brother Andrew appeared. Sim came hurrying forward on his short stiff legs crying on Andrew to tend the visitor's horse, Kate to lower the kettle to the fire.

"I hope I see ye well, Jamie," said Sim and stood mouth open like a man waiting the answer to an unspoken and much more significant question.

"You do, Sim, and the same to all here. I came to see Kate."

"No word from the Doctor?"

"None."

"Ah," Sim closed his lips. Andrew had tethered the horse and hurried back fearful that he might miss a word between the two men. James noticed how alike he had grown to his father; the same shoulders and arms shaped for burdens, the same evasive glance, artful and calculating.

"Your uncle Sam and me were out shooting today," said the youth.

"Yes? I'm surprised there's a gun left in the countryside. I thought they were all lifted after the commotion."

"Not from them that's loyal. Mr Burke gave us a magistrate's permit to keep ours for fear o' trouble——"

Sim shuffled round to rattle his knuckles over the boy's head. "Your gob's too big, ye whelp ye! Off, and find something to do. Off, I say!" Kate appeared at the door to call them in. What trouble, thought James, as he followed Sim into the house. There was one person in this family who could answer that. "Where's Hugh?" he asked as he sat down at the table.

"In the back meadow tending a heifer," said Kate.

But her father was more solicitous of the young man's query. "Well, send Andra to fetch his brother. Jamie wants to see him," and he turned to James with the air of one awaiting with pleasure any further request.

"Thank'ee," said James surprised. "What happened to the animal?"

"A heifer took a tumble in a ditch and got a founder. Hugh got her back on her legs. He's a poor cratur, Hugh, but he's good wi' dumb beasts." He waved to the food on the table. "Don't wait for the young 'uns. Reach forrit your hand." He watched the young man help himself then said, "You're not eating at the Doctor's table, these days?"

James stared at his questioner. "Surely Kate told you a month ago——"

Sim kneaded his brow. "Aye, aye, I knowed about ye leaving Legg's Lane . . ."

Andrew scurried in, breathless, and dragged a stool to the table. "Hugh's coming," he informed the two men and proceeded to stuff his mouth with bread and butter.

"So you've set up on your own?" said Sim. James, glancing at the youth, contented himself with a nod.

Andrew swallowed violently in his eagerness to join in the conversation. "You must know some right big dealers."

James awarded him a brief smile.

"—other than the Doctor," the youth added, his small eyes watching him intently.

"Aye, aye," breathed Sim and his fingers closed strongly on the visitor's arm. James looked from father to son. "What are you trying to ask me? This trouble you mentioned . . ." As he spoke the iniquities and evil disposition of the mis-shapen man in Legg's Lane came flooding back to his memory. "Speak out, Sim!"

"Och," muttered Sim, and withdrew his hand to knead and beat his temples. Andrew stuck to the issue. "Could *you* take our weaving and crops frae us?"

"I could not," said James firmly. "What devilment have you got yourself caught up in, Sim?"

The Purdies had no more to say. Gault couldn't or wouldn't serve their purpose. Sim pretended to hear his wife's voice. Andrew, eyeing their visitor in sullen silence, left the house. James was about to follow him and find his horse when Hugh and Kate arrived.

"You took your time," said James. But for the first time he was sincerely pleased to see Hugh Purdie. Together they walked out to a gentle slope above the farm. Smoke curled upwards from the habitations scattered below them. Men, women and children moved about their tasks or play. Their voices rose faintly to the two men on the brae.

"You don't appear to have many vacant lettings on your estate."

Hugh Purdie kept silent.

"And how is the self-appointed coryphaeus, Campbell? If that's still his place by the road, I see he's thrown out a weaving-shop behind his hovel."

Purdie stared morosely below him. "It's murder they're weaving down there."

James's levity vanished. "Campbell . . . ?"

"Christ," cried the youth suddenly, "for a well-read man, you're as blind as the next!" Regardless of the other's affronted face he seized him by the arm and pointed. "Look, will ye! What difference is there between Charlie Campbell's hovel and his neighbours'? Would ye strip off your fine coat and boots and live barefut among them?"

"Why should I?"

"Or rather, why need ye? There aren't four masters riding your back . . ."

"Explain yourself."

"What these men and women earn," said young Purdie heavily and patiently, "is split four ways. There's Burke the landlord, Ephraim Smart the agent, your friend the Doctor, and last, my father, who gets the crumbs."

"The Doctor?"

Hugh gave an abrupt gesture. "Och, it's a long tale . . ."

"Tell me."

"It's better not knowing. Marry my sister and get her out o' here."

"Tell me, Hugh."

"Well, let us keep on the move. Eyes are watching."

They descended through land so infested with rushes, whin and bracken that even land-hungry men had failed to put it to the spade. James stopped and rested his foot on a twisted root. "Your father's a frightened man, Hugh."

Hugh glanced around. "What did he tell ye?"

"Nothing. He asked me to find a buyer for his linen and crops."

Hugh laughed quietly. "What linen? Linen's dead and well you know it. If there's a loom clacking in this townland it's on cotton, and your friend, the Doctor, supplies the yarn. The pig and the stirk have taken over from the wheel and the loom." He put his pale face close to that of his companion's. "You're marrying into a family o' smugglers."

"Hugh, say what you have to say, simply and clearly."

"The Doctor came about six months ago and told my father that he had a ready buyer for any amount o' beef and pork and tallow and suchlike. All he lacked was the supply. In the next week cattle and pigs arrived to be raised and fattened."

"Given to Campbell and his like without payment?"

"Where would him and his like get money to buy stock? I can tell ye more. What was once our mealhouse is filled to the couplings with the best of oak casks and the finest St Ube's salt. And they're still there, for there was neither the space nor the secrecy to cure the stuff."

"It's not against the law to salt down a bit o' beef."

"It is, if it's going to be eaten by the Frenchies." He paused to watch the effect of his words.

"To France? Beef... tallow carried openly from this place to *France*? Past the excise and the military? You're raving, man!"

"Ah, God, James, it isn't branded for France! It sets out for Legg's Lane. Maybe up to four waggons full. Did *you* ever see any such great load arriving there from Ravara, eh? They wait until there's been a storm. Then, with Fearon or Darragh in charge, they go by the lough road, and about the clachan of Ardmillan they call a halt——"

"Do you or your father or Andrew ever drive?"

"They use Belfast men and carts."

"That's one small mercy."

"There's always a schooner lying close in, for shelter, ye might say. Given a high wind on the Irish Sea you can warrant a heavy night's work around Purdie's farm."

"And then?"

"They say a big boat lies waiting beyond the lough bar. I know no more. I know too much. What's the punishment for selling things to the French?"

"Hanging."

There was silence for a time. The beat of wings grew and passed as three swans toiled across the sky towards the lough.

"Does Kate know of this traffic?"

"She doesn't know where it's bound for."

"Then what has her frightened?"

"Not the Doctor's men. She has a liking for Mr Gordon——"

"What the devil is Aeneas Gordon doing here?"

"He's their book-keeper, isn't he? He comes to pay my

father. It's not them that know about the smuggling, but the ones that don't, that are the danger. Ephraim Smart, for one. He sees the squatters wi' live stock. They're doing too well. So he claps two rises o' rent on them in nine months—one for the squire, one for himself. And he's made my father rent-collector. If you don't, says he, I'll get Burke to clear the lot of ye off the land. Charlie Campbell and the rest are worse off than at the beginning. What money they get for tending the animals is taken away from them. They've lost their weaving, they have to share their potato crop wi' beasts they don't own, that they'll never own. It's like a factory. And the tether that's holding them is perilously tight, James. It'll part one o' these nights."

"Has Campbell threatened you?"

"No, no, there's worse nor him. They hate my father, they hate Andra, they hate me, no doubt. None o' us goes out alone at night . . ."

James ground the whin under his boot. "That accursed Doctor—he twists everything to his own ends!"

Suddenly afraid that the other might interpret this as sympathy for the whole Purdie breed, Gault turned and hurried towards the farmhouse. Their ramble had taken them beyond the squatters' shelters and as he picked his way among children, pigs, goats, dunghills and stinking pools, he felt a stirring of sympathy for the gaunt men and women who withdrew under their smoke-grimed lintels to watch him. How were they to know that this solidly-dressed man, collogueing with Sim and his sons, was not planning another burden for their backs?

He declined Kate's plea to share the evening meal. "I've lost almost a day's work." He raised her face. "Listen to me." He spoke quietly, choosing his words with care. "Make ready for the wedding. Avoid talking about what concerns only you and me. Your good sense will guide you as to how much you need tell your father and mother." The girl read in his expression what he did not want to put into words.

"Yes, if that's your wish, James."

He rode away, pleased with this amiable agreement, the thought of their imminent marriage. It was difficult not to feel that he was at liberty compared with those he had left. He had a sense of well-being in his snugly-fitting coat, the plunge and clip of the sound horse under him, the creak of good leather. But as he travelled, grey fears crept into his mind. To take Kate away from Ravara was his right. But had he not a duty towards her father and brothers? If their treasonable traffic was uncovered, the punishment would be harsh. Now that he knew more, Sim's questioning tore at his heart, yet he could puzzle no way, even at the risk of his own neck, to extricate the old man from the consequences of his greed. The Doctor took a cold delight in using avaricious men like Purdie and then ditching them. Wistfully, James recalled the pagan largess he had enjoyed in the old days. But those days were past. There could be no appeal now to the Doctor's forbearance. Forbye that, if I blab in Legg's Lane what I have learned today, I'm likely to come to the same end as Simmons the gauger, and all to no avail. He closed his eyes. *God, if it be Thy Will, show me the way.* He gathered up the reins, stirring his mount to a brisker pace.

Later that evening, after supper, he sat down and wrote to his father, advising him to have as little as possible to do with Sim, and adjuring him above all not to engage in buying or selling with the Purdie men. He was about to retire when Mrs Black brought him up a letter, just arrived by hand. He set it aside until he had undressed, said his prayers and got into bed. The letter, to his surprise, was from Mrs Hazlett. His company was requested on an evening as early as he might find convenient. The lady hoped that Mr Gault would be pleased to dine with her and Mr Hazlett and meet their wards, Sophia and Lawrence Morgan. It was a voice from a stable and gracious world. There was a smile on his lips as he extinguished his lamp. A pleasanter ending than might have been expected to such a vexatious day.

IX

"Mr Gault," said Arthur Maxwell, his eyes on the chimneys of the Linen Hall, "ye can't carry on your business indefinitely at damn windy street corners. Not for ever. You need an office."

"I'm well aware of my lack, sir," said James stiffly. "So far I've had no success in my search."

"Have you anything in mind, Arthur?" said Mr Hazlett.

"I have. A small office in Weighill Lane, with a yard to it, has fallen vacant in one of my property interests. It would suit you admirably, Gault."

Thus James, in little more than a week after leaving Legg's Lane, came into possession of his first counting-house. There were, he discovered, a number of human appendages to the property; a gang of alley rogues and their women who had frightened away the last occupant and turned the yard into a doss house—and Michael Alphonsus McGrattan. On the first morning he was so taken by his new office that he paid no attention to the laments, clamour and scoldings of the men and women, as they drifted in and out of the yard with the fruits of their begging and petty thievery. While Mr Hazlett, viewing the scene with distaste through the grimy window, was advising James to summon a constable, the young man was measuring the walls at arm's-stretch. Then, just before noon, having arranged to his satisfaction cupboards, a desk, oak fixtures, stools, scales, a letter press, James strode into the yard with a scowl as black as the ebony rule sticking from his coat and gave the rabble three minutes to leave his premises, bags and baggage. A few seconds short of that time he clapped the yard door on their parting maledictions.

"Never," he informed Mr Hazlett through the window, "call for help when you can do the task yourself. They think they have you scared, otherwise."

Mr Hazlett gestured behind him. "You have a caller."

A little wizened fellow sat perched on a stool, his heels hooked on the topmost rung. As James entered he jumped to his feet and stood to attention.

"Who might you be?"

"Michael Alphonsus McGrattan, at your service, cap'n," said the newcomer and threw a military salute.

"Aren't you one of the rogues I've just put out?"

"Me? Murder alive, I am not." He looked at Mr Hazlett. "This gen'leman knows about me."

Mr Hazlett gave a small smile. "He says he goes with the office."

"I worked for Mr Miskelly, the rope merchant, that left last week, an' Mr Callaghan afore him, an' Mr Leitch afore *him*, an'——"

"But all these tenants, I understand, pursued different businesses."

"That's right, cap'n. I checked at the quays for them, counted the stock, sewed bales, branded casks, ran errands, swept the place, clerked——"

"Clerked?"

"Faix, I can read an' write. Keep books."

"And what d'ye want from me, McGrattan?"

"Fonsy. Fonsy's the name, cap'n. The same as with the other gen'leman. A job o' work an' a shakedown in the yard loft. They gave me sixty pence a week."

"You can keep a simple stock book?"

"Try me, cap'n."

James studied the thin weather-darkened face, the startingly blue eyes, the nimbus of grizzled curls. He was disarmed against his will. This was an auspicious moment. His first employee. His scrutiny noted something familiar in the hue and cut of the tattered jacket.

"Were you in the Volunteers . . . Fonsy?"

Again the thud of the broken heels, the salute. "Sarvant to Major Hanna, the First Antrim Company, cap'n."

"I am not," said James carefully, "a captain. I am Mr Gault." He waved his hand in dismissal. "Very well, redd up the yard and be here at half-after-seven in the morning."

Fonsy started a salute, hesitated, then skipped out into the yard.

"Tomorrow," said James, "I'll begin moving my stock in."

"You'll do well, James."

"Aye, if I'm not added to Fonsy's roll-call."

"That's unlikely," said Mr Hazlett, picking up his walking-cane.

As time passed customers and acquaintances found their way to the premises in Weighill Lane. Among the latter came Spifford Lamont, drawn, it seemed to James, by jaundiced curiosity, Tom Adair the coal merchant, Louis Fitzgibbon, a young hardware merchant, with a proposition to share a cargo of timber and tools, Arthur Maxwell, full of affable good wishes, who turned haughty when profferred the rent. A tap on the door one morning and James found himself looking over Fonsy's shoulder into the eyes of the Doctor. "Not too early, Mr Gault?"

"The shutters are down, Doctor." James nodded Fonsy away and with a skip and a jump the clerk was out through the yard door. The Doctor came in followed by Aeneas Gordon. Across the way Matt McCoubrey leaned his bulk against the wall. James glanced through the window. What wayfarer had seen them enter? They looked around appraisingly. "Good fortune," said Mr Gordon. "Good fortune in your new premises, James."

"Thank ye. Now, gentlemen, in what way can I oblige?"

The Doctor raised a hand. "None, none. We stepped by to wish you luck." Then suddenly, "Who was that fellow just gone out?"

"My clerk," said James after a moment, "if that makes you any the wiser."

"A clerk, eh? Admirable, James. An old soldier, by his rig?"

Little escapes him, thought James. "He says he was a Volunteer."

"I'm happy that you've contrived to give employment to one of that admirable body, since treated so shabbily. Um . . . hum . . . and yourself, James? You take no part in town affairs . . . a man amid thriving and influential friends?"

"I'm a merchant, Doctor, no more."

The little man nodded. "The habits of barter do much contract the political mind."

James smiled in spite of himself. "I haven't the time to pursue both—or the wish."

"Business thriving, James?" asked Mr Gordon, and James, detecting a note too politely indifferent, took warning.

"I'm satisfied."

The Doctor peered into the yard. "You've plenty of room out there."

"I need it."

The Doctor lowered his hand gently on to the table, fingers bent like talons. "The truth is, James, we're overful at Legg's Lane. A load of cotton yarn arrived on us——"

"No." James shook his head. "No, Doctor, not in any circumstances."

"Damn ye, can't ye wait until ye hear what I have to say!"

"I read ye like a book. There's no room in my yard for aught that isn't mine."

"There's nothing irregular with the stuff, James," cried Mr Gordon. "We can show you the customs clearance."

"I need those sheds for my own goods. I've gone half a cargo from Glasgow with another merchant. The vessel's due in a week or less."

The little man's eyes glittered in his dark face. For a long moment he seemed at a loss. Then: "So this is the thanks ye offer your old comrades."

"I've never been behindhand in thanking you for past

favours. But," added James looking down on the other, "please to remember that I'm in business now, with my living to make, and other obligations to fulfil. And, gentlemen, I'm busy about it."

"Pretty Poll," whispered the Doctor. "And a long-standing debt to pay, you eloquent huckster!"

James saw the alarm and anger on Aeneas Gordon's face. His master, it would seem, had spoken out of turn. With furious glee the young man whirled around and tore open a cupboard. Mr Gordon stepped forward to restrain him. James elbowed him away. Plucking a cash box from the shelf he emptied its contents on the table. He took a leather bag and poured it on the heap. In a fistful he gathered up the coins set aside for Fonsy's errands. He searched his pocket to the last penny. The two watched him in silence. He pointed to the money. "Take what's due to ye." Neither moved. "Do I have to count it out piece by piece?"

As Gordon began slowly to scrape the coins together, James wrote out a receipt and slapped it with pen and horn on the table. "Your acknowledgment."

An embarrassed smile quivered on the Doctor's lips. "But, James, man——"

"You're outstaying your welcome. Sign."

The smile vanished from the Doctor's face. Seizing the pen he rent and spattered the paper with his signature. James picked up the receipt. "And what," said Mr Gordon after a silence, "do you hope to do with that?"

"Use it to recover *my* money," said James sharply.

Mr Gordon's face bore as close to a sneer as James had ever seen. "Then you've been in a fair way of roaring yourself out of a hundred and twenty-seven pounds. *That's* no proof that Mullan owes you as much as a farthing. Give me a fresh sheet and a pen." Mr Gordon wrote fluently for a space then pushed his work across the table. "That'll give you a toehold on him."

James watched them go. They've heaped coals of fire on my head. But a small monitory voice restrained him. When he looked out the Doctor and his companions had disappeared among the figures that hurried or loitered across the arched mouthway that led to the High Street.

Fonsy slid in, eyeing the room. "Your friend . . . the Doctor . . . he's gone?"

"You know him?"

"Who doesn't?"

"Fonsy, the Doctor was here on a matter of business. He's not a friend of mine."

"Oh, b'god, cap'n, Mr Gault, sir, don't say that! The Doctor's a great stick to beat our enemies wi'——"

"Now, what d'ye mean by that?"

"Them scum ye threw out o' the yard. They're round the lane again. They trip me and clod stones at me when I'm on an errand. But one glimpse o' the Doctor stepping in here and they've skipped. I tell ye, cap'n, he's better than tar water for vermin!"

"Fonsy, if you run into that class of trouble again, tell me. There are constables to protect you."

"Protect *me*?" Fonsy tried to stifle his derision.

"Here," James handed him an account. "My compliments to Mr Ritchie, and I'd like that bill settled."

"I'll bring the money back, cap'n."

"You'd better. Your wages are in it."

Two days later, at the corner of Castle Lane, he came on Nugent Mullan standing with several others, among them Clulow of the Ballast Office and Spifford Lamont. He exchanged unsmiling nods with the group then spoke in the leather-chandler's ear. "A word with ye, Mr Mullan."

"Readily," said Mullan disengaging himself. "I was looking for ye."

"To settle your bill?" Mullan's face showed that that had not been his intention. "You owe me a hundred and twenty-seven pounds. I need it."

"Keep your voice down . . ."

James stepped closer. "I'll be obliged by a speedy settlement."

Mullan's face settled into the brute sullenless James knew so well. "It's impossible—out o' the question."

"Make it possible, sir. I must be paid. I've settled in full with . . . the third party."

Mullan looked up sharply. "He came for it?"

"He got it. Now it's your turn."

"I tell ye I can't! I was coming to you for more credit."

It was James's turn to fall silent.

"Gault," cried the other in desperation, "let me have another hundred in goods!"

"You're out of your wits!"

"Then some of the ready and I can settle . . ."

"No."

"Nugent," called one of the men, his curious gaze on the two as he and his companions moved off, "we're for the White Cross——"

"Coming, coming! I've business wi' those gentlemen."

"Let us hope that it's profitable. You'll find me at 7 Weighill Lane. Bring me the money there, Mr Mullan."

With a malevolent glare the other turned and hurried after his companions.

*

Favouring dark clothes, he had rid himself of the green suit bought him by the Doctor. On the evening that he was to dine with the Hazletts he dressed with extra care, permitting himself, as the only touch of elegance, a fine muslin stock given him by Kate. He put on his cloak that had a touch of the cleric in its cut, took his stick, and set out for his host's house in Stranmillis.

He paused in the shelter of the tall laurels. His first impression of Pringle Hazlett's residence was that of a roseate richness; through the glass of the inner door came a glow of crimson hangings, foliage, tall gilt lamps. It was totally outside his experience. He could compare it only to Squire Burke's house. Standing in the doorway he realised that this house was much smaller. But the squire's entrance hall was like a stable, the door-posts smudged with filth, horse-dung on the steps. Here all was unsullied brightness and warmth.

A servant admitted him. Mr Hazlett came forward. "You're welcome, James." He smiled. "Your punctuality will be much appreciated by Mrs Hazlett."

"It's a night that encourages one to move briskly."

"Then have a glass of wine."

"I'm not a drinking man, Pringle."

"On an occasion such as this?" James felt as he took the glass that *his* tutelage had begun. "Now come and meet Mrs Hazlett and the children."

Early in his visits to such gathering-places as the Assembly Rooms James had discovered the value of reticence. At the beginning it had been a sensible precaution against *agents provocateurs* who, after the Rising, infested every assemblage. But as time passed he discovered that it was the attitude expected of a 'college man', a species not too plentiful on mart and quayside. In this manner he gained the acceptance, even the respect, of hard-faced men who could have bought him thrice over without thought. He suspected that just such a portrait had been carried by Pringle Hazlett to his wife.

He was introduced to Mrs Hazlett and the Morgan children in the garden room, and thought that he acquitted himself fairly well in the exchanges. He observed that his hostess moved with grace and that her long sallow face took on a plaintive expression when she thought that she was unobserved. Miss Sophia Morgan acknowledged him with much the same fine manners as her aunt, and her brother Lawrence greeted him with the pleasure accorded an adult who threatened to shadow his young days with schooling.

They moved between the tall, white, folded doors to the dining-room. James was seated at his host's right, opposite Mrs Hazlett. Sophia Morgan sat beside her aunt. The young man glanced at the array of heavy silver before him and felt his hands sweat. The butler, assisted by a maid-servant, served the soup and toast. James pursued a query of Mr Hazlett's until his host had picked up the appropriate spoon.

By such minute stratagems he made his way carefully through the gleaming sequence of forks, knives and spoons.

The conversation of the three adults was lively enough, Mr Hazlett reviving it with some small witticism when it threatened to falter. Gault was not at his best. He was puzzled as to whether it was for him to refer to the reason for this dinner party. Once or twice he had found Sophia's gaze upon him. A lamp set behind her dropped its light on her fair-brown hair, leaving her pale face in shadow. He was unable to read her expression but it seemed to him that what he had suspected as a faintly supercilious air had given way to a scrutiny of intense interest. After a time he avoided meeting her eyes. As for the boy, James couldn't decide whether it was good appetite or good breeding that held his rapt attention to the dishes set before him. He's put away more kitchen this evening, thought James, than a Ravara child would see in a month.

"I'm surprised to learn," said Mrs Hazlett, "that you don't favour the theatre, Mr Gault. And yet you so enjoyed reading *Jonathan Wild*. You see," she continued archly, "there are informers in the Assembly Rooms who note your enthusiasms."

"If all spies were as amiable this would be a happier world," said James.

Mrs Hazlett's face drooped. "When you have rebellion against order, and threats to property, the antidote has to be equally odious—to the miscreants."

"Perhaps," cried Sophia brightly, "Mr Gault prefers to follow the drama in the solitude of his study!"

The boy Lawrence turned round-eyed to his neighbour. "Have you a theatre in your house, sir?"

In the amusement Mrs Hazlett's reproof was dissipated. But James had learnt a lesson. He recognised also that the girl had come to his rescue. In gratitude he turned to her. She awaited his glance. She wore the triumph of one who had at least lighted a rocket of playfulness. He smiled and freed himself.

"When can you come to us, Mr Gault?" asked his hostess.

"Mrs Hazlett," said her husband with a tinge of impatience, "the question is rather how can Sophie and Lawrence best dispose themselves to meet Mr Gault's convenience."

"I but ask because Sophia is due to visit Sir Daly—her uncle, Sir Daly Morgan of Queen's County," the lady added for James's benefit.

"Should not the improvement of my mind come before even the gratification of visiting my uncle?" The girl spoke gravely. Mr Hazlett smiled painfully. Her brother sniggered. Mrs Hazlett rose. "Children, bid your uncle and Mr Gault goodnight. Gentlemen . . ." and Mrs Hazlett swept the girl and her brother from James's sight.

The two men went into the garden. Among the blacknesses and shadows cast by rhododendrons, daphnes and flowering cherries, James sauntered behind his host. A more pungent odour came to his nose. Mr Hazlett had drawn a long pipe from his coat and, lighting it, leaned his elbows on a low wall. "If my niece has put you off, I'll understand, James."

The young man glanced suspiciously at his companion. "I saw nothing untoward in Miss Morgan's behaviour."

"Sophie . . . Sophia, if you must. She puts on the grand air without encouragement." Mr Hazlett turned. "She and her brother are orphans. Their parents died of the fever in Jamaica. By rights, I suppose, they should be living at Cashon Lodge with their uncle, for Lawrence is heir to the baronetcy as well as his father's properties in the West Indies. But my wife, convinced that her brother would have reared them with his livestock, took them into my house. And indeed I haven't regretted it, James."

James having grunted in polite assent, Mr Hazlett continued. "Sir Daly will not have them leave Ireland. Not even for schooling. It's the only interest he takes in them apart from an invitation once or twice a year. Meantime he lives in mortal fear of the papists. He bars his front doors against them every night and takes their rotgut of poteen in at the back. The man's a fool. Lawrence will come to the title before the next five years are out."

The elderly merchant tapped the bowl of his churchwarden gently on the wall. "I'm not disloyal to my connection, James, but I have a concern for the children. I know the value of schooling. Your assistance would be mighty welcome. I hope you've been given no reason to go back on your generous agreement——"

"You make too much of a quip, Pringle! I enjoy lively spirits as much as the next."

"Good. I'll say no more." Mr Hazlett waved with the stem of his pipe. "Have you ever looked down on Belfast at this hour?"

"Yes. From another hill."

Below them the lights shone in broken rows and clusters. A single light, the most distant, crept at a steady pace across the darkness. The two men recognised it as the mast lantern of a vessel heading into the mouth of the river. In the town, lamps and candles set in windows pricked the gloom. Under a constellation of flaming torches, the fiery glow thrown back by tall gables, James could see men, like ants, working around a new house.

"*Belfast*," said Mr Hazlett slowly. "They tell me that in the old tongue it means the place where men crossed the river on their journeys. Now we've come to a halt on its banks. We are the dwellers at the ford. And prospering James, draining, raising, prospering."

The evening had gone to James's head. He smiled foolishly and murmured,

"He shall be like a tree that grows
near planted by a river,
Which in his season yields his fruit,
and his leaf fadeth never——"

"Apt, James, even in your dissenter's doggerel. 'Whatsoever he doeth, it shall prosper. As for the ungodly, it is not so with them: but they are like the chaff, which the wind scattereth away from the face of the earth.' "

"Do you really accept that, Pringle?" asked the younger man moved by genuine curiosity.

"Most certainly. Consider the happenings in this country a brief year or so ago."

"Those were the ungodly that the Psalmist had in mind?"

"How could they deny the charge? They were envious men who would have taken away what others had laboriously gathered together." There was a silence and then Mr Hazlett added, "That's the opinion you'll come to, my friend."

"I can keep a watch on my opinions. They don't have to chime with my beliefs."

"I see you're learning," said Mr Hazlett.

Abruptly James pointed to the distant figures. "Those men—what are they at?"

"Building a new town house for your landlord, Arthur Maxwell. Arthur has abounding confidence in the future, and he's in haste to live in it. I want to talk to you on that head. Let us go indoors."

They entered a small room to the left of the hall. "This is now my counting-house," said Mr Hazlett when they were seated. The young man looked around him. The walls were lined to the ceiling with volumes resplendent in gold, red and umber bindings. Small busts sat in niches, their snowy temples and locks unsmirched. James nodded in admiration. Does anyone open these books? he wondered. "It must be pleasant to make your deals in such surroundings."

"Wine?" said Mr Hazlett and, when James declined, poured himself a glass. "Bit by bit I'm retiring from business. At my age I find the markets too much. But I have careful managers of my concerns. And I continue to take an interest in the town's affairs." He studied his guest. "Next month the Lord Lieutenant comes down from Dublin. He'll be entertained at a dinner given by a number of our acquaintances. Arthur Maxwell is to arrange the affair. He is well-versed in such formalities—as befits a man in pursuit of a title. I'll be there. I've been asked to extend an invitation to you."

James stared at his host. It flashed into his mind that this was a trick. But who would trouble to trick an obscure merchant? To gain time he asked, "And what is the Lord Lieutenant's errand here?"

"To persuade our fellow-citizens that a legislative union with Britain would have something in it for them."

"Ah," said James, and withdrew into his chair. "These matters aren't for the likes of me, Pringle."

The older man slowly turned his glass. "I've never pried into your arrival in the town, James. The last year or so has been a time of strange comings and goings, and you are only one of many. But on this occasion I think it would be prudent to show your face."

"I'm greatly obliged to ye, but you'll permit me to refuse. I've moved into my first counting-house. I've a small but growing trade. I'm content with those for the present." He rose to go. In the hall he stole a backward glance. The garden room was silent. "You'll convey my thanks to Mrs Hazlett?"

He chuckled as he undressed. Invited to dine, no less, even if it was below the salt, with the Viceroy of Ireland. . .

But his sleep was restless. He tossed and turned, aware of a grimace in the shadows, a voice chiding him. Over breakfast, in the grey light, he gave shape to the creatures that had plagued him in the small hours; the sneering countenance of the Doctor, the captious voice of Hugh Purdie. Angrily he pushed his plate away. Were there any two individuals in this wide world who had less claim on his consideration? One, a murderer and blasphemer, the other, shrill in his denunciation of tyranny, but markedly absent when the fighting began. On reaching Weighill Lane his first act was to write an acceptance of the invitation and send Fonsy speeding with it to Mr Hazlett's residence.

X

HE HAD TO admit that his efforts as a pedagogue were not totally successful. He could have reported some progress on the boy's part. But Sophia seemed to be of the opinion that there was more to be learned in studying his face than in the book on her lap, in watching the movements of his lips than paying attention to the words that issued from them. This was provoking, for he came of a breed that thought it culpable not to expend all energy in gathering knowledge that could be turned to future advancement. But this wasn't a carrot that could be dangled before Sophia Morgan's nose. It was, he decided, his own fault. He should have looked closer at his prospective pupil before he agreed to Hazlett's request, for he knew very little about pretty young women, and could see no profit, or peace of mind, in knowing more. As it was, he had to use what wits he had to remain the teacher and not become the taught. Of one thing he was certain; he would accept no money for tutoring the Morgans.

Trade was moving satisfactorily enough at Weighill Lane. James had spoken the truth when he told the Doctor that he was sharing a cargo with another importer, if perhaps not quite accurate in hinting at its immediate arrival. He had met his provisional partner, Louis Fitzgibbon, a young Catholic merchant, at the Assembly Rooms, and taken a liking to him. To charter a schooner in Glasgow had been Fitzgibbon's idea, and as he claimed to have had profitable experience in such a venture, James went in with him readily. Unfortunately, in slapping down his debt before the Doctor that morning he had dealt a sad blow to his ready money. He was privately relieved, therefore, to learn that a dispute between the Scotch merchants and the owner of the vessel would mean a delayed sailing. As for that miscreant, Nugent Mullan . . .

It soon became evident that there was no settled opinion among those who were to entertain the Lord Lieutenant. Mr Sam Hassan, a prominent wine importer, whose interests often took him to London, claimed to have seen the scheme proposed for Irish trade should there be a legislative union. In his words 'it went to scarcely anything'. Someone reported Lord Charlemont, the Ulster peer, as having said that as good a plan could be drawn with a burnt stick on a wall. But Mr Arthur Maxwell, informed, assiduous, persuasive, would have none of it. Sam Hassan might be noted for his Old Red Port, but would he claim to be as well-informed on butter, tallow, pork, beef, wool, leather, all those commodities that Ireland could *export*? As for Lord Charlemont, he had always been a noted anti-unionist, and what other could they expect from that gentleman than an honourable if mistaken consistency?

"No, sirs," said Mr Maxwell, "we are men of independent mind. Lord Cornwallis comes north aware that we can decide that what spells good for the nation is to our good."

As his audience smilingly set the inversion to rights, Mr Spifford Lamont pushed his mirthless countenance over his neighbour's shoulder. "And what if this change should set up the Roman Catholics, eh?"

Mr Maxwell paused until he had everyone's attention. "Gentlemen, we are islanders. We are acquainted with the purgative power of the sea. A pestilence in a sluggish stream is rendered harmless once it is swept into the great ocean. So it will be with the papists, Spifford. Here they outnumber us three to one. Given the union and they will be diminished and lost in the Protestant millions of Britain." He ran an exulting eye around his listeners until suddenly he met the expressionless face of Louis Fitzgibbon. James, seated at the table, saw him falter. Then he had hurried forward to seize the young merchant's hand. "My dear Mr Fitzgibbon—my dear sir—need I assure ye, no offence intended . . . why, sir," and seeking inspiration he eyed the men of independent mind, grocers, brewers, linen-drapers, corn-chandlers, "*why, sir, you're one of us!*" Fitzgibbon bowed gravely and relinquished the other's hand.

But James, nettled, said, "Two years ago we had rebellion in this country to break the last connection with England. D'ye think those men will now tolerate a union?"

"What men?" Mr Maxwell blew out his lips in amusement. "Peasants and weavers, in the main. I'm happy to inform ye that the lower orders no longer trust their betters to lead them. So lay your orders, my dear Gault, there'll be no rebellion." And away he went in his smart fustian coat, trailed by his cronies. Confound him, thought James, the dog deserves a title. Then he fell to worrying if his question had been a prudent one.

Mr Hazlett arranged to call for James at his lodgings and drive with him to the reception. That afternoon the young man dismissed Fonsy and walked leisurely back to Mrs Black's to prepare for the evening. As he dressed he mused on the events that had brought him to take his place among the leading men of his circle. When he found himself dwelling on the more flattering aspects of the story he thought of the long months as a fugitive amid the ugly secrets of Legg's Lane. But to chasten himself he recalled that he had turned passively away from the supreme call of his life. He would never be a minister of the Gospel. But surely he could make amends by living among his fellows a life of righteousness, honest dealing, and above all, humility? He found such a prospect attractive. Might he not indeed have been called to this scene for that purpose? He hummed a tune as he adjusted his neckcloth, a psalm tune.

As he bent to the glass he heard a horse and vehicle enter the quiet street. It was too early for Pringle Hazlett, and too heavy in hoof and wheel. He glanced out of the window. There was something familiar about the man clambering down from the country cart. When he turned, James recognised him as a distant neighbour, Tam Orr of the Island. He was looking up and down the houses in a bewildered manner. James threw open the window and called, "Hey, Mr Orr!"

The countryman looked up, relief in his face. "Is that you, Jamie Gault?"

"Yes."

"Ye may come down. Your father's deid."

"Wait . . . wait."

In the street James gazed into the middle-aged man's face. "You said . . . ?"

"Your father's deid."

"When?"

"This morn, as I understand it. Kate Purdie came over the fields tae our house wi' the news. I said I would tell ye."

"It was kind of you, Tam."

"Heh, I had an errand tae the town anyway. Can I gie ye a lift back tae Ravara?"

"No, thanks. I'll . . . I'll ride out."

"Aye." Orr climbed up again. He lifted the reins and looked down on the young man. "I'm sorry for your mither and your Uncle Samuel and yoursel'. Hup horse!" The heavy cart lumbered away.

James changed into simpler clothes. He left a letter for Pringle Hazlett with Mrs Black. At the White Cross Inn he hired a horse. As the Viceroy was sitting down to dine with Arthur Maxwell and his fellows, he was breasting the Castlereagh Hills in the darkling evening, ruminating on the treacherous similarity between humility and self-flattery.

Men and women, touched by the flickering firelight, drew back as he entered, making room for him beside his mother. She looked up and laid her hand in his. He took it, then it was withdrawn. She was giving consolation, not asking for it. The Reverend Loudan, seated opposite, in rusty black coat and tow wig, could convey to her words of comfort, but not knowledge of death. Simply, the time had come for the departure of the man she had worked beside and lain beside for thirty years. James nodded to the faces, half in light, half in shadow, and saw the sharp ferret-blink of curiosity in their eyes. Here was Jamie Gault, the scholar, now grown rich in some strange way in the distant town.

His Uncle Sam sat outside the fire's glow with Sim Purdie. At the table were two or three elderly women in black, their noses red with weeping. One was his father's sister, Aunt Maggie Gaw, from Saintfield. Her husband, William, musing over the burning turf, sat with his hands and the head of his stick lost in his silken beard. He broke the silence without lifting his head. "This is a sair homecoming, Jamie. Aye, sair homecoming."

" 'Tis, uncle."

"Yous'll miss him." He lifted his splendid head and looked around challengingly. "Yous'll all miss him." A soft sigh of assent rose in reply.

Dr Loudan leant forward. "Will ye go down to him?"

James followed the minister through the cluster of young men at the door, among them the Purdie brothers and young Dan Echlin of Rathard. Their muttered condolences brushed him like fingers as he left the kitchen. Behind him, his Uncle William Gaw came lumbering down the narrow dark passage. Encased in pine boards, Robert Gault stretched his length like a candle. His son touched the coarse fibre of the linen nightgown. Be merciful to him, Lord, for he was a good man.

"He was a good man, was Rab," said Uncle William close to his nephew's ear. "A good man."

"He was, uncle."

"He hadna much when he married your mither. But if he had been blossomed wi' siller and fruited wi' gold, he couldna ha' been a better man."

"He wouldn't have been so good," said Dr Loudan testily.

"Ah," said Uncle William, stepping back, offended. James glanced at the broad stupid face that belied the prophet's beard and felt pity for him. He guided him to the door. "It was kind of ye both to come so far, uncle."

"Ah, sure, we could dae nae less . . . nae less," and the old man, leaning on his stick, crept away.

Dr Loudan scowled in self-reproach. "I'll give him the kind word before I go."

"He means well," said James soothingly. "I'm sorry, minister, that I couldn't be here earlier."

"All's been arranged. The grave's opened. I'll be here for the lifting of the coffin at eleven in the morning." The minister nodded towards the dead man. "Say your goodbye until you meet."

By that hour the neighbouring men had gathered in the Gaults' cottage. Their heads bowed under the minister's prayer, they darkened the room and the passage, and flowed out into the clear light of the farm close. The prayer finished, they turned to shuffle out, impeded by late-comers searching for the hand of James or his mother. A hand-clasp speaks for those with few words. The coffin, in the grasp of men skilled in burdens, was steered out of the house and into the daylight. In the lane, men who had travelled from more distant parts, stood watching silently. Sam was at his elbow. "Who'll take the first lift tae the road wi' us, Jamie?" James beckoned to Sim Purdie and Frank Echlin, a recognition of old neighbours. The four men took the coffin on their shoulders from those who had carried it out, clasped each other by the waist, trimmed their stride and bore their burden away towards the road, uncoiling and drawing the mourners after them.

Three or four neighbouring women, among them Kate, had helped the widow prepare food for those coming back from the churchyard. James led the girl outside. "Thank ye, Kate, for sending Tam Orr with the news."

"I wish it had been better." She made to move away, then paused. "But it takes the like to bring you back."

"Ah, is that fair, Kate——"

"Yes," she cried with a flash of anger. "You haven't been here for weeks. I'm forgotten!" As always, when she was roused, the hair above her temples seemed to lighten in hue and stir as if breathed upon. He had never been sure if it was a trick of the light or if her scalp contracted at such moments, but trick or not, it never failed to fill him with unease and an answering anger.

"You're not forgotten. I've been busy. I've now lodgings. But I told you that . . ."

"And no more. It's like watching somebody climbing a distant hillside. If you've found a place why can't ye take me to it?"

"She's an old widow with room only for one lodger. She couldn't take in a newly-wed pair."

Sullenly she looked around her. "What's going to happen to this place now your father's gone?"

He smiled. "Why, d'ye want to see me back here?"

"I was wondering."

"My mother's here—and my uncle Sam."

"Aye, but it's yours by right." The look on her face, more than her words, chilled him. For a fleeting moment he saw Sim, her father, peep out of her eyes.

With an effort he rid himself of what he had seen. "What use would this place be to anybody who didn't labour it with his own hands? Our future lies in Belfast. I work hard every day to that end. When you and I take our place in the life of the town it'll be in our own house. You understand that, my dear?"

"Kiss me, Jamie, my love."

Before he left for the town he drew his mother aside. "You'll never want for money. I warrant ye that. You see to it that Sam quits running the fields with young Purdie, and that he does the heavy tasks about the place for ye."

"Ah, son, what odds is tasks when there's only the skin o' your ribs between yourself and the next world?"

James's fingers closed on the hand resting on his horse's shoulder. "Mother, it is for the Lord to determine when we enter the next world." His grasp changed to a caress. "You taught your faith to me. Draw on it now for your comfort."

As he rode home he pondered on the folk he had left and how they figured in his life. What more could he have done for his mother? As for Kate, she wouldn't thank him in the future, if he brought her into his circle through the door of a humble lodging-house. He turned quickly from the memory of that look. What of Sim and her brothers? Barely a word with them beyond the needs of the funeral. They must know now that I can't free them from the tribe in Legg's Lane. And yet I would give much to know how they stand with the Doctor . . .

To address Miss Morgan by her first name, was, James discovered, a strategic advantage. It indicated his seniority and the relationship of teacher to pupil. Recalling that one of his favourite sages, William Law, had been a tutor to young ladies, he dipped into *A Serious Call to a Devout and Holy Life*. But the Englishman's Flavia and Miranda proved birds of a very different feather to Sophia Morgan. Also there were admonitions in the work that now upset and irritated him. He snapped it shut and put it at the bottom of his trunk.

He worked with his pupils in a corner of the study. Their uncle never appeared on these evenings. The squeak of furbelow and silk informed them of Mrs Hazlett's approach. She did not come often and stayed briefly, not wishing, she said, to interrupt their studies to the smallest extent.

One evening he arrived to find Sophia alone. She rose quickly as he entered and something in her manner filled him with misgiving. He looked around. "Your brother . . . ?"

"Lawrence is confined to his room. He has a chill."

"I'm sorry to hear that."

She stepped close to him. Undoubtedly she was paler. He met her scrutiny calmly. He even managed a playful scowl. He was the tutor. But her whole expression and bearing was so charged with an intensity that his gaze fell away, gratefully, to her pens and papers spread on a small stool. "Sophia, if you——"

"Are you much given to sympathy?"

"Eh?" he looked up with a foolish grin. "A running nose is not a pretty thing——"

She frowned impatiently, standing erect before him, her tapering fingers spread on her bosom. Helpless to resist, he looked at her again. "James Gault, I love you."

He put his hand very carefully on the back of a chair. Dry-mouthed, he said "No, Sophia, this is impossible . . . I have never led . . . it is quite out of the question . . ."

Her head drooped, her fingers still outspread on an offer that had fled like a bird set free. A sad little smile came on her face. "You could have put it more gently, Mr Gault," she said in a low voice, and stepping past him, left him. In the distance he could hear Mrs Hazlett approaching. He ran down the steps, led out his borrowed horse, and rode away.

Next morning the rising sun warmed his fresh-shaved jowl as he ascended the Castlereagh Hills. He did not draw rein until he had reached the Purdies' farmstead. Kate, called from the house, heard her lover, to her gratification and surprise, beg her hasten her preparations for their wedding.

XI

FROM AMONG HIS 'property interests' Mr Arthur Maxwell found a house for James. It had a neat parlour, two small bedrooms, a kitchen, a dairy and a stable. It sat in a kitchen garden fenced off from a sloping meadow overlooking the river Lagan. The yearly rent was nine guineas and the town was only two Irish miles away.

James told none of his Belfast acquaintances about his approaching marriage. His standing among them being what it was, he had no wish to disclose his meagre origins, or those of his bride. The thought of the voracious flattery with which Sim Purdie would greet people like the Hazletts or the Adairs, made him prickle in cold sweat. In the days before the wedding he kept a close watch on his actions and words. Nothing would give more delight to Tom Adair, a man of overbearing geniality, than to muster a fleet of carriages and descend on the rustic ceremony. Then he learned to his relief that he had nothing to worry himself about. By chance, Kate and he had chosen a wedding-day to be marked by a more portentous union; that of the legislatures of Great Britain and Ireland. The merchants gathered in the Assembly Rooms would have a great deal more to occupy themselves with, on the first day of August in the year 1800, than a humble country wedding.

It was with surprise and some annoyance, therefore, that James saw a back clad in fine broadcloth among the frieze jackets gathered in Sim Purdie's kitchen. He found his hand taken in greeting by Mr Gordon.

"Thank ye, Aeneas, we . . . it was kind of ye to come."

"I could do no less," said Mr Gordon. His gaze was on

Kate. James had never seen such animation on the ex-lawyer's face, such a glow in his eyes. Great God, he thought in mingled astonishment and derision, the dried old scobe has fallen in love with Kate. "You're a fortunate fellow, James."

"I'm well aware of it."

Mr Gordon turned away. He moved through the thronged kitchen, sharing a glass with Sim, exchanging a smiling word with James's mother and Kirsty Purdie who sat together. He has been the Doctor's emissary here many times, thought James, watching him. The bridegroom was hedged in by a circle of young men, neighbours and old school-mates when Mr Gordon, waiting his chance, approached Kate. He held out his wedding gifts—a locket, the fine chain of which ran down and settled in the girl's palm like golden water, a small curiously-chased pistol, a Dublin silver cream jug.

"They're too much, Mr Gordon."

"They're no more than some geegaws I came on. But this," he turned the pistol butt so that she could read *Aeneas Gordon* incised in the silverwork "this is personal. All I can give you of other and better days."

She flushed under his gaze and bobbed her head. Then, hiding the gifts in the folds of her sleeves she hurried to her room where she hid them in her travelling trunk. Later, when she showed the locket and jug to her husband, he viewed them with displeasure. "They're too valuable," he said curtly.

Kate looked up with candid eyes. "Are they? I know nothing of such things. Will I give them back? Mr Gordon said they were but—" she hesitated over the unfamiliar word, "but *geegaws*."

"Ah." James's face cleared. He could well imagine Gordon rummaging the boxes and cupboards in Legg's Lane for such things. "No, no, keep them, love." But something warned Kate to say nothing of the pistol with the name in filigree. When she came on it by chance she would run her finger over the silver fittings and wonder how she could find out what it would fetch.

James had avoided any discussion on the value or nature of Kate's dowry. From Sim he learnt that it was made up of some pieces of good furniture, a substantial quantity of household linen and two hundred guineas in gold. James had known of the furniture and the abundance of linen was traditional. But the size of the sum of money astonished him. He guessed, not without a quirk of guilt, that his betrothed had driven a hard settlement with her father.

In the neat rooms and scented presses of the cottage on the river bank, Kate found a place for her furniture and linen. Satisfied in bed and board, James set off each morning on his two-mile journey to Weighill Lane. Kate filled her day arranging and re-arranging in house and garden. She made friends with Mrs O'Neill, the lock-keeper, and at a fallen willow found a colony of water birds. These she fed most afternoons in the long hours. But as time passed the impression grew on the young wife that she had travelled a long journey and hadn't yet arrived. The town, with its bustle and company, remained beyond her reach.

*

James's marriage had made such small demand on the attention of his fellow-merchants that he had to acquaint those he thought worth the confidence with his changed status. His long serious face, and the fact that he had married a woman unknown to their circle, from some obscure townland, discouraged curiosity. Even Mr Hazlett, met in Fountain Lane, had greater news to impart than to receive.

"James, I've been looking for you. I've something to tell you. My niece has suddenly flown off to her uncle in Queen's County."

"Miss Sophia?" James eyed the other circumspectly. "Is there aught amiss?"

"No, no . . . but it was a thankless action . . . when you had put yourself about to instruct her . . ."

"Your niece has little to learn from me," said James evenly.

"These young 'uns are so confoundedly thoughtless . . . you're not vexed?"

James took his friend's arm. "My dear Pringle," he said with warm conviction, "think no more of it. It was only a small service that I could do for you. Indeed, I'll have to relinquish your nephew to more competent hands. I've a wife and a home to care for since we last met."

"Eh?" Mr Hazlett stopped in the thronged street. "And you gave us no word?"

James urged him on. "Circumstances never permitted my wife to get acquainted with anyone in the town. We could see no sense in dragging people out, Pringle. A remote wee kirk . . . where our people worshipped."

"Aye, but Mrs Hazlett will think it strange." Mr Hazlett himself thought it strange. But he had long recognised that young Gault was one of those who kept themselves to themselves and he valued such men. It spelled discipline, a practical head. And it was becoming increasingly important to Mr Hazlett that James Gault should reveal no inconsistency or weakness in his life, that is, his public commercial life.

"You are no longer at your lodgings?"

"No. I've rented a house about two miles up the river."

"Your friends will expect a house-warming."

James laughed. "It's an old house, Pringle."

"But you've a new wife. It'll give Mrs Gault a chance to meet your friends."

"The Assembly Rooms would be better suited."

"As you wish, James. We could make up a little affair of six or eight. Dinner at the Donegall Arms, then cards, perhaps . . ."

Their news shared they walked arm-in-arm along the High Street. To the wharfmen and market hucksters and stall-women who impeded their way, accosted them, bumped their elbows, pushed by them, they were two merchants deep in business. But the words they exchanged were few and as unimportant as the feathers blown along the gutter.

Mr Hazlett was trying to vizualise, without much success, what sort of woman could have attracted James Gault as a wife. The news of Sophia Morgan's flight completely filled the mind of his companion. It had not been an impudent young hussy who had faced him that evening, but a woman, deeply, painfully, in love. Great God, he thought, how could I, in ignorance, have so hurt a fellow-creature? And try as he would he could not rid himself of a sad-sweet pang, that he had missed, irreparably, something precious in his life.

The 'little affair' turned out to be even more modest than Mr Hazlett had proposed. James had no relish for a dinner at the tavern, Kate lacked the costume, and both held card-playing in abhorrence. James suggested that they should take tea some afternoon with Hazlett, Tom Adair, Fitz-gibbon, and their wives, inviting Arthur Maxwell as a mark of esteem for securing them River Cottage. Kate agreed. As yet they were no more than names to her. Then she added. "I want Mr Gordon asked."

James had half-expected this. Nevertheless he closed his eyes in exasperation. "Kate, I've rid myself of that crowd. If I remember right, you begged me to. I'll not be dragged back among them!"

"Mr Gordon isn't the Doctor. He's a gentleman."

"He's well enough. But I tell you this isn't the place for him, among these people——"

"Aye, they're *your* friends. But I want to see a familiar face, next Thursday."

"My hope is that they'll become your friends, also," James sighed. "Am I expected to carry the invitation to Legg's Lane?"

Kate showed no outward sign of her victory. "You could send that craytur, Fonsy."

The party met at the Assembly Rooms at the appointed time. Coming in, Kate was nervous and subdued. But the simplicity of her dress gained her the sympathy and therefore the goodwill of the ladies. The admirable colouring of her hair and skin won her the approbation of the gentlemen. Mr Maxwell and Mr Tom Adair, the coal importer, applauded her genuine delight in the aquatint designs and coffered ceiling that enhanced the principal room. She had also the attention of two men standing in the doorway of the card room.

"That's Gault's new wife," said one.

At the mention of the name the other shrank back. He peered over his companion's shoulder. Something in the girl's movements and face caught his attention. She stirred a memory that he was unable to define. Then Nugent Mullan gave up with a shrug. He lifted his glass as if in a toast. "Hell burn them both," he murmured and drained it. "I'm away home."

If the tea party, James decided later, was not a sweeping success, at least nothing was lost. Kate held her tongue and behaved discreetly under the worldly eye of Mrs Hazlett. Mrs Adair was, as usual, running over with her own joviality, and young Mrs Fitzgibbon was too modest in manner and means to have opinions worth considering. The arrival of Aeneas Gordon caused some perturbation among the men. Even the lightsome Arthur Maxwell, chattering away to the ladies, looked put out. But as usual, Gordon, in his neat black clothes, behaved admirably. His conversation was pleasant and addressed to the company at large. He neither offered nor encouraged confidential asides with his neighbours at table. This strange fellow, thought James, watching him with interest tinged with envy, has known circles far beyond that of the decent self-satisfied merchants in this room.

"You hadn't met Mr Gordon before?" he said in a low voice to Louis Fitzgibbon.

"No," said the young man. "He seems a very amiable gentleman."

"Nor his friend . . . the Doctor?"

Mr Fitzgibbon shook his head.

Truly, thought James, this town is growing larger.

Mr Maxwell, to his unconcealed satisfaction, had been elected one of a dozen commissioners appointed to supervise the new municipal law for the paving, cleaning and lighting of the town's streets. This piece of legislation had cost the Town Corporation over twelve hundred pounds; each commissioner had to be in possession of personal estate valued at two thousand pounds (Kate noticed that apart from Mr Gordon, who was smiling faintly, the others shifted as if in annoyance). So did Mr Maxwell. He hurried on: ladies and gentlemen could be assured of walking on, or being carried along, unsullied thoroughfares. Mr Maxwell drew breath. What did the company think of that?

Mrs Hazlett and Mrs Adair complimented each other on the prospect of walking abroad without having their skirts fouled. Kate, appealed to, agreed warily, having as yet little experience of the town's streets. But Mr Maxwell wasn't satisfied. "What do you think, Tom?" he demanded of Mr Adair.

"What do I think?" said Mr Adair turning from pretty Mrs Fitzgibbon. "I'll tell ye what I think, Arthur. I think if Ireland ever names a national dish it should be the pork steak. We must be the only people that cut up our pigs so prodigally."

Mr Maxwell stared, Mrs Adair shook and twinkled to her bugle laugh. As if stirred by the thought of more solid and succulent food, everyone got up, declaring that it had been a very enjoyable afternoon, that it would be only the first of many, and in the meantime the young couple could rest assured of everybody's felicitations and friendship. James drew Aeneas Gordon aside to tell him that he had recently ridden out to Ravara.

"I hope you find them in good health?"

"But not in ease of mind. Hugh Purdie tells me that the Doctor has contracted his father to deliver foodstuffs to the French."

Mr Gordon glanced carefully behind him. The others were moving off in search of cloaks, hats and canes. "He's a very loquacious young man, your brother-in-law," he said smoothly. "If such a traffic exists, it's certainly much more indirect than he puts it."

"It'll be as straight as a piece of rope to a government agent. I want it stopped."

"And what will Sim Purdie think of that?"

"You—or he, must find another customer."

"That's easier said than done. You're over-anxious. We're not alone in the trade. Napoleon, they say, is trampling over the face of Europe in English-made boots."

"Aeneas, I want the arrangement broken . . . for Kate's sake."

Mr Gordon paused. He looked at the younger man for a moment. "I don't know what goods are moving this week. But I'll see to it that they're the last. Here's your friend, Mr Fitzgibbon. I'll leave you. My thanks to you and your wife."

Fitzgibbon and Gordon bowed as they passed. The young merchant held up a letter. "Word, James, that our cargo is due from Glasgow in the brig *Irish Oak*, before the end of the month, given wind and weather."

"And no French frigate," said James gloomily.

"Heh," cried Fitzgibbon surprised, "that's no way to take the news!"

"Of course not, Louis. It's good news. When are we due to settle the bill?"

"Twenty-one days after unloading. We'll have the profit safe by that."

Kate lay beside her husband, her eyes following the lanes, roads and broad highways in the cracked ceiling of their bedchamber. She had much to think over. While the company chattered and gestured, she had watched and noted their words and movements, bringing away a hundred memories and impressions unobserved by James, and that lay, no doubt, far outside his perception. Even while she talked with Aeneas Gordon her eyes stole little glances at the women, watching them help themselves to tea, hold the cup, cut bread-and-butter, offer cakes, address the waiters. Her ear recalled the pronunciation of words, the smiling inquiries that had nothing to do with feeling, the polite giving way to a contrary opinion. Mrs Hazlett she recognised as a *lady*, but she and Mrs Adair were too old to imitate. For the time being it would be better to follow the costume, speech and behaviour of the young Fitzgibbon woman . . . wasn't it the world's wonder to have a papist as a friend . . . She quivered under the sheets as she rebelled, momentarily, against the need to put herself to school to any of them. The life she knew lay far beyond the ken of the Harriet Hazletts and the Jessica Fitzgibbons. Mrs Adair, with her comfortable laughter, had never seeded potatoes until she wept and cursed the agony of frozen fingers that must go on fumbling long after sense of touch had gone. None had followed the harrow all day in sodden clothes or scraped dried meal from their forearms long after nightfall. They had shivered at the word 'rebel' among their parlour cushions. She had lain in bog holes to evade the rebels or their pursuers and learnt to load a pistol so that, if need be, she could turn it on herself. But all that, thanks be, was in the past. Now she could look forward with a sharp eye and a sharp relish. Hasten slowly m'lass. And the first step was to get this man snoring at her side to move into a house in the town. A slated house . . . a house fit for such acquaintances as Mrs Hazlett, whose brother, James said, was a greater landlord than Mr Burke.

XII

THE *Irish Oak* drew so little water that it was possible to work her right up to the Town Quay, saving James and his partner the expense of discharging into lighters in the tortuous channel to the port. It was with satisfaction and a feeling of importance that James watched the stevedore's gang swing out the casks and hump up the sacks and bags from the hold. Stacked on the quayside, the cargo made a fair show; chests of fine Malaga lemons, hogsheads of scale sugar, tea, coffee and olive oil, barrels of pearl ash and Teneriffe barilla, bags and jars and boxes of spices, cheeses, liquorice and cream of tartar.

"You've a mixed bag, cap'n," said Fonsy as he surveyed the growing pile of merchandise. Mr Fitzgibbon, invoices flittering from his hand, a copy of that day's *Belfast News-Letter* sticking from his pocket, was hurrying here and there among the porters. He paused at Fonsy's words. "The tide was on our side too, James," he said gleefully. He took the newspaper from his pocket and shook it. "The buyers will have had our advertisement with their coffee. We can expect them any time." He hurried away after a back bowed under a chest of tea.

Fonsy scratched his chin. "Y'r pardon, cap'n. But you're not thinking of selling from the quay?"

"Yes, Fonsy, that's in the advertisement."

"And you with all the grand storage in Weighill Lane?"

James laughed. "And all the grand money saved on haulage warm in our pocket."

Fonsy considered his master and then looked upward. He pointed over the town. From above Divis Mountain the west wind was unrolling a dark sheet across the sky. "Well," said the ragged odd-jobs man, "your customers will have to lift their feet if they're gonna be here in time."

A windblown dash of rain struck James's face. Like a burning spark it startled him into life. The peasant lad who had saved many an armful of corn or kindling from the destroying rain saw what was about to happen to the rich merchandise spread on the quayside. "What's to be done, Fonsy?"

"Cart them to the store, for sure, cap'n."

"Ye fool, there's nearly a hundred tons there! Can we get them under cover? That shed—" James pointed to a store lying back from the quay.

"That shed," said Fonsy in a huffed voice, "is choked full o' mess beef and pork waiting a ship the-morra."

A skift of rain came sweeping over the roofs, freckling the water in the dock, drumming on the brim of James's hat, rolling like hailshot on the piled casks and kegs. Fitzgibbon came hurrying back. A glance at his face and James knew that he had sorely overrated his partner's judgment and experience. The black clouds mustered over the town. Then down came the torrent, lancing and splintering on the cobbles, driving even the pigeons and gulls to shelter. Mr Fitzgibbon made an irresolute gesture towards the shed and moved in that direction as if seeking shelter for himself. James was outraged. "Come back e're that!" he bellowed above the tattoo. "There's work to be done!"

Fonsy, his hair plastered in a triangle between his eyes, the water spouting from him as from some riverside animal, was pushing sacks below casks and kegs, a frenzied grin on his face. "Tar'plins, cap'n," he screamed, "tar'plins, tar'plins!" They borrowed two from the *Irish Oak*, a third from the stevedore's hut. Splashing ankle-deep, their nails broken by the flapping covers, they dragged the tarpaulins over the merchandise. As James tucked the last corner in, the downpour wavered, the clouds drifted seaward, the sun reappeared and the pigeons fluttered back to the yellow meal scattered on the cobbles. But not one customer came ambling in from the town.

The two partners gazed morosely at the sodden heap. A rivulet of olive oil ran across the stones carrying with it streaks of pearl ash. It gleamed in the sunlight like a wide sardonic grin until it dripped over the quay's edge.

"How much have we lost?" said Fitzgibbon at last.

James gave a gesture of angry bewilderment.

"The sacks that's caked wi' the wet are goners," volunteered Fonsy. "The boxes an' kegs are all right."

James surveyed him with a melancholy smile. "Away back to the counting-house and get yourself dried out. You'll be getting a founder, man."

"Faix, cap'n," said Fonsy squirming in gratitude, "sure, I'm web-footed."

"Off ye go when I bid ye. But first, what's your advice?"

"What I said at first. Get it round to Weighill Lane."

"When you've a dry shirt on, hire two carts. Do you go with McGrattan, Louis, and put the word about that we're selling from my store."

Handing the keys to Fonsy saved him having to look at Fitzgibbon. He felt that he had been put upon, and the knowledge that his partner was as likely to suffer put no bridle on his resentment. Damme, hadn't Fitzgibbon claimed to have shared in such shipments before?

There had been some talk about the inadvisability of going into business with a Roman Catholic. He heard it in varying degrees of emphasis from the Market House to the White Cross Inn. Injudicious, said Arthur Maxwell, the guardian of citizens' rights: sell to 'em, buy from 'em if you must. But . . . Dan Ritchie, the grain factor, as Orange as his maize, finished Maxwell's admonition. "But don't be putting the idea into their heads that they'll ever be our equals, by the Lord God!"

James listened in silence or avoided a direct reply. What troubled these men wasn't a threat to their theology, so much as the old aching fear of the reconquest of their territory. On that stood all their gear, spiritual and temporal. He thought himself freed from such a fear, and, with some satisfaction, counted it to the liberating influence of the university.

But that didn't absolve Fitzgibbon and his crazed handling of their cargo. To have landed goods on an open quay without discovering whether or not there was cover available if the weather broke! He was as great a fool himself. He kicked the pile, heard the jangle of broken glass, saw the oil spew out redoubled. Looking around him guiltily he pulled the tarpaulin close. The rain had started again when a couple of waggons rolled on to the quay, Fonsy seated beside the driver of the first, Mr Fitzgibbon, his expression betraying that his guts had taken a shaking, on the tail board of the second. In a dozen or more laborious journeys, under the pouring rain, the carts dripping as if coming from a distillery, they shifted the cargo of the *Irish Oak*, or what was left of it, to the storehouse in Weighill Lane.

*

James dropped his pen and studied the column of figures dully. "Yes, that's it. About a hundred and fifty guineas . . ."

Kate spread her hands on the table. "Of a loss?" she said unbelievingly.

"Of a loss," her husband echoed.

"But, Jamie man, how did ye let it happen? It's impossible to lose that much money!" In her agitation she sprang up and ran to the sideboard where she stood with her back to him.

"I've gone over the calculations till I'm blind. Maybe you'd like to try your hand?"

She spoke over her shoulder. Her face was flushed, her auburn curls showed vibrant gold in the window's light as if they changed hue in her passion. "For Jesus sake, m'man, is it only a matter o' ciphering——"

"Kate!" he cried in a shocked voice but she topped him shrilly. "God forgive me for the swearing, but if we sit here till the screech o' dawn will we figure that loss away?" She swung round on him. "It's a judgment on ye for going in with that papish, Fitzgibbon!"

Having already trodden that path in his own mind, James was quick with an angry denial, but not without a twinge of superstitious fear. "There's no mystery to it! The rain ruined the stock and Louis Fitzgibbon stands to lose as much as I do. I thought," he added lamely, "you liked Jessie Fitzgibbon."

She sat down again. "James, don't try to put me off. My liking Mrs Fitzgibbon's of no consequence. She doesn't sit in my lap. I tell ye that ye won't prosper in any dealings with people of that persuasion. Push your affairs with people of our own kind and don't make a martyr o' yourself with our money."

The word *our* trembled as a query on his lips. He looked into her hard black eyes and swallowed it. "Who have you been talking to, Kate?"

" 'Talking to?' " She laughed at him. "D'ye think I was reared in a pigeon's nest? No, m'man. I've my feet on the ground and keep my eyes and ears open. And when you're at it there's that other papish craytur, Fonsy . . ." she left it unfinished, watching him.

"Fonsy?" He had never given a thought to the religious persuasion of his odd-jobs man. "How d'ye know he's a Catholic?"

" 'Michael Alphonsus McGrattan'." She drew out the syllables with a grimace. "You'd as lief find holy water in an Orange lodge as one of that name."

"And I'd as lief not have him around me if I knew he was an Orangeman," he said in a flat cold voice.

"Hire them that it pays ye to hire—and get rid of that fellow!"

"No!" He struck the table. "Fonsy's my right hand. If I had listened to him I wouldn't be in this fix today. Fonsy stays and that's an end to it!"

"And where," she said at last, "are ye going to lay hands on the money to meet this?"

There and then James made up his mind that she would have to be his partner and confidant. "I don't know, Kate."

She clenched her hands on the table-top. With foreboding he met her gaze. "Ye could raise something on the tenant-right at Ravara."

He stared at her. "And what of my mother?"

Her eyes slid away. "Aye, indeed," she sighed.

"You can't be serious, Kate?"

"Can ye think of anything better?"

"I would be hard put to it to think of anything worse." His smile was not without malice as he added, "She would have to live with us."

Again the sigh. "Aye, that would be the way o't." He wasn't prepared to put his mother on the roadside. He watched her relinquish the idea. "But the place owes ye something. Unless, of course, you're going to let it go to your Uncle Sam——"

"There's nothing there, girl. When my father was alive the three of them could barely scratch a living out of it."

"You've the money to find." She spoke softly, her hand on his arm. "Ride out tomorrow and try. The corn's cut and gathered. If you got it milled you could raise maybe ten, fifteen guineas. Every weethin' helps. And you could pay them back when you see daylight again."

He agreed with little enthusiasm and less hope. In his mind's eye he saw the thatched cabin crouched on the edge of that dark spongy bog from which most of the poor wealth of its peat had already been gouged.

But the hearts always lifted in him when he climbed the Castlereagh Hills on a sun-filled morning. The wind was so mild today that in the distant fields trees stood motionless, but by the roadside the leaves of ash and beech fluttered and flittered around the errands of small birds. A boy, feet braced wide on the floor of a turf cart, jogged past, favouring James with a wink, his breath employed in mocking thrush and blackbird. Beyond the village of Ballygowan the undulating plateau stretched before him to Strangford Lough, the smoke from the cottages leaning away south-east like stalks waiting for the sickle.

The dark mass of Lusky Woods where he had trespassed many a time seemed altered, misshapen. Tracks and fox pads that he had explored through the undergrowth now lay open to the sun. The fleshy odour of sawdust hung in the air. He smiled sardonically as he cantered under the arched boughs. Mr Burke was laying an axe to his liquor bills. He overtook Hugh Purdie beyond the demesne gates. The young farmer turned guiltily at James's hail. He had the haunted look he always wore when he had been on an errand to the landlord's house.

"I see ye well, Hugh?" said James ignoring the other's expression.

"Aye. And your care?"

"Well, thanks be. I'm on my way to my mother's." James slipped down from his horse. "How was the harvest?"

Purdie chuckled sourly. "*You* should know. The Belfast merchants are asking forty-one shillings for a hunner-weight o' oatmeal. What would ye take from that?"

"That it's in short supply."

"And ye would be right. 'Twas a poor crop."

They walked for a time in silence, the horse plodding meekly at rein's length. "I did as ye asked me, Hugh. I got word to Legg's Lane."

"I know." Purdie tramped the road beside him, head lowered.

"Well," said James sharply, "isn't that what you wanted?"

"They've left us with our crops on our hands——"

"You never see any of the Doctor's men, now?"

"Ne'er a hair of one of them."

They had travelled from under the gloom of the trees. "God be thanked for that," said James lightly as he remounted. "Hard work will find ye another buyer. Try the markets in Downpatrick and Killyleagh. Give my kindness to your mother. Tell her Kate's well."

"James . . . !"

The rider looked down into the youth's face. "No, Hugh," he said coldly. "I can offer you nothing in the town. I'll go now, for I've to be back before dark." He urged his horse forward, angry at Purdie's piteous look, angrier with himself for his harshness.

His uncle was piling a heap of new-cut boughs in a corner of the close. Even the white flesh of axe-chips had been neatly gathered together. The cobbler turned to greet his nephew. He waved at the tree-trimmings. "From the Squire's bounty."

"I saw that they had been felling as I came through. You didn't have to take that in lieu of wages?"

"No. Ephraim Smart told us we could take them for kindling."

"My mother?"

"She's inside. She's not been at herself these last days, Jamie."

James stooped to enter the cottage. His mother sat crouched over the fire, beside her a steaming bowl of tea as black as bogwater. He knelt and put an arm around her shawled shoulders. "Sam tells me you've been ill."

She turned to greet him. He saw, with a sense of shock, how aged she had become. Her hair hung in tails round a face that was seamed and darkened, as if she had sat for days over the turf smoke. To be brisk and spotless had been her first concern when her husband was alive. She patted his arm gently. "I'm all right, son. I'm only brissling my shins at the fire."

"That stuff you're drinking—is there no milk in the house?" Heedless to her voice he strode out to the close. His uncle had shaken out a handful of fodder before the horse. "Uncle, my mother's ailing—why didn't you send for me?"

"For why, Jamie? She's on the mend now."

"Shouldn't she have a woman in?"

"Damn-it-skin, Jamie, d'ye see Jeannie Gault sharing her kitchen wi' another woman?"

His uncle always had an answer, the answer that invariably spelt the minimum of effort, of exertion. They went into the house. His mother had made some effort to tidy herself.

"You took me unbeknownest, son. And look," she held up a coarse white jug. "We've lashins and lavins o' milk."

"Good," said James. "The cow's giving well?"

"And Hugh Purdie leaves over a can every other day."

"That's kind o' Hugh," said the young man, his voice muted. "I met him on the road. He tells me the crop was poor."

"Poor?" echoed his uncle. "A jenny-wren could have sat on her haunches and ate the top pickle o' grain. It was *that* poor."

James remembered his errand. He looked around the familiar kitchen, its roughness blunted in shadow. "How are ye for money?"

"Well enough."

"Times are hard but our wants are small, Jamie."

"Sam's had a brave turn at the mending, lately."

"The neighbours had to draw the cut timber for the landlord," his uncle explained. "Their harness might have been fit enough for a plough or a harrow, but once they yoked the animals to a tree trunk bust went collars, brichen and belly-bands!" The cobbler threw back his head and laughed. "The patches I put on are stronger than the owld harness, now."

"It's an ill wind . . ." said James smiling, as Sam took himself outside highly pleased at his good fortune.

He put his fingers into his fob pocket and brought out a couple of guineas. "For you, mother."

"Ah, you needna, James." But she took the money and reaching up dropped it into a lustre jug on the mantelshelf. She stood for a moment surveying her son. "And Kate, is she tending ye well?"

"And why not?" he asked with an irritable smile.

"No sign of a child yet?"

"No, mother."

"Ah, the Gaults were never a great breeding race. Ye dinna look yourself at all, James."

"We all have our cares."

"It was them rebelly men, son. They put your feet on the wrong road."

"That's past history."

Drawing her shawl around her, she sat down. "It was the only thing your father and me never agreed on."

Surprised, James knelt beside her. "I never heard him say anything of that."

"Heth, son, it wasna a thing ye told the world. But he always held ye did the right thing in principle."

James rode away from the cabin and its two ageing people who, every day, patiently balanced a fistful of meal, a couple of potatoes, a drop of milk, against privation. He pressed steadily past the scatter of hovels on Sim Purdie's land, noting from under the brim of his hat that every shelter had its heap of twigs and white splinters. With a grim smile he wondered what scale Sim would employ to measure the labour in return. Grateful to the thickening darkness, he raised his mount to a gallop past the farmhouse, his cloak drawn up, his ears sealed to any hail of recognition. Beyond the last bush on his father-in-law's land he dropped to an easier gait.

*

Kate drew her embroidery back into her lap. "If you were to sell off cheap what you have at Weighill Lane, could you clear yourself?"

"I would have to wait too long for buyers. But that's not the worst of it. If I cut below the buying price I'm gathering another load for my back. Forbye . . . it would do my credit in the town harm."

She nodded and he felt that he was merely voicing what she had already discerned. "And you've no deals on hand that would raise the money?"

He pushed a spurting coal into the fire with his toe. "None."

"You're beat, Jamie man?"

"I can see no way out, Kate."

She put her linen aside, rose and left the room. He heard a drawer being opened. When she came back she had a small leather drawstring bag in her hand. She seated herself at the table. There was the chink of a coin. He raised his eyes. With the money from the bag she was building small pillars of gold on the table. At last she was satisfied. "There," she said, "a hundred and fifty guineas."

"Your dowry money, Kate!"

Her left hand was still cupped around the money, filling him with a sudden unreasoning anger.

"I'll make a bargain with ye, James."

He eyed her silently.

"We move into the town."

He relaxed. "That's not a hard bargain to meet."

A hand still shielding the money she leaned over and picked up the newspaper. She began to read from it. "Mrs McCreery of Ann Street had returned from Dublin with printed calicoes, black and coloured velvets, Norwich muslin shawls, beads, bugles and fancy feathers . . ."

He laughed in spite of himself. "Kate, Kate, you can visit Mrs McCreery's emporium any day you wish."

She tossed the paper aside. There was no smile on her face as she looked at him. "If that woman can go into trade, so can I. I kept my father's books. I'll keep the books at Weighill Lane. That's the second half o' the bargain, Jamie man." Carefully she pushed the money across the table. "Take that and settle your debt."

XIII

Mr Arthur Maxwell, it was credibly reported, had been summoned to Dublin Castle to receive the industriously-sought-after and long-awaited accolade. To the clerks, hucksters, carters, porters, stall-women, message-boys, workless weavers and suchlike of the town's streets and alleys, the news (if they heard it) was of as much consequence as a skift of rain. To the new knight's fellow-merchants and their wives, if they stuck to their caustic opinion, the news would be received in the drawing-rooms with derision and contempt. But their faces, the sum total of which, mustered in the Assembly Rooms, made up the public face, bore only complaisant good-humour and quirks of gratification at the thought of rubbing shoulders with a knight and his lady. The wits could wait.

For Maxwell, as Kate and James discovered, had a wife. They met her at the celebratory ball, a faded, creased little woman, like a piece of taffeta that had lain in a drawer too long. Kate quickly put her out of mind, being much more taken with the ladies of her acquaintance, Mrs Hazlett and her fine manners, and on this occasion, Mrs Adair and her jewels.

James had little appetite for the banquet and its speeches and was sorely tried by the dancing that followed. He had gone to the affair with two ideas; to speak to Nugent Mullan, who was much in his thoughts lately, and to ask Arthur Maxwell about renting a house in the town. But on this evening his debtor wasn't present, and the new knight, according to Pringle Hazlett, had rid himself of his interests in Belfast.

James was disappointed. "What will he do now? He seemed a man of considerable property."

"He is to settle in England," said Mr Hazlett.

"To look after his properties at Liverpool and Bristol," said Tom Adair with a grin.

"His East India trade," added Sam Hassan, an amplification that afforded Mr Adair further amusement.

James looked from one to another in perplexity. "I didn't know he was in that trade."

"Sir Arthur's East India trade, James, is in human flesh and blood," said Mr Hazlett.

James stared at his friend. "A slave-trader?"

"That's it."

"My God, that's incredible . . . it's impossible. It's a damnable business!"

"How d'ye think he made his money, simpleton?" said Tom Adair. "By renting out cottages and back lane stores?"

"He'd spend a twelve-month of such rentals in one trip to woo the satrap in Dublin," said Sam Hassan. The wine-merchant stood up. "Here are the ladies. So lay in to his vittles and liquor, Gault, for they come, as you might say, off broad backs," a remark that gave James little stomach for the dishes set before him and a strong repugnance for the loquacious figure at the top of the table.

The need to accept his wife's money had planted Mullan and his chronic debt in the forefront of James's mind. His powerlessness to deal with his debtor had never left him. It gnawed at his self-esteem. It possessed him as he went about his business and troubled his sleep at night. Even the satisfaction of paying over to Fitzgibbon his share of their mutual loss left him with a sense of guilt. If Kate had offered her help with a tender, even a kind, word! She had pushed the money at him as if he was a stranger. The recollection of how she had shielded the coins until she had struck her bargain filled him with resentment not far removed from hatred. Yet, as the days passed, a word, a thought revealed in some act of affection, freed him from his bitterness towards her.

But these moods varied too often for his comfort; painfully he tried to reconcile himself to this duality of feeling towards the woman he had married.

Two days after the banquet he overtook his debtor in the Cornmarket. "A word with you, Mr Mullan——"

The other turned on him violently. "The same pestering question?"

"When are you going to give me my money?"

The leather chandler smirked defiantly. "Never. Now ye have your final answer."

"I'll been patient with you, Mullan. I'm going to have you taken up for debt. At least I'll save other merchants."

James had only a confused idea of what he meant by the threat. But a glance at his adversary made it clear that he had, inadvertently, laid his hand on an effective weapon. The colour drained from the sodden face. James watched the struggle between hate and mounting panic.

"I am . . . d'ye know who I am, Gault?"

James stood silent.

"Curse ye, ye can't mean it!"

"I mean it."

"It'll be the Bridewell for me."

James nodded coldly. "I'm aware of that."

"But Great God, how could I raise that much money?"

"Ye can afford to run with those that have it."

"I'll have to sell up!"

"Sell up and give me my money."

Mullan stared at him piteously. "Christ, Gault, my wife and children——"

"—at Weighill Lane." James took a final glance. The barb had gone deep. He turned and walked away.

He now set about fulfilling his part of the bargain. Mr Hazlett, delighted that his young friend intended to move into the town, promised that he would keep his eyes open for a suitable house. In less than a week he was able to report that a friend of Mrs Hazlett, a Mrs Masterson, would be happy to consider, not lodgers, but someone to share her house at No. 7, Talbot Place. He offered to introduce James to the lady.

On their way to Talbot Place Mr Hazlett told James something of Mrs Masterson. The widow of an attorney who had practised long and successfully in Dublin and the north of Ireland, she continued to live, with stubborn pride, in a house that suited neither her convenience nor her purse.

"It's not so much a matter of money," Mr Hazlett corrected himself, "for her husband left her well-provided for. But large houses need to be warmed and lighted by more than faggot and candle. I would reckon that there are up to a dozen apartments in the place, but Mrs Masterson makes no use of more than two or three."

Number 7, Talbot Place, was a handsome four-storey house set back from the street, the area between house and street neatly pebble-paved. Above the adjoining wall showed the black winter branches of the orchard. A young serving-girl admitted the two merchants. As she took their hats and canes Mrs Masterson appeared from a doorway at the end of the hall. The light falling from the staircase window revealed to James a woman of imperial build with a heavy florid face, the expression on which, at that moment, was far from amiable. She acknowledged Mr Hazlett's introduction with the slightest of bows. Opening a door to the right of the hallway she led her visitors into an apartment, where the flames of a lively fire opposed the dropping gloom and set outposts of dancing light on the knobs and legs of chairs, sofas, tables and cabinets. Reaching the hearthrug she rounded grandly on James.

"You understand, Mr Gopp, that I don't take in lodgers." She closed her eyes as if to hear the imputation spoken aloud was too much for her. "If you and Mrs Gopp come to reside at Talbot Place you undertake to rent part of the house as your private establishment, with your own furniture and linen and domestic arrangements. That is clear to you?"

"*Gault*," murmured Mr Hazlett and went on to inform the lady that Mr Gault was quite clear on the matter, that only pressing business and social reasons compelled him to leave the pretty cottage rented him by Sir Arthur Maxwell, and that Mr and Mrs Gault were keenly aware of their good fortune in being offered occupancy of such an estimable house in the town.

The fire playing on her sarcenet-clad buttocks, Mrs Masterson thawed visibly. "You will have an apartment of this size," she informed James with an almost affable wave of her hand, and as the young man noted apprehensively that the walls were a great distance apart, she added, "and one overlooking the garden only a little smaller. At the rear there are the usual kitchen offices. Now, upstairs," said Mrs Masterson stepping into the hall, "are four rooms which you may put to use as best suits you and above that two garrets for your in-servants." She led them along a paved passage to the rear of the house. Here a door opened on the garden. "You will excuse me not going out. The winter mists don't treat me kindly. But there you can see the stables and the coach-house. All these I keep in good repair." James, peering through the fruit trees, saw the dark mass of the buildings.

"I can have a horse!" he whispered to Mr Hazlett.

"You can have six," said Mr Hazlett.

"And there are quarters above the stables for your coachman," said Mrs Masterton closing out the night mist.

"And the yearly rent, ma'am?" said James as they followed her along the flagged passage.

"Such matters you discuss with Mr Lucas, my solicitor," cried Mrs Masterson, her voice rolling out like a bow-wave as she forged ahead of the men.

They were given their hats and sticks by the little maid. "My friend Gault," said Pringle Hazlett, "will be very happy to call with Mr Lucas. But *I* have to carry word back to Mrs Hazlett. Come, ma'am," with a hint of impatience, "what's the rent?"

"Thirty guineas," said Mrs Masterson.

James was silent.

"And I hope," added the lady her eye suddenly shrewd,

"that your friend finds the figure suits him. Mr Lucas tells me that the town is growing so, that the building of houses for the better classes is lagging far behind. Mr Gault and his wife," and the lady bowed to the young merchant with tart amiability, "could travel farther and fare worse."

The men bowed in reply. The maid closed the door on the figure of Mrs Masterson.

James stood motionless in Talbot Place. In-servants . . . coachman . . . "Great heavens, Pringle, that's three times as much as I pay for River Cottage!"

"The consideration," said Mr Hazlett linking the young man as they walked away, "that it is also more than three times as desirable a residence will have little weight if you can't pay the rent. But think: first, its convenience to your business, the markets, your acquaintances; then its certain that Maxwell will have sold up the cottage and you'll have to shift anyway, and not least your wife's wish to live in the town. You could find a cheaper place, but that house," Mr Hazlett turned to point with his cane, "is fit to raise a family in."

James didn't answer. Mr Hazlett spoke again. "Your friends know that you lost on the Glasgow shipment. But that mustn't geld ye. A young man like you deserves better. So, if you'll let me help you—whatever you reckon——"

"No, no!" James spoke abruptly, then recollecting himself, softened his voice. "Thank ye kindly, Pringle, but I'll weather this upset."

"James, credit, like fire, makes a good servant. It's yours for the asking."

The younger man made a gesture of flat rejection. "Now, friend, please not to mention that again."

Mr Hazlett was not a bit huffed. "Certainly not, now I know your feeling. Damme, I'm well-satisfied in ye!" and the elderly merchant, to James's surprise, jigged a few steps on the flagstones. "I like a man that isn't easily put down. Now, let Mrs Gault see Talbot Place and I'll be disappointed if we're not fellow-citizens within the month!"

*

Nugent Mullan was not to be envied his awakenings. With returning consciousness came the terror that today the bailiffs were already searching for what paltry belongings he had in town. They wouldn't have to get off their horses to do that. Then they were galloping the six Irish miles to Comber to distrain his sticks of furniture, his miserable stock of a few curled and mildewed bends of leather, half-a-range of Northampton boot uppers, even the bench, last and hammers that had been the honest tools of his craft, until he had hidden them from the sight of his well-to-do acquaintances. What would happen to his family if he was thrown into a debtor's jail? Could they seize the huckster's grocery by which his wife kept their three children and herself alive? There were times when the yeo sat on his bedside, head in hands, and felt the warm tears trickle through his fingers.

These were not questions that he dare ask his drinking companions so well-versed in the processes of the prosperity or the calamity of others. They could toss a coin on the sodden tables of the Donegall Arms or O'Hare's Wine Vaults so that he might carry on the pretence of paying his whack of the liquor. Ask them for the same guinea to put jackets on his sons' backs and they would chuckle at his waggery. Ask for a loan as small as ten guineas and their faces would fall, they would withhold their coins, talk over his head, wink and move away to keep forgotten appointments, leaving him alone with the bottle's dregs.

Painfully he set himself to puzzle out the beginnings of this debt that threatened to destroy him. He had first met the swine Gault in Legg's Lane in those glorious days when a man put on a uniform every morning, spent the day with his troop hunting out some cursed rebel, and the night in liquor set up by a frightened tavern-keeper. Jesus, if he had only kept his fingers on the valuables that came his way then! . . . I got goods on credit from that hell's cinder in Legg's Lane . . . I got that often enough . . . the bastard's never asked me yet to settle in full . . . for services rendered. Then what? . . . then this James Gault appears . . . for some reason I disremember the stuff gets charged to me in his name . . . now he haunts me for a hundred and twenty-seven guineas. If he's bluffing? Even if he's bluffing one well-aimed question would break me in this town like an eggshell . . . I know my friends, Christ help me . . .

Although he made an effort to keep to his well-worn round, the markets, the eating-house, the dram shop, the frightened man, unsure when and where the blow might fall, took to skulking in the lanes and alleys. The thought of being lifted by the law officers as he sat among his cronies, filled him with a shudder of shame and fear. At times he wandered around the quays, half-tempted to beg a working passage to anywhere that would carry him away from his trouble, but the thought of his wife and children always drove him back to the town again. Loitering at the mouth of an alley one morning, he saw the Gaults pass on the thronged pavement.

James and Kate had just parted from Mrs Masterson and the house in Talbot Place. Concealing her excitement and delight, the girl, under the older woman's guidance, had inspected all the apartments, from parlour to garret. She had hidden her astonishment at the sight of spring water piped right into the kitchen, showed some disappointment that her husband and she would use a side door and not the main entrance. But, all in all, she declared herself satisfied with the prospect of living at Talbot Place.

"But the rent's too high. Twenty-five guineas is the offer Mr Gault and me had fixed on."

"I do not," said Mrs Masterson grandly, "haggle over such matters."

"Then, ma'am, we're of a mind. Twenty-five guineas is our figure."

Mrs Masterson eyed her. For the first time that morning she experienced a doubt as to whether this young person, a peasant in speech plainly, if not in dress, might be so easily put down. She shifted her gaze. "My solicitor, Mr Lucas, will be pleased to settle details with you."

Once clear of Talbot Place Kate danced on air. It was a splendid house! Yes, yes, the size of the rooms had put the heart across her. But they would manage somehow. Jessie Fitzgibbon had waxed the floors that they couldn't yet afford to carpet. James held his tongue. And they would have room to set out their furniture at last, wouldn't they? Not creep round it as if they were in a junk store.

"I didn't know we had decided on twenty-five guineas rent," said James genially. "You ran the risk of a refusal from Mrs. Masterson."

"I tell ye I was stiff with fright, James, when she didn't answer readily. I was praying harder than at any time in my life." She stopped and crossed her arms over her breast to convey to her husband the intensity of her plea. Mullan, lurking in the shadow, saw the betraying gesture. His eyes became fixed in his head. His mouth fell slowly open. So *that's* who she is! The lass I made strip to the pelt on the night after the battle. Christ in Heaven, Gault's wife!

James laughed in spite of himself. He took her arm and hurried her on. "Well, you've saved us five guineas."

"It'll be put to good use, m'man."

"You've spent it already?"

"It'll pay Aggie McDowell's wages." Her husband gaped down on her. "You don't think I'm going to tend that big place my lone? I'll fetch her up from Ravara as soon as you've signed for the house."

"Ah," said James weakly, "weren't you school-friends? Doesn't she call you—"

"Aggie'll learn her place. To get away from that hive o' brothers and sisters, she'll learn anything. And she's a good girl. Now, let us get to Weighill Lane and have a look at the ledgers."

James summoned his man out to the storeyard. "In a day or two, Fonsy, Mrs Gault will be taking over the books."

"Is this me finished, cap'n?" said Fonsy glumly.

"It is not. You'll give more time to the store. I can't be

expected to be here every time a cart comes in or not. And take a look at that back wall. The floor's wet."

"Rain's the boy!" said Fonsy with a grin.

"It is. As I know too well. Get the repairs done if need be. And, Fonsy, if Mrs Gault wants an errand run, you go just the same as if I asked."

Fonsy thumped his heels together. "Cap'n!"

"Did the man I named, Nugent Mullan, leave a message?"

"No, cap'n, not this day neither."

He would give Mullan another ten days. If no money had been paid by that time, he would put the law on him. But, by the Man Above, he hoped that he wouldn't have to put a hand to that lamentable task.

It had been a long time since Nugent Mullan walked the streets of the town so purposefully. He strode past his usual haunts, waving away the hails of two or three familiars standing at Bridge Street corner. A carrier left Smithfield Market for Comber at noon. He had to get away, alone, to gather his wits.

His children were loose in the fields. With his wife in the lean-to, were a tinker couple bartering for a piece of salt ling or a bowl of meal. He bolted himself into his cobbler's shop and sat down to ponder his discovery. There was something, he felt, hidden in that chance encounter that could be turned to his advantage. But the link eluded him. He beat his forehead in exasperation. It wasn't in how he had put shame on the girl . . . she had been one of many. And yet out of all those days and nights of wrecking and rutting and looting and bloodshed he still remembered her . . . as he lay sleepless, his brain aslop in his skull after a punishing day's boozing, the weight and smoothness of her breast in his hand came back to stir him . . . her menfolk at muzzle-point he should have lifted her to an outhouse and played her in the straw . . . and he would've too, if it hadn't been for that damned Englishman, Treefall . . .

But there was no profit in spreading the story of how he had made Gault's wife-to-be strip naked before him. Then what was the shadow of hope that kept evading him? 'Gault's wife-to-be'? From a pigeon-hole frame on the wall he took a bundle of papers, beat off the dust, and unrolled it. He ruffled through the pages until he found what he sought. '13.8.98 Killinchy: townland of Ravara—' yes, Sim Purdie, and in the same townland, by God, the name Gault! '*Gault, Robert, Dissenter, cottier farmer, wife Jeannie, brother Saml., cobbler. Last-named reported by Yeoman Capt. Mullan as insolent under previous searching, but now put no confidence in Capt. Mullan's observations. All inhabitants elderly. No reason to believe in treasonable activity here. No arms found*—' With a stubbed forefinger Mullan retraced the concluding words: '*Gault couple have one son, James, a clerical student. Claim that he has been attending Glasgow College for past year. Signed: Treefall, Major: York Dragoons.*'

Nugent Mullan sat with the paper crushed between his knees, a grin of joy on his face. He had found what he needed. Hadn't he been the wise man to filch these reports from the quartermaster's office! James Gault out of the country for the length of a year. He reappears shortly after the Rising. And where can this clerical student be found? At the home of his father and mother? No, but scouring cobbles and running errands for the most treasonable and bloody-minded villain in Ireland! To hell with the Doctor's tale that the dog got sick of his books and threw up his studies. He had come back to fight. If he was important enough for the master of Legg's Lane to conceal then he must have held rank in the United Irishmen. That was treason enough, and yet his persecutor had escaped transportation or the rope!

He replaced the papers and began to pace the earthen floor of the shop. Canny, Mullan, canny . . . how best to use this? Gault is well-thought-of in the town and these damned merchants have become so prosperous and overbearing that they not only wear the Law, but weave it. I only want to muzzle the dog, not hang him . . . if I inform against him and his friends get him off, they'll grind me under their feet.

Mullan heard the voices of his children as they trooped into the house. If I can't frighten Gault, I must put a scare into that wife of his . . . Christ knows how, but it's my only chance . . .

James signed the Talbot Place lease in Mr Lucas's office. The rent, he was gratified to discover, was twenty-five guineas. A waggon of furniture, loaded by Fonsy and a muscular urchin, had left River Cottage for the town. At the cottage Kate finished packing a box of pots and pans and delph that could be done without for a week or so. She drew a last handful of straw over the top, then pushed the curls back from her damp forehead. Throwing a cloak around her shoulders she took a bowl of scraps and crossed the meadow to the fallen willow that overhung the river.

She amused herself tossing the crumbs among the redgold twigs so that they fell to the little black moorhens rather than to Mrs O'Neill's ducks that always came breasting downstream at the first flutter of her apron. Their drab domesticity aggrieved her. At last, to her delight, the three swans that had been undulating in mid-stream were tempted closer. She threw, at the full arc of her arm, a crust in their path. As she drew back, smiling, she saw the rider leave the track and turn his horse's head towards her.

The horseman had ridden quite close before she realised that, in some way, he was known to her. Had she not seen him at the Assembly Rooms? An acquaintance of James? No, he came from a darker, more distant scene, heavy with a fetor of sweat, terror and death.

He dismounted, looped his rein over his arm, and touched his hat. "Mrs James Gault?"

Kate nodded.

"Mullan, ma'am. Nugent Mullan."

"If you're looking for Mr Gault, he's in the town," said Kate turning again to the river.

"That I know. My errand's with yourself. The guts o' the matter is that your husband says that I owe him a sum o' money and holds a bill as evidence against me. I deny the debt. I want him to drop the claim and give me that paper receipted."

Kate stared at the intruder in mounting astonishment. "You've come a long journey on a poor errand——"

The sudden malignance in his face silenced her. "The road to prison is a worse journey, lass," he whispered. "And that's your husband's plan for me if I don't pay him a hundred and twenty-seven pounds."

Startled at the figure, Kate gave little attention to the rest of his words.

"A hundred and twenty-seven pounds?"

"That—or the debtor's gaol."

She thought of James's losses. She thought of her broken dowry money. "Then pay or go to prison!" she cried beside herself in a sudden rage.

Mullan planted his hands on the tree trunk and pushed his face closer. "By Jasus, not me, woman. It's James Gault that's for the dock and it's me that'll put him there. He's strutting the streets when he should be under the sod wi' the rest o' the perfidious curs that fell at Ballynahinch. *He's* in debt. He hasn't paid yet for his treason."

She was about to speak, faltered, and stared at the man in silence. "My husband never had a hand in any such business," she said hoarsely. "He was in Glasgow—at the college."

Mullan showed his teeth in a grin. "He was skulking in Legg's Lane. I know all about him, Mistress Gault, so you can quit lying to me. He took the United oath and the price for that's the gallows—" he showed his teeth again, "—though I hear the Royal Navy's looking for able-bodied men. Now, mark me, I've the proof, and the ear o' the government. Unless I get that paper signed, or some certainty that your husband has given up his scheme to ruin me, I'll lay it in the right quarters."

He took the rein from his arm. The girl watched him in silence. He need have said no more. A glance at her pale face and he knew that he had wounded and frightened her.

But he turned as he was about to mount. "There was a night in your farm close at Ravara when I gave you and your old father a taste of what I can do."

The girl laid her hands on the willow tree to steady herself. She did not speak. The leather chandler looking over his shoulder noted with dull surprise that the hair around her bloodless face was a lighter hue of gold than he had thought. But it was the pallor of her face that struck him. It was as if some terrible coldness, starting in her heart, was spreading through her whole being. Her eyes like blue ice stared into his. He flung himself on his horse and cantered up the meadow towards the track. Looking back he saw her stand there, her hands still resting on the tree, her face fixed on him. At the top of the incline unease forced him to glance back again. He could have sworn that the distant figure had moved neither finger nor eyelid since he rode away. With an oath he turned his horse's head towards the town.

XIV

James locked the door of River Cottage for the last time, swung the gate to, and clambered into the gig beside his wife. As they moved away Kate glanced across at the leaning willow. She had avoided the place since that morning. Flowering hoops of water on the surface betrayed the presence of small birds among the submerged branches. In the river the swans kept abreast of the ebb. Large and small they were waiting for her. With a shrug she turned her face to the Belfast road.

"What ails ye, girl?"

Kate started. "Nothing, there's nothing wrong with me, James."

He slapped the horse's rump sharply. "I thought you would be full of yourself on *this* jaunt."

"I'm happy, James." Feeling that this wasn't enough she turned to him. "Our bits o' furniture will be lost in those grand rooms."

"Ah," said James relieved, "give us time and we'll furnish them like any gentleman's house." Recollecting himself he added in a more subdued voice, "When we've the money."

From various vantage points Mrs Masterson had watched the Gaults arrive and settle in. To her friend Mrs Hazlett she expressed the opinion that young Mrs Gault was not perhaps all that one might have hoped for in a resident of Talbot Place. Mrs Hazlett, having tasted Kate's deference and amiability, thought that Mrs Masterson judged too harshly.

"Oh, I grant she's not a savage Red Indian. But it seems, these days, that one can scale the best society in the town with a warehouse ladder."

"Elizabeth," said Mrs Hazlett with a touch of impatience, "I doubt if that young woman wishes to scale much beyond her own establishment. But if she hurts your susceptibilities, instruct her better. You have both the curiosity and the time."

"And the familiarity with good society," said Mrs Masterson blandly, adding that she would be happy to do as her friend suggested.

"Then let us give our attention to the soup kitchen money."

Kate, concealing her fear from her husband, turned every street corner as warily as a wild creature. Unacquainted with the town, she had no way of knowing where Mullan lurked or when he might appear. The thought of meeting him filled her with such revulsion that only the drive of duty, as she saw it, of tending James's books forced her to leave Talbot Place every morning. Safely in the counting-house, she spread the morning's work on the desk before her, but her mind was only half on the bills, invoices and ledgers. She watched her husband go about office and storeyard. Time after time, she was about to speak, to tell him of the menace that hung over him. Each time she drew back. In the confusion of her mind only one thing was clear. She wanted to inflict a cruel injury on Mullan. How that could be done she did not know. Nor did she want to examine whether her eagerness for revenge was greater than her fear for James's safety. To tell him would be to give in to Mullan's threat. As she stood at the desk her whole being rebelled to the point of retching at the thought of further humiliation at Mullan's hands.

Fonsy discovered that one of his duties in the new economy was that of bag-carrier to his mistress. Kate discovered that he knew the reputation for fair dealing or rascality of every owner of shop, booth or stall. One morning, leaving James in the office, she set off with Fonsy for the booths in High Street. At the corner of Pottinger's Entry she stopped quite still. Nugent Mullan stood in a doorway across the street. She watched him, vixen-eyed.

"That man in the thickset coat," she said with a guarded gesture, "isn't that Mr Hassan?"

"Faix, no, ma'am," said Fonsy. "That's a person by the name o' Mullan, Mr Nugent Mullan."

"I thought that might be Mr Hassan's place of business."

"That, ma'am, is O'Hare's Wine Vaults."

"And what would a person be wanting there at this time o' the morning?"

Fonsy cackled. "That's where Mr Mullan does most o' his business."

"And what's his business?"

"Leather chandler, I heard tell, ma'am."

"Of no interest to Mr Gault, Fonsy?"

Fonsy hesitated. "None, ma'am."

She glanced cautiously at the man across the street. Scratching his head under his scruffy wig he seemed lost in contemplation of a vessel newly arrived at the quay. Satisfied that she had allayed any curiosity in her attendant's mind she handed him the shopping bag and slipped into the throng around the stalls.

But she was to learn, before the day was out, that Nugent Mullan was well aware that she was in Weighill Lane. About mid-afternoon James left the counting-house. As if his departure had been a signal Kate heard footsteps rapidly approach the office. A letter was flicked under the door. It was addressed to *Mistress Gault*. Slowly she stooped and picked it up. Opening it she read *The magistrates are sitting on Friday. If goods not delivered by 11 of that morning I have business for them. N.M.*

The letter drooping from her fingers, she felt she had been struck a heavy and stupefying blow. Then, coming alive, she swore in anger and self-disgust. She had allowed herself to think that her persecutor might not, after all, be determined in his threat. This ultimatum came as a relief. It gave shape and certainty to what had been but a shadowy menace. Friday, he said, and this was but Tuesday . . . She crushed the letter and dropped it in the stove.

One or two small matters were discussed with James when he returned. Her day's work was finished. She closed the books. "Before you come home," she said, "I want you to hire the gig for tomorrow morning. I'm for Ravara."

"I won't be able to go with you."

"I'm going alone."

"And what takes you there?" he asked disapprovingly.

"To get a set o' delph from the farm and bring back Aggie McDowell. I'll want the gig for eight o'clock. Don't be late for your dinner," and before he could say anything further she had left the counting-house for Talbot Place. An extraordinary change had come over her. She no longer hesitated at every corner to peer furtively up the street but stepped out boldly like one with a purpose and a destination. A loitering buckeen in the Corn Market admired her light step. One glance at the set pallor of her face and the stoniness in her eyes persuaded him to continue his amble unchecked.

Next morning, shortly after breakfast, James watched her drive off. He returned thoughtfully to the house. With Kate out of the way for a few hours he had no further excuse for putting off the unpleasant task that had been growing larger and more vexatious with every passing day. Reaching Weighill Lane he told Fonsy to stay in the counting-house until his return about midday. A pair of eyes watching from O'Hare's Wine Vaults noted with satisfaction the cheerless expression on the young merchant's face as he crossed the High Street.

He trod the cobbles where Kean and he had lain that night to evade the pursuing soldiers. Many a time since he had passed the spot without as much as a glance. Today he slackened his step. And what wonder, he thought glumly as he walked on, when I'm bound for that place again?

The small door of the smiddy opened to the pressure of his fingers. He looked inside. The fire, smouldering under the great bellows, was untended. He crossed to the storeroom door, sniffing again the mingled odours of cooling trough, wet slack, and a sweetish pungency the origin of which he well knew. He knocked and the door was opened by a stable-hand unknown to him. He suffered the silent scrutiny for a moment.

"Is the Doctor within?"

The door widened and James could see, over the ostler's shoulder, that the Doctor was indeed within. In one hand he held a jeweller's leather and in the other a silver figurine on which he had been blowing his breath. He considered his visitor for a moment. "By God's Hanged Son," he said at last, "see who's here!"

Two figures turned obediently. Poll, in his familiar corner among the casks and bales, glanced blankly at James, then went on with whatever occupied his fingers. Mr Gordon, at the hearth, leaned forward, his face reflecting his master's surprise. The Doctor indicated a chair. "Come in, Mr Gault," he purred. "Come in, my good sir, and take the weight off your legs."

"I'll take little of your time," said James seating himself. "My business is brief."

The Doctor replaced the silver ornament on the mantel-shelf, Mr Gordon smiled encouragingly, the ostler, sensing the chaffing note in the Doctor's greeting, sprawled comfortably on the long bench. The Doctor's eye caught the movement. "*Imigh as seo, a mhadaidh,*" he hissed into the fellow's face, "*agus fan amuigh go nglaoife me ort!*" The man stumbled to his feet and with a sour glance at James took himself out to the alley.

The dwarfish man gestured to Poll, then took a seat opposite Aeneas Gordon. "And now," he said with a gentle smile lifting the corners of his mouth, "you have business with us, Mr Gault?"

James listened for a moment to the clink of bottle and glasses behind him. "It's more in the way of information. As you know, Nugent Mullan owes me a hundred and twenty-seven pounds. I have asked him to settle this debt. He refuses. That being so . . ." he looked from one to the other of his listeners. Neither spoke. ". . . that being so I have no other recourse than to take him to law. I thought I would tell you of my intention."

"That's considerate of ye, Mr Gault." But there was an interrogative lift in the Doctor's voice as if he awaited more from his visitor. James accepted the glass from Poll. He bowed and drank and studied the man across from him. Surely the oiled hair was less refulgent, the cravat a shade less white and crisp? The Doctor bent to reach his glass again to Poll's bottle and it seemed to James that a fine grey dust dimmed the chocolate-red of the cloth between the heavy shoulders. The rings winked as wickedly as ever, but only pulverisation could extinguish *their* fire.

"Aye, considerate," said the Doctor harshly, "but you've more to say, Gault?"

James recognised the end of the truce. "While there's no doubt about Mullan's liability," he said, looking into his glass, "I acknowledge that there are certain weaknesses in my claim—the considerable time that has elapsed since the debt was incurred, and, more important, the unverifiable nature of the bill bearing his name."

Aeneas Gordon the lawyer, nodded. "Let it rest at that, James," he said softly.

The young man drew himself up indignantly. His expression angered the Doctor. "Booh, booh, booh! All these big words. Come to the point, man!"

"I would be obliged," said James as calmly as he could, "if one of you gentlemen would accompany me before the magistrates and support my claim."

Head sunk between his shoulders, the Doctor stared incredulously at the young man. "By my soul," he whispered, "I believe the fellow means it. And I thinking all the time that he was here to assure himself that his hide would be safe if he took Mullan to law!"

"Such a thought," said James with great contempt, "never entered my head."

"Well, give it a trot through your skull now," said the Doctor viciously, "before you open your mouth again."

"Why, you foolish old man," cried James forgetting his design in his angry amazement, "d'ye think you're looking at some poor devil with a throat fit only to cut? I'm a citizen and merchant of this town——"

Mr Gordon waved him down. "Don't cry till you're hit," he said sharply. "You were long enough in this household to learn that no member of it sets foot in a court of law. Above all," added the ex-lawyer with a sad grin, "the two you're asking now."

"You won't help me, then?"

"I tell you, don't come here looking a deponent. But," and Mr Gordon glanced at his master, "we might see our way to return you the money you gave us."

"Forced on us in your counting-house," said the Doctor.

"Thank you, but I don't want to recover it that way."

"Tell me, Gault, what d'ye hope to gain by this pursuit of Mullan?"

"My money, Doctor."

Mr Gordon stared at him. "God help your wit, James, d'ye really think Mullan has it to pay you back?"

"He has a business . . . a leather concern."

"He may call himself a leather chandler but he's a cobbler by trade. I doubt if he's made a pair of shoes, or an honest penny, for years."

"Yet he can afford to run with Ronald McKissock and Spifford Lamont and solid men like that," said James stubbornly.

The Doctor swung round. "Mullan's a carried man, you poor simpleton. His friends buy him liquor and throw him the odd suit o' clothes to cover his back. All this against the time when his word could save a store from looting. But those great days are over for Mullan. So go and have the misfortunate dog clapped in gaol. It's your duty as a Christian merchant and a good citizen."

For a long moment James looked from one man to the other. "Can I believe this, Aeneas?"

"You've been told the truth about Mullan's affairs."

"And I'll tell you more," said the Doctor. "If Nugent Mullan had had the wherewithal, you would've been left the bones to pick. He owes us nearer three hundred guineas."

Gault examined the head of his cane. It was hard to doubt their good faith. It was impossible not to be moved by their goodwill. "I have to thank you for the offer to return my money," he murmured. "It is . . . generous."

"Will you take it?"

"No."

"And what of Mullan?" said Mr Gordon.

James shrugged. "What can I do? Scratch him out of my reckoning."

The Doctor rose and took his hand. "Well said. I knew there was a sensible man behind that black Presbyterian mug." The little man looked up at him. "If you're pressed we'll rent a bit of that yard of yours."

James relinquished the other's hand and took up his hat. "It behoves me to have my yard doubly busy now, with my own transactions, Doctor." He turned at the door. "I bid you good day, gentlemen," he said and bowed.

They may have fooled me, he thought, as he retraced his way over the grimy cobbles of Legg's Lane. Yet I can't believe it. And he felt his spirits rise suddenly and inexplicably. What extraordinary creatures we are. We harass and torment ourselves pursuing some gain or in the righting of a wrong, real or imaginary. Then how often we accept with something close to equanimity the discovery that what we want is unobtainable or is no longer worth the labour. There is now no need, thank God, for all the vexatious business of dragging Mullan to court. But, uncharitable as it may be, I'll reserve for myself the satisfaction of keeping him on tenter-hooks.

He opened the counting-house door to find Pringle Hazlett awaiting him. "I hope," said Mr Hazlett, "that you're not hurrying out again. I've business I want to discuss with you."

"My time is yours," said James. "Go out and get your dinner, Fonsy."

When they were alone the elderly merchant settled himself in the desk-chair. "As you know, James, I have interests outside linen. Indeed, since the decline in that trade, I have put my money into several concerns in the town. Among them is a bakery in Winetavern Street and a tallow refinery behind Hanover Quay——"

"Campbell and McBurney's?" said James surprised.

"It still trades under that name. I bought it from the late Joe McBurney's nephew when he had almost scattered what his uncle had gathered. However, both it and the bakery now thrive." Mr Hazlett paused to give due weight to what was to follow. "James, I'm getting old and I'm getting tired. I want you to keep an eye on these two concerns for me."

"Sure, I know nothing about bread or tallow, Pringle!"

"I've experienced journeymen in both places. It's the buying and selling, and taking on labour, that need looking after. I'll pay you eight guineas a month to furnish me with reports and extracts of the trading figures. Does it interest you?"

"It interests me. But what will your men think of the idea?"

"You're my agent. That's enough for them. What d'ye say?"

"I'll try my hand at it, Pringle."

Mr Hazlett eased himself from the chair. "I'm pleased that you've agreed to this. You did yourself no harm in my eyes when you set to and cleared that loss on the *Irish Oak*. I liked that." Fortunately, the piece of mirror at which Mr Hazlett was adjusting his hat was so small that he was unable to see his companion's face. "Now what about clinching our little agreement at the White Cross with a plate of Irish lamb and a glass of Irish whiskey?"

The opportunity to make nearly a hundred extra guineas a year! He closed his eyes and uttered a brief prayer: *O Lord, accept my humble thanks for your goodness and mercy to me. And forgive me my obduracy and uncharitableness towards my debtor, as I forgive him.*

*

Kate carried the pieces of the dinner set from the house and placed them carefully in two hampers on the floor of the gig. She was aware that her brother Andrew was watching her, counting every dish that she bore over the threshold. Exasperated, she turned and called him. He appeared in the doorway, surprise and guilelessness gleaming in his small eyes.

"Fetch me more straw from the stack."

Returning obediently with the straw, he leaned over and peered into the gig. "We'll want them baskets back."

"They'll come back when I'm finished wi' them."

The youth took another long look. "I suppose it's in order for ye to take that delph wi'out my father being here?"

"He bought it for me from the old rectory sale, so ye suppose aright." She took a handful of the straw. "Where's Hugh?"

"Cutting rushes in the bog meadow."

"Away and fetch him. I'm going soon." He lingered mutinously. She turned on him, her face sharp with anger. "Do I have to speak twice to ye, boy?"

She waited until she saw him slouch through the kitchen garden, then sped lightfoot to the house. Reaching unerringly into a dark corner above the door she brought down a powder horn. Returning, she dropped it into one of the hampers. Then she hastened across the close to the barn. From the top of the wall where it joined the roof couplings she dragged down a box heavy with broken latches, rusty files, nails and harrow teeth. She fumbled in this debris until she found what she sought. From her skirt pocket she took out the silver-butted pistol. She ran the three balls cupped in her hand into the mouth of the barrel. Discarding one she dropped the other two into her pocket with the pistol. She thrust the box among its cobwebs and walked back to the gig. There was sweat on her forehead although the air was cool. She looked at her bruised rust-marked fingers and with the back of her hand brushed the damp curls from her face.

Hugh came round the corner of the house, his brother on his heels. He had a sickle in his hand and with a whetstone he made small corncrake noises on the already keen-edged blade.

"Did I bring ye from your work?" For the first time the girl smiled.

"I was near finished, anyway. Are you waiting till my father gets back from Downpatrick?"

Kate didn't answer. Her cold gaze rested on her younger brother until he turned and retreated to the house. "I've to call at the McDowells. I'm taking Aggie to the town."

"Ah?" Hugh was alert. "For a bit o' a trip?"

"She's coming to work for me."

"So she'll be going away from here." It wasn't a question. He spoke as if he were voicing his thoughts aloud.

Kate frowned. "Yes," she said at last. Then, "I'll say goodbye to my mother." She went indoors, past Andrew still loitering in the doorway. Kirsty Purdie was seated at the hearth. She raised her head to speak as her daughter bent and pecked her cheek. Kate stepped back, her hand raised. "I've no time, mother," she said and ran from the house towards the gig.

"Isn't she the strange lass," said Mrs Purdie listening to the departing wheels.

"Aye, she's the strange lass, all right," said her son Andrew from the door and spat into the close.

Kate drove steadily towards Lusky crossroads. She avoided the Gault farm. If she had few words for her own mother she would have less for the old woman crouched in the cottage in the bog. The road skirted the hovels that surrounded her father's house. From the corner of her eye she saw the women and children pause to watch her drive by. She had been absent long enough to be repelled by their filth and rags and drooping hopelessness. It would not have needed a fastidious nose to believe that a stench rose into the clear air. She turned away her face, stroking the whip along the horse's flank. The world's for them that can stand up and lay hold of it.

On her journey from the town she had called with the

McDowells to bid Aggie be ready to go back with her. At the crossroads she turned the horse's head in that direction, the gig lurching along a rutted track with a ruff of shaggy grass running down the middle of it. The McDowells' cottage sat below the level of the track, but at the head of a meadow, that swept down to a little lough. Many a time, on their way home from school, Kate and Aggie and their brothers and sisters had sported on its rushy banks.

Aggie and her mother and her two little sisters stood up as she entered the cottage. They watched her with silent apprehension. Aggie wore a shawl and an old battered bonnet of her mother's. Her possessions, knotted in a red spotted handkerchief, sat on the table. A jutting hardness in the bundle prompted Kate to rap it with her knuckle. She untied the knot and found along with the girl's Bible and bits of duds, a couple of cakes of oaten hardbread. "Dear Heavens, girl," she said with an angry laugh, "where are ye for, Ameriky?"

Dumb, Aggie glanced at her mother. "We didna want to gie ye the trouble o' getting her a meal, Kate," said Mrs McDowell humbly.

Kate was silent for a moment. Then, "Pick up your bundle, Aggie," she said in a brisk voice. "It's time we were on our road."

At this the two small girls threw themselves on their sister with lamentations and weeping. Kate went out and climbed into the gig. At last Aggie appeared, her arms encircling the children, her voice assuring them that she wasn't going to Ameriky at all, that she was only going a dozen miles away, and that soon, soon, she would be back to see them. Tearfully, doubtfully, they freed her to climb into the gig. Mrs McDowell stepped close at the other side of the vehicle. "You'll be good to my girl?" she said, looking Kate levelly in the eyes.

"You have my word for that, Mrs McDowell," said the young woman, picking up the reins. "She'll never regret coming to me."

Already a pale star hung in the sky when the gig turned on to the Belfast road. The talk was lively enough as Aggie told her school-friend the news of the townlands. Amused at times, Kate turned to glance at her companion, noting the fair fluffy hair under the old bonnet, the bright eyes, the delicate skin, a testimony to pure spring water. They came to the brow of the Castlereagh Hills, below them the lights of the town. Kate's mood changed abruptly. "Call me 'ma'am', Aggie," she said brusquely, cutting short the girl's narrative. "Address me as 'ma'am', always."

"Yes . . . ma'am," Aggie shrank back in her seat. As they wound down the steep hill she made an attempt to recapture the earlier mood. There was no response from the woman beside her. The girl was intelligent enough to know that she was not at fault. She studied her mistress, saw her pale tense face as she crouched forward, her hands dragging with unnecessary force on the steady sure-footed horse. Whatever had wrought this sad change in Kate Gault lay down there in the lights they were approaching. Little Aggie was ill-schooled in such unhappiness. She thought of the people she had left. Her father would be home now from his labour at the road-mending. Soon he and her mother and her five brothers and sisters would be sitting down to their supper of potatoes and salt and herrings. She clutched her bundle and wished dearly she was back with them. When at last the gig rounded into Talbot Place, Aggie McDowell's face was wet with silent tears.

Fonsy, no doubt, could have got her the information she needed. After careful thought she put the idea out of her head. She could trust only herself. On that Thursday morning, James, by great good luck, had to attend a meeting of the Chamber of Commerce at the Market House. When he had left the counting-house she took a sheet of paper and wrote *I have what you asked for. Will give it you at the Bridge Key this night.* She folded the paper and sealed it.

For a long hour in the grey morning, she stood, half-hidden, at the corner of Weighill Lane. At last she saw

Mullan come out of the Vaults with two companions and disappear up the High Street. Returning to the office she draped Aggie McDowell's shawl over her head and crossed the street. A cellarman was trundling a number of small kegs on the footway. She sidled up, holding her shawl close to her face. "I hae a message for Mr Nugent Mullan frae m'mother."

The cellarman, a small wiry fellow, a younger edition of Fonsy, looked up. "You've missed him, girl."

Kate revealed the letter. "What'll I dae wi' it?"

"Ye maun gie it tae me," he replied, mimicking her country voice.

Kate handed it to him. He turned it over, looking with curiosity at the seal.

"We canna write," she said coolly. "The schoolmester set it doon for us. Will Mr Mullan be back?"

"This evening for sure. His Orange lodge meets here tonight."

This was unexpected. She felt the sweat prickle on her back. "At what time does he leave that?"

"About ten o'clock. Why, are ye looking an answer?"

"I dinna know. It's just tae tell him we canna pay for the shoon till after Killyleagh market."

"B'god," said the cellarman, amused, "he'll break his heart o'er that. I'll see he gets your letter."

Kate held out a sixpence. He pushed her hand away. "Awa wi' ye, lass," he said in his broadest voice, "and haud on tae your siller till ye get hame." And with a show of strength as unexpected as his words, he swung a keg chest-high and went staggering into the tavern.

"When you've the dishes washed," she said to Aggie, "the plates and saucers go on the dresser. The cups on their hooks. The cutlery in this drawer."

"Yes, ma'am," said Aggie.

"I'm going to Mrs McCreery's shop for some things I need," she said distinctly. "If Mr Gault asks, that's where I am. You understand?"

"Yes," said Aggie hesitantly, puzzled that what seemed so simple should require such insistence. She watched her mistress put on her cloak and slip silently from the house. That woman's sick in herself, she thought, returning to her work.

Kate's story of her errand had been a ruse. But she had gone only a few paces along Talbot Place when she realised that it would be prudent to go to Mrs McCreery's shop. She must leave nothing to chance. Avoiding the main thoroughfares she walked swiftly by George Lane and Poultry Square to Ann Street. There were two or three customers in Mrs McCreery's emporium. Under the soft light of the shop's lamps two girls searched for stockings, whispering and giggling as they picked up and rejected; at a counter an old woman matched buttons. Mrs McCreery was tying a small package for a fourth woman. The customer paid her money, lifted her purchase and turned. Kate recognised her as Miss Mary Ann McCracken of Rosemary Lane, who, only a few years before, had walked by the side of her rebel brother, Henry, to the very foot of the scaffold. Passing, Miss McCracken bowed pleasantly to the pale-faced girl. Kate's eyes followed the erect modestly-dressed figure. There went a brave and fearless woman who had not turned back. She drew a great breath like one revived. Mrs McCreery was before her.

"What can I get for madam?"

"I was looking a muslin dress for my servant."

"I haven't such things made-up, ma'am," said the draper, surprised.

Kate glanced around. Above her a clock ticked slowly. "That I know. If she called on you, can you give her the material?"

"She'll choose the pattern?"

"Yes, the cloth for two, if she sees what pleases her."

"I stock the newest colours."

Kate glanced at the clock. It read five minutes off the hour. "And charge to Mrs James Gault of Talbot Place."

The shopkeeper signified her recognition of the name.

"Thank you, Mrs Gault. Please to tell your girl to ask for me."

"That I'll do. Good evening to you, Mrs McCreery. My chair is waiting."

She slipped into the gloom of the street, then turned sharply towards the Bridge Quay. A schooner lay tied close up, its stern throwing the stone bridge into darkness. She took her stand on the quayside, half-hidden in the shadow of the vessel. A minute or so after the hour the side door of the Vaults opened and shut. It was done so silently and swiftly that only a fleeting slit of light betrayed whoever had entered or come out. She heard heavy footsteps on the cobbles on the other side of the channel. Nugent Mullan appeared on the crest of the bridge, hand on the parapet, looking down on her. She saw with a swift shock of rage that under his Orange sash he wore a yeomanry jacket. He descended the bridge's slope and walked along the quayside towards her. Grim and dark-faced he stopped to survey her. "You're on time, ma'am."

The woman was silent. "Well," he said sharply. "What ha' ye brought me?"

"This," she said drawing the pistol from her sleeve. It was then, seeing astonishment and fear dawn in his face, that she first realised fully what she was about. The weapon was heavier than she had thought. With a shout of "Murder!" he started towards her. She steadied the barrel with her other hand and pulled the trigger. There was a roar and a spurt of flame. In that moment, when every image and sound was monstrously dilated, she saw the swift pucker in his tunic low on the left side. He slid his hand down to the wound, horror on his face, his mouth working to shout again. Moaning in rage and terror she sprang forward and hurled the pistol in his face. The wretched man stumbled back, his heels caught on the low coping of the quay, and he somersaulted into the black depths. She heard his skull strike the vessel's hull with the thudding crack of a turnip splitting on a barn floor.

Doors were opening, windows lighting up. Kate gathered her skirts and fled across the quay to the sidewalk. A man and two women came trotting out of Church Lane. One of the women caught Kate by the arm. "It came from over there, girl," she said, pointing to the stone bridge. In cunning obedience Kate turned with them back to the quayside. People were crowding on her heels, shouting to those on the other side of the channel. A town watch came puffing over the bridge, halbert at the charge, ready for anything. The swarms met, stopped, gazed around them. There was nothing. The cobbles lay damp, glistening, bare under the feeble lights.

"There was a shot, sartinly," a man said to restore his own and everybody's confidence.

"There was a shout afore the shot," said another.

"I heard no shout."

"There was a shout . . . a man's . . ."

A hatch was thrown back on the schooner and a squat figure grew out of the deck, lantern raised. The seaman came to the gunnel to peer down on the crowd. The town watch elbowed his way to the front.

"Was a firearm discharged on board your vessel?"

The seaman leaned forward, hand to ear.

"Did ye fire a gun?"

The man shrugged, muttered, drew his wool cap over his brows.

"He's a furriner," the watch informed the crowd.

"Bloody dutchie!" cried a youth at the back.

The seaman considered the faces below him for a moment, then dropped a long spittle into the darkness. They watched him turn, saw his light disappear, heard him shoot the bolt of the hatch behind him.

Kate clung to the bridge parapet as the crowd melted away. I mustn't be alone here. I must leave with them. She drew a deep breath. Was there already an unthinkable taint in the stench that rose from the emptying channel? Her hand to her mouth she hurried up the High Street after the stragglers. In Castle Place she hired a chair to carry her home.

In the broad morning light they discovered Nugent Mullan, an arm hooked drunkenly over a mooring-rope. As they raised the body a sharp-eyed citizen spotted the silver-mounted pistol as the mud closed over it.

XV

THE NEWS OF the arrest of Aeneas Gordon for the murder of the leather chandler Mullan was received with surprise and incredulity. Around the coffee tables that morning little else was talked about. But, to James's watchful eye, a surprising number of his fellow-merchants showed disquiet in their faces and a general uneasiness in their behaviour that could have had little to do with Gordon's plight. I wouldn't have suspected, he thought to himself, that so many of these upright fellows had had dealings with the crew in Legg's Lane. To Mr Hazlett he expressed his blank disbelief in Gordon's guilt.

"I know the man. Such a deed lies as far outside his nature as . . . as it would yours."

"He could have been driven to an unnatural deed, James," said Mr Hazlett taking a pinch of snuff.

"No." His denial was so emphatic that he felt obliged to continue. "Not three days ago," he said, leaning over the table, "I had occasion to speak with Gordon about some money owed me by Nugent Mullan. I took his advice to pursue the wretched fellow no further. He was penniless. If Gordon's view of him was not high, it was not without pity. No, Pringle, Gordon is not the murderer. Why," he asked, the query striking him, "do the authorities think so?"

"The pistol, of course, and the knowledge, now admitted by everybody, that Mullan was well-known in Legg's Lane. Don't be too zealous on Gordon's behalf, James. His long association with certain persons won't stand to him if he's brought to trial."

To this James made no reply. But, having learnt the nature of the evidence, he hurried home to tell Kate. "A pistol—a pistol with his name on it!" he cried. "Why, any sneak thief could have had it!" He waited for her to speak but she kept her head bowed over her plate. "Aeneas has only to prove that he was elsewhere. And that," he continued with a sardonic smile, "shouldn't be impossible."

She raised her head. "For God's sake, Kate," he cried, shocked at the pallor of her face, "the man's innocent!" He stared at her in sullen anger. He had always viewed the regard between Aeneas Gordon and his wife with amused tolerance. But to reveal such anguish as this was out of all sense and unseemly in a young married woman. He rose abruptly from the table, taking the newspaper to his easy chair. "He'll be set free tomorrow," he declared from behind the sheet.

But Aeneas Gordon was not set free on the morrow or the next day or the next. Meantime the leather chandler's death remained the main topic among the important citizens of the town. Mullan's former associates expressed their satisfaction that *someone* had been taken up for the crime. But James felt that they were savouring the catastrophe more than sorrowing over the abrupt demise of their crony. There were a few individuals who had only scant acquaintance with the accused man and his alleged victim, but that little led them to the sorrowful conviction that a God-fearing town would be well-rid of both. And there were those, among them James and Mr Adair, who held firmly to the opinion that Aeneas Gordon was incapable of the deed of which he was accused.

The Spring Assizes were little more than a week away and Gordon was to be held in custody until brought to trial. This information was put about by two or three gentlemen who now appeared in the Assembly Rooms. They were usually to be found in the company of Nugent Mullan's former companions and they bore a remarkable similarity to each other in the southern twang of their speech and the drab hue of their clothes. Outside those who introduced them to the Rooms no one seemed to know their names. The waiters referred to them as 'the gentlemen from Dublin', and more accurately behind their backs, as 'the Castle spies'. In their presence, James discovered, men were inclined to hold their tongues on the matter of Gordon's innocence.

"They've an old score to pay off," said Mr Adair. "Or maybe a number of old scores. There was that poor devil, Simmons the gauger, found in Dalton's Meadow with his throat cut. And a merchant, Poots, I recall."

Poots . . . Habakkuk Poots . . . Kean borrowed his name and papers . . . "But I understood that the man Poots came from Fermanagh or Derry?"

"His body was found not a quarter of a mile from Legg's Lane. And there were others . . . others. And now it's Nugent Mullan, a man of no consequence, but a yeo and an Orangeman, and such, for the moment, those in Dublin Castle smile on. No doubt the Attorney General would rather have another person in the dock on Monday morning, but he'll not let second-best slip because of that. If Gordon hangs it will have been that master of his who put the rope round his neck."

James thought otherwise, but kept silent. He could well imagine the rage and despair of the Doctor. One of his comrades in deadly peril from which, it seemed, neither intrigue nor violence could save him. The young merchant was not taken by surprise, therefore, when Peter Darragh appeared next morning in Weighill Lane. As Kate was in the office, James called the ostler into the yard. The man handed him a letter. '*Base treachery*' it ran '*has put the life of a friend in jeopardy. Your word that he dined and spent that evening in your company can free him and fill the heart of an unworthy old man with undying gratitude, Deus vobiscum. Luke Bannon.*' James's hands trembled as he refolded the letter and handed it back.

"The Doctor wants ye to write."

"There is nothing I can write, Darragh. I was in other company that night and the gentlemen who were there wouldn't bear me out. I'm convinced that Mr Gordon is wrongly charged. But there's nothing I can do to help him."

It had been in his mind to attend the trial. Tom Adair's words made him hesitate; the Doctor's letter drove away the idea completely. But he was not left unaware of how matters were going with Aeneas Gordon. Hassan, the wine merchant, and Fitzgibbon, had been at the courthouse. They joined him at his mid-day meal. A cellarman from O'Hare's Vaults, they said, had come forward to tell of the peasant girl who had left a letter for the murdered man. A fragment of paper found in the yeo's pocket was produced in court, but so fouled with mud that it was unreadable. Mr Fitzgibbon was of the opinion that defence counsel could have made more of the odd circumstance of the sealing wax on the cover. They were also able to tell James that Mr Justice Torrens and Aeneas Gordon had been contemporaries at the Dublin Bar, indeed friends, until Gordon's lapse, disgrace, and disappearance from the capital. And that his Honour had little relish for the task before him.

"And Gordon?"

Mr Hassan held up his hands. "I don't understand it. He admits to the pistol but seems unable to explain how it got out of his possession. Mr O'Driscoll, who's for him, was full of hints and prompts of it being lost, or stolen, or mislaid. But his client wouldn't be coached. He simply stared across the court as if he had lost all interest. In the end counsel gave up."

Within the last few days a coldness had grown between James and his wife. She moved about the office, silent, shrunken, as if she had been wounded inwardly. On the day of the trial he sent her home early and stayed on in the town. At the Assembly Rooms he came on Tom Adair, straight from the court. After this brief adjournment, Mr Adair told him, everyone expected the verdict.

"And what of Gordon's . . . friends?" asked James studying the wall.

"Ah, yes, the Doctor arrived. We heard him in an anteroom. But Mr O'Driscoll declined to put him up as a witness."

"*Heard* him?"

"Heard him cursing and raving when he got O'Driscoll's answer. Justice Torrens and his fellow-magistrates were very forbearing. They held up the proceedings until the hullabaloo died. The man I felt for was poor Gordon. Damme, James, there's something cursed odd about this affair. Gordon seems set on his own destruction. I wish O'Driscoll had let that villain take the stand!"

They were joined by Mr Fitzgibbon. He had arrived at the courthouse in time to see the Doctor, twitching and gibbering, half-carried back to his conveyance by a huge sullen fellow, while two vulpine creatures skirted their master until he was safely lifted aboard. The rabble at the entrance, cess-men, bailiffs, coachmen, loiterers, had gazed after him in silence, as if at some nocturnal beast of the deep forest that had appeared among them in broad daylight.

Shortly after seven o'clock the verdict was on the streets. Aeneas Gordon had been found guilty of the murder of Nugent Mullan. He was to be hanged on Thursday morning at eight o'clock from a gallows erected in High Street at the scene of the crime.

Early on that morning James left Talbot Place for his counting-house, alone. During the night Kate had been disturbed and feverish. As he came down Weighill Lane he saw through the arch at the end of the lane that at the execution place a crowd was already gathering. Fonsy stood under the arch. James summoned him and handed him a packet. "Take that sample of barilla to Mr McAllister."

"Murder alive, that's away round in Arthur Street, cap'n!"

"That's right," said James, smiling, in spite of himself, at the outrage on his storeman's face.

"But they're for hanging a man out there in ten minutes' time——"

"You won't be there, Fonsy. Nor will I. Away you go."

Satisfied that his messenger was slouching away from the High Street, he closed the door firmly on the growing murmur and cries of the crowd. But at the first stroke of the courthouse bell he laid down his pen and sat motionless with bowed head and closed eyes.

The quivering death-knell widened over the town's roofs and entered the small gable window of the room in which she stood. Each stroke fell on her like a blow driving her backwards until she dropped on her knees at the bedside. She clapped her hands to her ears, crying out her terror and guilt in broken phrases and entreaties. *Oh, God, oh God, forgive me and spare me!* Laments, promises, great wordless sobs poured from her in a flood of tears until she was brought up, eyes staring, hands rending the bedclothes, by the rattle of Aggie's bucket and mop on the landing.

James worked quietly through the morning at his desk. Fonsy sulked in the yard. Trotting all the way back from his errand he had had the scant satisfaction of seeing, from a distance, the dead man dangle from the gallows. He and his fellow-citizens had been deprived of even that when a knot of men, recognised by Fonsy as from Legg's Lane, arrived with a signed paper and a covered cart, and cutting down the corpse, drove off with it.

There was a tap on the office door and Mr Hazlett entered. In his hand he carried a roll of papers.

"Well, Pringle," said James gravely, "he's gone."

"Eh?" It took Hazlett a moment to catch the other's meaning. "Ah, yes, Gordon, poor wretch. I met Tom Adair. He's now convinced that he was guilty, having watched him in court."

James was about to speak but the elderly merchant claimed his attention by plopping the papers on the desk before him, while he regarded him with a benevolent smile. "I've seen the first reports of your stewardship, James. You found the bakery and the tallow works in good shape?"

"I would call them thriving. You've two good managers, there."

"Well, James," Mr Hazlett pushed the handful of documents across the desk. "Both concerns are yours."

James, astounded, stared at the other man. Mr Hazlett returned his gaze calmly. "What are you saying, Pringle?"

"I'm offering you the bakery and the refinery, lock, stock and barrel."

"But I haven't the money for them, friend!"

"No doubt. I'm offering to sign 'em over to you, if you'll take 'em. I'm tired of 'em."

"But you could sell them."

"That I could, but I don't want to. I want you to have 'em. I've more money than I need for the years left to me. And I've no children."

Unbelievingly, James touched the deeds with a finger. "There's your niece and nephew."

"They're my concern no longer," said Mr Hazlett with sudden bitterness. "The boy, Lawrence, has entered into his patrimony. At least, Sir Daly, his uncle, has given him a home at Cashon Lodge, and promises to manage his schooling. And Sophia, as you know, is married——"

"I did not know!" cried James involuntarily.

"No? Shortly after she fled from us. To Mr Stephen Langrishe of Dublin, a worthless cub in my opinion, but heir to a title, and moneyed, James, moneyed," added Mr Hazlett with a grin. "So you need not concern yourself about my relatives. What d'ye say to my offer?"

"You've given it serious thought, Pringle?"

"Yes."

"Well, what can I say?" replied James soberly. "Thanks is a poor word."

"You accept them, then?"

"My dear friend, with all the gratitude of my heart."

"I told you I liked your way of going about business. Bring the papers and we'll settle the matter in Joe Lucas's office."

The fall of a hammer on wood kept time with their steps along the lane. They passed under the arch, now deserted, into the High Street. James stole a glance at the gibbet standing beyond the stone bridge. But the figures on it were alive, their hammers dismantling the structure, spar by spar. On the sidewalks and along the quays were groups of idlers, left by the ebbing tide of the crowd. He picked up, from their chatter, that, all in all, it had been a satisfying spectacle, even if the calm demeanour of the principal actor had lent it an unfortunate brevity. There was a cheerfulness among his fellow-merchants as they stood around, fingers in fob-pockets. They had seen the officers of their town mete out punishment to the wrongdoer with all the morality and scrupulousness of the Law. Even their lesser brethren, the hawkers and stall-holders, had a good word for the Law this morning. Their booths were bare and their pockets chinked. The mob, bulging High Street around the gallows, had sustained itself on apples and sweetmeats and roast potatoes and boiled pig's cheek as it waited for the flight of Aeneas Gordon's soul.

XVI

Sim Purdie quitted this life at five o'clock on a dewy September morning in the year 1802, some ninety minutes before his first grandchild entered it. The departure was easier than the arrival, and the door at Talbot Place was opened to Hugh Purdie not by Kate as he had expected, or Aggie as he had hoped, but by the midwife.

"Ye took your time," said the woman, holding out her hand. Then, in answer to the young man's puzzled frown, she demanded, "Aren't ye from the 'pothecary's?"

"No. I've business with Mrs Gault."

"Your business'll have to keep for a day or two. Stand there till the serving-girl attends ye." A moment later Aggie came hurrying to the door. The two young people were so pleased to see each other, and had so many questions to ask and answer, that Hugh's horse had destroyed a clump of ornamental grass before Aggie came to her wits sufficiently to show Hugh the way to the stables. She told him that Kate had given birth to a son and that the father had left a short time before to close the storeyard and would return within the hour.

The young man's grief for his father was not so consuming that he could not give his attention to Aggie's talk of her life at Talbot Place. If, in innocent vanity, she coloured the events of her days rather brighter than they really were, she had an equally guileless listener. As he nursed his cup of tea in the wide kitchen, Hugh turned over in his mind such terms as 'ma'am' and 'master and mistress', applied to his sister and her husband by the girl who had, a year or so ago, been their neighbour and schoolmate. For the first time he began to have an inkling of how well-found and important the Gaults had become in the merchant society of Belfast.

"And now," said the girl, "the farm's yours, Hugh."

He stared at her for a moment then looked away. "I dunno," he mumbled.

"Well, like, it's none o' my concern," said Aggie embarrassed, "but I thought that's how things went wi' the eldest son."

"Aggie," he cried, turning to her, "I don't want the cursed place!"

He saw the disappointment that shadowed her face, but before either could speak James was heard in the hall. "It's the master," said Aggie springing up. "I shouldn't have brought you in here!"

"Where should I be?" asked Hugh, nettled.

"I should've asked ye to call back or put ye somewhere else wi' a picture book to look at."

Hearing voices, James came into the kitchen. He stood swinging his doorkey and staring at Hugh in surprise. "Aggie," he said without looking at her, "there's a package on the hall table for Mrs McBratney, the midwife, and when you're up inquire from her how your mistress is now." The girl gone, he continued, "Well, good news travels fast."

For all the smile on his brother-in-law's face, Hugh felt himself an interloper. "I'm glad for you and Kate," he said coolly enough. "I came on a different errand. My father's dead."

It was James's turn to be at a loss. "Come in here," he said at last, leading his visitor across the hall to the sitting-room. "I'm sorry to hear this. When did he die?"

"This morning."

"Sit down, Hugh," said James recollecting himself. "How's your mother taking it?"

"Well enough. I didn't think I would be bringing her back news of a grandchild today. How's Kate?"

"She was ill, Hugh. But the doctors tell me there's nothing to fret about—both are doing well. I'm afraid you won't be able to see her."

"I understand."

"Leave it to me to break it to her. When's the funeral?"

"The day after tomorrow."

"You understand that I won't be able to get out before that."

"I know rightly, James."

Aggie reappeared. "Mrs McBratney says the mistress is a lot easier and sleeping."

"There," said James turning to the young man, "you can take that word back with you."

He didn't see Aggie again. James accompanied him to the stable and bade him farewell in Talbot Place. As he rode homeward he realised glumly that only half his errand had been accomplished. He had wanted to talk to Kate, to tell her that Sim had left no word about the farm, that Andrew was behaving already as if it was his. Lacking the acquisitive appetite of his father, and guiltily aware at times of the lack, he wanted his fiery-spirited sister to spur him on, to tell him what to do, above all to settle matters between himself and his brother. Last night, when his father had scarcely grown cold, Andrew had slipped out to see Ephraim Smart, the land agent. Even before he had left home that morning, the kitchen was filling with Andrew's cronies, each bobbing his head dutifully at the open coffin, but with an eager eye on the plentitude of whiskey and tobacco his brother had laid in against the wake. And outside, Charlie Campbell and the other squatters, from the entrances of their miserable hovels, were watching, watching.

When James entered the Purdie house the mugs and tumblers had been washed, the bottles and kegs carried to the back room, the hearth swept clean. But the brisk fire had failed to draw all the fumes of tobacco and liquor up the wide chimney. His nostrils wrinkling, he threaded his way among the neighbours in search of Mrs Purdie. She had taken to her bed again.

"I'm sorry for your trouble, Kirsty." It was no more than the trite word of a neighbour. "And Kate, a' course," he mumbled. He could find nothing more to say on Sim Purdie's end.

"Aye, he's gone. How's the wee fella?"

"They're both doing well, Kirsty."

The woman on the bed sighed. "He never complained, Jamie. He was at his work all that day. Then, in the evening, he just snapped like an auld stick."

He reminded her of God's Will. Then, "What about yourself—will I send in Hugh or somebody?"

"No, I'm for rising now. Has the clergy come yet?"

He left his mother-in-law and went back to the kitchen. Andrew Purdie, in the midst of a group of neighbouring men, watched him as he passed. At the door he met Hugh. He held out his hand to the young man. "He went quick at the end, Hugh."

"Aye, sitting at that table. He fell forr'ad, vomiting up blood on the money."

The other, wary of being caught in any domestic trouble in the Purdie family, looked away. "The money?"

"He was counting it when he died. Andra washed it clean." There was a lurking smile on the speaker's lips.

James stepped past him out to the close. Hugh followed. "Your mother was asking if the Reverend Quinn had arrived yet."

"Not yet." The young man detained him. "James, will you and your uncle take the first lift o' the coffin with Andra and me?"

James scraped impatiently with his foot. This small show of authority both touched and irritated him. "If you've no nearer kin, Hugh. Now, I'm going for my mother. Has she been over to see Kirsty yet?"

"No, but your uncle was here this past two nights, mourning deep with Andra and his friends."

As James crossed the close towards the road he noticed that the entrances to the squatters' dwellings were closed. Not a living creature stirred around the hovels; even the goats and dogs had disappeared. Yet he felt that he was being watched from the chinks and holes in the crazy structures. In the distance he saw his mother and Sam approaching in the turf cart. The manner in which his mother sat akimbo from his uncle told him that they had been quarrelling. He could make a fair guess at the reason. When the cart came to a halt, he saw that his uncle's face was a testimonial to two days and nights of liquoring.

"I was on my way to meet you, mother."

"You're like Royal Charlie," the old woman said crossly. "But better late than never."

"I thought you might be at the Purdies. You've heard about the arrival of your grandson, eh?" he smiled, humouring her.

"It was left to Hugh Purdie to bring the news."

"I couldn't get away until today. It wasn't easy for Kate."

"How is the girl?"

He hid his annoyance at her trick of refusing to name her daughter-in-law. "Better, mother, better."

"I suppose I'll see the boy afore he's growed up, or I'm dead."

"When Kate's herself again, I'll come and fetch you."

The old woman muttered something that he couldn't make out. "How's all there?" she said, nodding towards the Purdie house.

"Kirsty seems well enough."

"I would ha' been over earlier but I hurted my leg. So I've had tae trust to this sot here," and she nodded over her shoulder, "tae yoke up and not cowp us intae a ditch."

Behind her back, Sam, all forbearance, was pantomiming his innocence to his nephew. She rounded on him. "Drive on, ye pachel, drive on, or the man'll be in his grave before we're there."

As they were about to start off again they saw the rector's gig, driven by his man, turn into the Purdies' close. "Wait till that man's got in," said Jeannie Gault and obediently her brother-in-law drew rein.

"Where are they burying Sim?" asked James.

"In the family plot at Ravara Meeting House, a' course," said his mother. "But the Church av Ireland man'll say the prayers. Trust Sim Purdie tae have two ladders tae Heaven's loft."

When the Gaults entered the house the Reverend Quinn, Rector of Killyturk, stood at the head of the coffin. Jeannie Gault slipped in to join the women seated around the walls, James and his uncle took their stand behind the men crowded on the kitchen floor. As the rector's prayerful eulogy rose to the beams James stole a glance at the bowed heads: the Orrs, McCareys, Echlins, McIlveens, Hannas, Gillespies. In the close, out of sight if not out of sound of the Protestant prayer, stood the Catholic neighbours, the Murrays, Lennons, Mageeans.

The Reverend Quinn closed his book softly. There was an awkward shuffling, a reaching for hats, and, among the older men, for ashplants and blackthorns. It was a brave long step to Ravara churchyard. Mr Quinn sought out the widow, anxious to clasp the hand that would pay the Purdie tithes in the future. The coffin was carried out and set on the shoulders of the Purdie brothers and their fellow-bearers. The men fell into a straggling line, neighbour with neighbour, and the rector placed himself at their head. Kirsty Purdie stood in the doorway to see the last of the active, tireless scheming man who had wed her thirty years before. James could hear the younger women busy already among the pots at the hearth. "Youse'll come back!" cried Kirsty plaintively. Back to the funereal meats, the bacon, mutton, yella-meal bread, weak ale, burning poteen.

The sun shone brightly but without warmth on the graveyard. The dark-clad men cast a sharp shadow as they lowered into the hole the neighbour who no longer needed fit weather for his sowing and winnowing. A wind, streaming down from the drumlins, sheened the dank grasses of the place, flattened the mourners' shaggy coats to their backs, and made the Reverend Quinn clap his prayer book to his wig. Sim Purdie was buried shallowly above his ancestors. As the sexton piled on the last shovelfuls, James wondered idly that such a meagre body could displace so much soil. But he knew that by the autumn, the mound would have subsided, and its raw earth been vanquished by the quicken-grass and convolvulus that infested the place.

The Reverend Quinn had placed the well-heeled coffin-bearer as the son-in-law who had married the daughter Kate and led her back to the Presbyterian fold. Gault, that was the name. There was a whisper, too, of his having been out in the Rising. If that was true, Mr Quinn, as a magistrate, speculated on how he had escaped punishment. But they say that the fellow is now a thriving merchant in Belfast. Old Purdie had chimed it often enough. And the rector was not one to hold past indiscretions against a man to whom the Lord had clearly shown His approval. This could but result in a greater abundance of money in Purdie hands, and the Purdies were of his flock.

"This is a grievous occasion, Mr Gault, um . . . um . . ." Behind his words the Reverend Quinn examined James with supercilious curiosity.

"Nothing can be sadder, sir, than the death over which there is no grief," said James soberly.

"Eh? . . . true, true. I understand that you and Mrs Gault are to be congratulated on a happy event. I trust that she is not too put down by this bereavement?"

"Thank you. I'm confident that Mrs Gault accepts her father's passing with Christian fortitude, in the sure knowledge that he's gone to a far better place."

Mr Quinn blew out his cheeks. He felt as if his pockets had been picked. "Proper and commendable. Convey, sir, my felicitations and sympathy, appropriating each to its congruent event."

James accepted the charge.

They were walking towards the graveyard gate. Ahead of them, with two of his companions, was Andrew Purdie. James saw him look back once or twice.

"With your concern in Belfast," said Mr Quinn suddenly and with apparent frankness, "it's not to be supposed that your wife will be much interested in the disposal of her father's goods?"

Ah, thought James, here we come to the real matter. I can hear the speiring voice of Andrew Purdie in this. "I must confess, Mr Quinn, that I don't know Mrs Gault's thoughts on that. Which is understandable," he added dryly, "when you consider her present condition and that the word of her father's death was as unexpected as it was sudden."

"Aye, of course, of course," said the other, concealing none too happily, a surly note. He's finished with me now, thought James. Then, as the rector quickened his pace to walk with more congenial company, it struck James that this was the time to rid himself of the Purdie brood for good and all. He overtook the cleric in a stride or two. "Mr Quinn, I have given more thought to your question. I think I may say, with confidence, that my wife has no interest in her father's farm, other, of course, than to see her brothers prosper on it."

"Ah," said the other with the air of one recalling his question. "Of course . . . a most commendable sentiment." With a faint bow, James dropped back. The mourners had travelled only a short distance along the road, when he saw to his satisfaction, Andrew Purdie at the rector's elbow, listening closely to what that gentleman had to say.

*

Kate Gault believed unquestioningly that the dead could see into the hearts of the living. Her father now had knowledge of the murder she had committed. There were others, her mother, James's mother, who were likely to die before she did. To them also would come this omniperci-pience vouchsafed to the dead. On the night following Sim's funeral, James, fatigued by a day on horseback, slept heavily. His wife lay beside him, awake and motionless, planning her tomorrow, a day to be filled with penance, humility and service to others.

On the Sunday morning following Aeneas Gordon's execution, as she sat silent and stricken in her pew, she had heard from the pulpit the words *There is now, therefore, no condemnation to them that are in Christ Jesus*. They burned in the blackness of her mind like a taper. Of what the Reverend Alexander McCashon had said before this, of what followed the words, she was in total ignorance. She had closed her ears in desperate fear that some qualification, imperative and uncompromising, would snuff out the gleam of light. From that hour she turned her whole being and will to the stubborn tilling of the righteous life.

James, at first, was puzzled at the change in his wife's speech and behaviour. But he sensed that some influence, deep and pervasive, was at work in her life. He cast about for a cause. He refused to entertain Gordon's death as the explanation; she had seen death among her neighbours often enough. The example of the well-to-do ladies who set aside an hour a day to tend to the deserving poor of the town? It would need more than that to alter the ways of his sharp-witted Kate. Nor, in all charity, could he see Alec McCashon, goodly man as he was, divining the spring. But he welcomed the change like a man whose path, inexplicably, had grown smooth.

Kate awoke every morning to consciousness of her misdeeds, past and current, and in the evening thanked God that he had granted her another day in which to make some small atonement. If she ever doubted the nature of her release, she ran from her doubts. As time passed she was troubled less and less by these fears. She was regular in her church attendance and bought Aggie new outdoor clothes so that she might accompany James and herself. She took on much work at the church, acting as sort of unpaid deaconess to Mr McCashon, and busying herself in the welfare of presbyterian lasses, drawn to Belfast by the expanding mills. Because of her ability to tot a column of figures, she was enlisted on the Committee of the Charitable Loan, a group of ladies and gentlemen who sold rice to the living poor at the greatly reduced price of threepence a pound, and supplied free coffins for their dead. There were times when she found it hard to subdue her temper and waywardness. Observing that many of those who came before the Committee were exhausted or starving, the women sometimes pregnant or carrying children in their arms, she asked that a chair be set for the suppliants. Older and wiser heads were of the opinion that this was against the whole spirit and nature of the charity. Although she continued to tend the Committee's funds with care, she did not appear again at their distribution. Without consulting Mrs Masterson, she had ornamental shrubs dug up at Talbot Place, and the ground planted out in vegetables for the public soup kitchen, thereby imposing an almost insufferable strain on the charitableness of that lady. Kate readily accepted that there were those who retired to sleep at peace with the world. She, it seemed, was not to be one of them.

XVII

HIS FATHER GONE, Andrew Purdie took a step long calculated. From the November hiring-fair at Killyleagh he brought back a ploughman and a serving-girl. His brother received the news in angry astonishment.

"Why didn't ye tell me what ye had in mind!"

"I thought ye would see the need yourself," said Andrew as he slipped the brichen from the horse.

"What do we need wi' the girl?"

"My mother's had no help about the house since Kate went."

"And what do we want wi' a ploughman at this time?"

"He can step intae the barn and swing a flail until the ploughing's due, can't he?"

"I mean what land is there to plough that you and me couldn't have opened?"

"There'll be work for him in seasons." The younger man looked up. "I'm for putting the squatters off the farm."

Hugh stared at him. "Are ye, by God! And where are ye for putting them?"

"Ah, we'll settle that some way," said Andrew smoothly. "Are ye wi' me?"

Hugh hesitated. Aggrieved as he was, he did not want to be pushed into a seeming alliance with the tribe of miserable creatures camped in the fields. "Why d'ye want to get rid o' them?"

"We can put our land tae better use. I hear tell the English are going tae war again wi' the Frenchies. There'll be money in crops and pork."

"Charlie Campbell will have something to say on the matter." His brother shrugged. "You'll find them harder to move than ye think." He walked away, knowing himself half-committed to whatever plot his brother was hatching.

Andrew Purdie knew well the task ahead of him. But he had inherited his full share of Sim's obstinacy and guile. His father's body had been barely cold before he had been trotting across the turf bog and along the dark yew walk to the house of Ephraim Smart, Mr Burke's agent. He got little change out of that lank, lugubrious, cunning man.

"The land was rented to your father. He never had written permission from me to sublet. So the Squire's not going to fault ye, if ye try to get rid of the squatters."

"Aye," said Andrew cautiously, "but how dae I get rid o' them?"

"I thought ye had the answer to that, Purdie."

"It's Mr Burke's land. Could ye not law them off it?"

Mr Smart gave a guffaw. "And loose twenty or thirty able-bodied vagrants on the district? B'jasus, Mr Burke would thank me for that!"

"If I come by a way tae shift them, you'll stand by me?"

"If ye can get more money out o' the land, the master'll be happy."

"Dam-it-sowl, Mr Smart," protested Andrew, "I'm not for risking my throat wi' Charlie Campbell and his crew to line the Squire's pockets! These men and women are scraping away at the soil like fowl. If I met Mr Burke, accident-like, and told him it's my intent tae put good heart back intae his land, I'm thinking he would be happy wi' *that.*"

They studied each other shrewdly. Smart saw a younger version of his old accomplice, Sim Purdie. All in all, he had found it a profitable arrangement. He rocked back on his heels. "Aye, no doubt. I tell ye what. Work the land and if ye show a return—satisfactory to all parties—I'll see you're not hindered."

He called after the departing youth. "What's your

brother's mind on the matter?" Andrew Purdie didn't even trouble to turn to reply.

There had been dispute in the Purdie household over the final disposal of Sim's remains. Andrew wanted the Reverend Quinn and a new grave in the episcopalian churchyard. His mother, with uncommon stubbornness, held out for Dr Loudan and the family patch at the Presbyterian meeting-house. Hugh had ridden off to carry the news to the Gaults. His compromise, when he returned from Belfast, of Mr Quinn and the family grave, was grudgingly accepted by mother and brother. Andrew took it upon himself to carry the request to the rector. It was late in the evening when he arrived. Having first won the rector's agreement to read the burial service in a dissenters' burying-place, he then set about sounding him on the problem of the squatters. The young farmer discovered that Mr Quinn, as a magistrate, was even more strongly opposed to eviction by force than Ephraim Smart, and for the same reason.

"Then what's the best thing tae do, y'r honour?" Like his father, Andrew Purdie crouched slightly when he stood before his betters.

"Ah, what, Purdie? Undoubtedly your holding could be put to better use. It's likely we'll be at blows again with the Corsican charity boy. If events turn that way his majesty's forces will need provender as well as men."

Andrew stood twisting his hat. When he looked up there was a gleam in his small eyes. "Men, sir? I heerd tell o' press-gangs lifting men at Newry port. There are some brave likely lads nesting around my place. A word from an important gentleman like yourself . . ."

From behind his desk the Reverend Quinn lifted his hand. There was mingled admiration and contempt in his voice as he spoke. "His majesty's recruiters will not snatch Irishmen from their hearths at my behest. For that matter, Purdie, they mightn't know where to stop, eh?"

The young man didn't trouble to hide his scowl of disappointment. "I'm no further forr'ad, then."

The rector stood up. "These people arrived on your land at the time of the '98 Rising?"

"And every one o' them a curst rebel, I'll warrant, sir!" cried Andrew with renewed hope.

"Your father gave them refuge for all that."

"Only out o' the goodness o' his misguided heart, Mr Quinn, y'r honour, sir."

"But they paid rent all these years?" Mr Quinn waved his hand, "I take it that Squire Burke's agent, for all the lack of formal permission, has benefited from this sub-letting?"

"That he has," said Andrew sourly. "Indeed to God, sir, there's no gain in it. The owld man was getting soft towards his end. Some o' the squatters he let fall intae arrears, but Ephraim Smart still got his money."

"Well, Purdie, you strike me as an honest young man. But all I can offer you is protection to collect your rents," the cleric looked keenly at the young peasant as he dismissed him, "whatever those amount to now, *or in the future*."

Morose and downcast, Purdie had trudged more than half of the moonlit journey homeward, when the meaning of the rector's parting words dawned on him. The suddenness and simplicity of the answer so overwhelmed him that he had to steady himself against a twisted thorn by the roadside. A red moon rode high overhead. He stretched his clasped hands towards it. "Lord God," he whispered, "I hae it, I hae it!"

That night, in the privacy of his room, he laboriously printed out a notice. In the morning he sought Ephraim Smart and laid it before him. "Put your name tae that."

The agent examined it. "I've seen a better fist, Purdie," he said with a grimace.

"I'm no scholar, Mr Smart," said Andrew coldly. "It'll serve."

But the land agent was plainly taken aback at what he read. "The Squire would never make a demand like this, man."

"And what need is there for the Squire tae know, Mr Smart? It's nothing more nor to frighten them off. Or mebbe," he added with a sneer, "ye think they'll find the money?"

"What if I don't sign it?"

"Then I'll take every wheel and animal and hunt for another place where the landlord knows an industrious man when he sees him."

The other smiled acidly. "I might let ye go, Purdie."

" 'Tis your choice, Mr Smart. When I'm gone ye could order up a company o' militia tae shift Charlie Campbell and his cronies."

There was silence. Smart drew the document towards him. "Well, I've warned ye, Purdie. If the Squire and meself don't see more money when these creatures are got rid of, you'll be given notice to quit." For answer he received a defiant stare. Lifting his pen he scrawled his name to the paper and Andrew pocketed it.

"When are ye going to tell them?"

"At the right time. When they come tae pay or cry poverty."

The right time came. About midday Andrew affixed the notice to a post overlooking the shanties. '*Take note,*' it ran, '*starting from this gale day all rents for plots sub-let on the holding of the late Sim Purdie, deceased, are riz by two-thirds. Take note that lying rents will be suffered no more. Settle or quit.*' Signed *Ephraim Smart*, agent.

Scurrying back to the farm, Andrew climbed to the byre loft. From a peephole he saw a tall figure in flittering rags approach the notice. The squatter read what was there then turned and ran from door to door until he disappeared among the hovels. The watcher clambered down from his spying-place. Methodically he went about his preparations. He rolled two casks into the close and laid planks from one to the other. Then he set out two chairs as if at the place of receipt.

Ephraim Smart, fearing that his employer might gather

his drunken wits together before the scheme was played out, and distrusting his fellow-conspirator, had twice ridden over to the farm earlier in the day. When he appeared the third time he was accompanied by a stable-hand. He looked up at the darkening sky. "No sign of them yet, Purdie?"

"Narra a whisper."

The agent stared sombrely at the dark and silent huts. "I don't like it. I'm sending for Mr Quinn, the magistrate."

Andrew held his tongue. His concern was not to collect rents but to rid himself of his unwelcome sub-tenants. If there were going to be ructions let his betters face them. He watched in silence as Smart's man rode off on his errand.

"What does your brother say of this?"

Andrew looked away. "The new plough-hand and him went tae Killyleagh this morn."

"I asked ye what he thought!"

"He knows naught o't. Why are ye concerning yourself wi' him?"

"His name's on the lease too, now. Ye didn't discuss your plan with him?"

Andrew sniggered. "*My* plan? *Your* name's on that notice, Mr Smart, sir."

Smart took a firmer grip on his whip. "As God's my judge, Purdie, I'll hunt ye from this place without a boot to your foot if anything happens this night that turns the Squire against me."

The smile went from Andrew's face. "Naught can happen if we stick thegether," he said in a low sullen voice.

Smart shivered. "I'll step in and take a warm at the fire." The rattle of an approaching cart halted him. Seeing that it was only Hugh and the plough-hand returning, he continued towards the house.

Hugh, clambering down from the cart, stared at his brother's preparations in puzzlement. "What's this? My father always took the rents in the kitchen."

"It's a dry night, Hugh."

"How will we see to count the money?"

"The moon'll be up."

"They like a sight o' the hearth. It's a sharp evening."

"It'll be warmer," said Andrew with a grin.

It was the servant-girl who first saw the sparkle of the torches. They came coiling out from the huts, a wavering line of light in the darkness. As the voices of the bearers grew, the girl ran to her employers. But the approaching glare already engulfed the farmhouse in black and crimson shadows. Smart emerged from the kitchen to join the brothers.

The squatters trudging into the close fell silent at the sight of the three men. The only sound was the tread of their steps as they shuffled into line beyond the trestles. Counting women and children they totalled about forty souls. Every third man bore a torch, a grease-soaked rag on a staff or a splinter of resinous wood. The flames spurted and spat above them, lighting up the pale wasted faces, soiled bodies and ragged clothes. No one spoke. The stillness of the white watchful faces made the hair creep on Hugh's head.

"There's something wrong here——"

"Hold your peace, Purdie," said the land-agent in a low voice.

"We hae raised their rents. I've a feeling they're not for paying them," said his brother in the same tone. Raising his voice he called, "Well, lads, what's holding ye? Who's first tae step forr'ard?"

To Hugh, the glare fell on his face and those of the two men beside him like an accusation. A voice spoke from the crowd. "Where's your rent book, Mr Smart?"

Caught thus, the land-agent glanced down at the bare planks.

"It's not rents you're looking," the voice went on chidingly. "It's evictions, isn't it?"

"Who's speaking?" demanded the agent. "If you're a man—" Andrew Purdie grasped his arm. The brothers were well acquainted with that voice.

A man stepped from the throng. In his hand he carried

Andrew's notice. Gazing at the ragged figure Hugh wondered enviously, yet again, how this man Campbell could come from squalor bearing such an air of dignity and fearlessness.

"There's no need for talk, Mr Smart," muttered Andrew, his head lowered.

"Aye, Andrew Purdie," cried Campbell harshly, "there is. Who's your spokesman, the penman who wrote this," he held up the notice, "or the tool who put his name to it?"

Everyone stood motionless as the clatter of approaching horsemen was heard on the road. Into the close came the Reverend Quinn, followed by his servant and Ephraim Smart's stable-hand. Then an officer, whom Hugh recognised as Mr Narcissus Poots, a squireen from near Strangford, heading a posse of six mounted yeos. The rector tossed his reins to his servant and strode forward into the torchlight.

"How are matters, Mr Smart?"

"We're about to come to the night's business, Mr Quinn."

"You're acquainted with Lieutenant Poots?"

The snub-nose in the epaulettes, whose disdain seemed as manifest for those on one side of the trestles as the other, bowed briefly.

"Have they paid up, yet?" asked Mr Quinn.

Smart looked at him surprised. "Not as yet, sir."

"You raised their rents, Purdie?"

"Raised, Mr Quinn, y'r honour," said Andrew touching his forehead. "Up two-thirds."

Mr Quinn's eyes opened wide and he put his hand to his mouth as if to stifle an ejaculation. "Very well, Mr Smart," he said, "get on with it. Who's that fellow?" indicating Campbell who stood alone in the close.

"Their spokesman, Charlie Campbell."

Campbell took a step nearer. "We hope you're here to see justice done, y'r honour."

"Address yourself to Mr Burke's agent," said the magistrate turning away and drawing his cloak tighter. "And hurry on with the business."

Campbell held out the notice. "It's beyond our power to pay this increase. We don't believe it's seriously meant."

"We don't jape about rents, Campbell."

The squatter smiled wryly. "You understand me well enough, Mr Smart. We don't believe ye hope to get the rents. What you're seeking," and he turned to indicate his fellows, "is to clear these people to the roadside—or to hell, as far as you and yours care."

The men and women behind him murmured, swayed as if a wind had passed through them, moved forward a step or two. The yeo nearest to Hugh shifted his carbine. "Papish rebels. Gie us the word, sir," he said in an eager whisper, "and we'll whitewash the walls wi' their blood." Pettishly, Mr Poots waved him to silence.

Mr Quinn decided to take a hand. "Give me that notice." He took it from Campbell, studied it, and laid it on the planks. "There's no mention here of eviction or clearance. Only warning of an increase in your rents——"

"God Almighty, sir!" cried Campbell. "Raised by two-thirds! There are poor creatures here who can barely keep alive!" Again the crowd murmured and crept nearer, the torches guttering in their hands. Mr Poots shifted restlessly.

The magistrate stubbed the notice with a finger. "The law permits the landlord to raise the rents as he thinks fit. I advise you to pay."

Andrew Purdie thought he heard commiseration in the speaker's voice. "But they winna dae it!" he cried in rage and fear. "There's ones that havena paid my father for two years past!"

"Two years?" said Mr Quinn in simulated astonishment. "Here's a different tale." He turned on Campbell. "It would seem that your landlord has been more than lenient. If you expect more, you expect too much, and should not be indulged."

"Is that your final word?"

"As a magistrate . . . yes."

"And what have ye to say as a man o' God?"

"That you're an impudent fellow!" cried the rector firing up.

This was more to the liking of Lieutenant Poots and his troopers. They flexed themselves like men readying for action. The crowd, straining to hear what passed between Campbell and his opponents, sidled nearer. Here and there men relit their cold torches from those of their neighbours, but their glare was diminishing in the calm flow of the rising moon. "What's the answer, Charlie?" cried a hoarse voice.

The magistrate signed to Ephraim Smart to deliver the verdict. "The new rents must be paid, Campbell," said the agent.

"We can't pay."

"Then you know the consequences. Pay or go."

"It's beyond the powers o' mortal man to pay these rents!" In desperation he looked from one stony face to the other. "Mr Smart, the winter will be on us soon. Will ye put our women and childer out to wander the roads? Andra Purdie, ye wouldn't have the holding ye have today if your father hadn't put us to labour it. We sowed for farthings, but your family reaped gold!" He turned to the rector. "Your honour, ye were put in authority to protect us from the wolves——"

The rector turned his back on him, drawing his cloak to his ears. Campbell watched him. "Great God," he said, "is there none to protect us from the shepherd?" He turned to face the squatters. "No mercy!" he cried in a loud voice. "No mercy!"

A deep howl of anguish rose from the men and women. They came stumbling and running out of the milky gloom, their faces so wrought on by despair and hatred as to be unrecognisable to Hugh. "No mercy!" shrieked a woman dragging a child at her skirts, and the voices of the others, like torches, caught alight, until men, women and children were screaming "No mercy! No mercy!" at the men huddled before the farmhouse.

The squatters, their thin arms straining from their rags, were overturning the planks and kegs. A spluttering torch rolled to Hugh's feet. "They're putting a light tae the hay-shed!" squealed Andrew, clutching the rector's arm. The reverend gentleman shook him off. "Mr Poots," he said with a dry mouth, "put a scare into them. Fire over their heads."

The trigger-fingers were ready. Hugh, half-stunned by the roar of the volley, saw Poots level his pistol deliberately and empty it into Campbell's body. The squatter's leader, arms outstretched to restrain his followers, reeled and fell on his face.

"Murderer!" screamed Hugh, mouth agape. "Murderer!"

"Silence that cur, one of ye!" Mr Poots snarled, and a trooper obligingly smashed the butt of his weapon into the young man's face, sending him sprawling on the ground. Hugh lifted his head. Before him was a red darkness. My God, he thought, I'm blinded. He staggered to his feet. No one paid any attention to him. He opened one eye gingerly. Acrid smoke shrouded the troopers. The night breeze stirred it and he saw Campbell's body stretched on the ground, and beyond it the tumbled body of a woman, her skirts rucked up on her pale thighs. Beside her a child, whimpering, pulled itself upright against the barn wall, fell down, dragged itself up again, fell down again, each time leaving a dark streak on the whitewash. Noisily the yeos were reloading, but their quarry had gone. Hugh could hear the cries and running feet as the last of them fled the place of death. The Reverend Quinn ran his eye over the still bodies. "More practice at the target needed, Poots," he said with a wintry smile. "More practice needed." Hugh stared at the well-clad back with revulsion, then turned and fled also. Past the house, across the meadows, until, exhausted by fatigue and loss of blood he fell down beside the track that led to Belfast.

After a time he sat up. The only sound in the flat, moonlit country was the distant bickering of rooks, disturbed by the gunfire, settling down again in Burke's Woods. By the roadside he found a peat-hole, its water silvered like a mirror by the moon. He bent to study his bruised and swollen face. A flap of skin hung over one eye. Blood had crusted black across his nose and into the socket of the other eye. He dipped his hand in the pool and laved his mouth, chin and neck, careful not to wash away the bloodstains. His protest against greed and murder had been meagre and too late. But when a timid man turns bold on behalf of justice he must content himself with any recognition. He carried the marks of the yeoman's blow like a trophy of war.

But, three hours later, as he clung weakly to the pillar of James Gault's door, there was none of the hero or martyr left in Hugh Purdie. The wound in his head had been torn again by a low-hanging briar, his breeches and hose carried the filth of a dozen black ditches, he had been apprehended by the town watch at the Linen Hall. The constable now stood behind him, lantern raised and staff at the ready, loath to believe that such a bloodied vagrant could be kin to Mr Gault of Talbot Place.

"Knock again," said the constable.

Hugh knocked again. He was not at all certain that his brother-in-law would take him in. The last time they had met was two months before when James and Kate had driven out to Ravara in a hired curricle to present little Robert Hazlett Gault to grandmothers Gault and Purdie.

"There's somebody stirring," announced the watch stepping back to look at the window above them. A light was borne down the stairs throwing vast whirling shadows of a figure in nightgown and tasselled cap. They heard slippered steps in the hall, then James Gault's voice.

"It's the watch, Mr Gault, sir. I've a man here——"

"It's Hugh, James!" cried the young man.

There was a pause, then the sounds of bolts being withdrawn. The door opened to reveal James, flickering candle in one hand, stout warming-pan in the other. He gaped in astonishment at the muddied blood-stained figure on his doorstep.

"Ye know this man, sir?" asked the constable.

"Yes, help him in. There's a fire in the kitchen." The ceiling lamp lit, James tch'd tch'd irritably as he examined the battered face. "Dear, dear, man, what befell ye?" Then he became aware that they had an interested spectator. "Constable, would ye knock up Dr McKenna, give him my compliments, and tell him I'll be with him in five minutes time?"

The man dispatched, James's mood changed. "I'll hear your story later," he said curtly. He set a dish and a jug of milk on the table. "You'll find the breakfast porridge on the hob. Don't make a noise to waken the women. I'll be down when I've got some clothes on."

As they drove back from the doctor's, Hugh told his story. To James, pleasantly conscious of the birds awakening in the trim gardens and the clip-clop of his horse's hooves echoing back from the sleeping houses, this tale of greed, collusion and murder, a mere dozen miles away, seemed horrible and incredible. He stole a glance at the bandaged figure beside him. The account rang true enough, but he was conscious of an irritable feeling of defeat, that Hugh Purdie, to achieve his long-wished-for migration to the town, had turned the affair to his own purpose.

Aggie was heard in the kitchen and her master went to her. "Hugh Purdie has arrived from Ravara. Go upstairs and prepare a bed in the attic. Don't waken your mistress. I'll tell her." Aggie, in her flight upstairs barely glanced at the bandaged youth crouched on the hall settle.

"And what," asked Kate as they sat alone at breakfast, "is he going to do?"

"Going to do?" repeated James a shade too vigorously. "Get his wound healed and then go home."

Kate made a noise in her throat.

"I hope you agree with me on this, wife?"

"I do, Jamie man. For reasons other than yours."

Hugh Purdie came downstairs later only to confirm James's fears. He refused flatly to return to Ravara.

"Maybe you'll tell us what you intend to do," said James in a cold voice.

"Why, for sure, James. I'll find work and a place to live." He smiled slightly. "Don't concern yourself. I won't be beholden to anybody."

"D'ye know what you're leaving?" demanded Kate, leaning across the table. James heard a note of acerbity in her voice that had long been absent.

Her brother laughed almost gaily. "Fifteen guineas in a seed bag, a good frieze coat and a handful o' books!"

"You've worked hard on that land all your life," said Kate. "You're leaving what's rightly yours."

"I want none o' it."

She struck the table. "Half a farm, ye poor silly garsun!"

"There's blood on that land, Kate." His voice was calm and decided. "I won't set foot on it again."

She stared dourly at him, then rose. "Set me out a list of your belongings. I'll send for them."

Hugh shrugged, then claiming to have news of the McDowell family, went to hinder Aggie in her duties in the kitchen.

"Can you find work for him?"

Hearing Hugh's declared intention to strike out for himself James was relieved and a little ashamed. But he had still no high opinion of his brother-in-law's resoluteness. "I'll cast around," he said evasively.

"Couldn't you get him a start in the bakery?"

"No," said James gloomily, his mind turning to his own troubles. "The journeymen wouldn't have him. They talk of nothing now but closing their ranks and combining for more money."

"What sort of world is it," said Kate, "where the servants can order the master?"

But two or three days later Hugh Purdie returned from his first outing in the town with the news that he had found employment as a loom-mender and that he could lodge over his master's shop as a sort of watchman. Kate looked at her husband inquiringly. Although he thought it a mean enough job, James was happy to put a good face on it and congratulate the young fellow.

Before Hugh left Talbot Place that evening, the newspaper was delivered. James came on the report of the affray at Purdies' farm. As he read it out Kate was filled with superstitious dread as she heard names of people known to her set out for the ear and eye of the world.

Disturbance in the County Down

On last Thursday evening during the collecting of rents in the townland of Ravara a large number of ill-disposed persons attacked Mr Smart, agent to Mr Arthur Burke of Lusky Woods, and his tenant, Andrew Purdie. Mr Quinn, a magistrate, with Lieutenant Poots and a small force of militia, were rapidly summoned. The mob having failed to burn a hay barn became so threatening that Mr Quinn was forced to order his men to fire over their heads. Campbell, a ringleader of the malcontents, was shot dead. We understand that his deluded followers, suitably cowed, have now fled the district.

"That wasn't the way o't!" cried Hugh, springing to his feet. "It wasn't like that at all! Nobody threatened Smart, nobody tried to burn the hay—'Fire over their heads'! Where's the mention o' the woman they killed and the child maimed—?" He stared with abhorrence at the paper in James's hand. "So that's a newspaper? God in Heaven, doesn't it have to show the truth? What I told ye was the truth. But that . . ." he stumbled to silence, pointing.

James said nothing. He had a high regard for the truth. There were times, recalling his earlier vocation, when he felt he had a clearer understanding of its nature than had most of his fellows. But the market-place had taught him that to stick too slavishly to a precise narration and description of events might possibly hinder, rather than help, the interests of prosperity and order. There were two sides to every story. And people of the class of the magistrate and the newspaper proprietor, no matter how venal they might be, were better fitted to promote those interests than the horde of the empty-handed, aptly represented at his table this evening, he thought, looking sourly over his paper, by his fool of a brother-in-law.

XVIII

When Hugh Purdie came to collect his belongings from Talbot Place his sister appealed to him to allow James to find him better employment than that of loom-mender.

"For why? He seemed pleased enough when I got it."

"Well, he's of another opinion now," said Kate evasively. "He would rather see you at something where you could use your penmanship."

"That's kind of him, but I don't want a high stool. I'm picking up the trade of carpentering where I am."

"James's opinion is that you're fit for something better," said Kate shortly.

"Our friends always advise us when they begin to despise us."

"You're an ungrateful cub!"

"And you're growing into a fine lady with a bad memory for where we all came from, sister," said Hugh with a smile that robbed his words of some of their edge.

He didn't appear again at Talbot Place until James's conscience was pricked at the thought of him alone in the town at Christmastime. Aggie, to Kate's mild surprise, knew where he lodged. So he came to share dinner with Kate and James. In his pocket he brought a cleverly-carved wooden mannikin for his nephew. He sat down to table, neatly dressed, his sister observed, in a good thickset jacket and worsted breeches.

"Things are going well, Hugh?"

"Ah, yes." The town fascinated him. Every morning, it seemed, someone was laying the foundations for a new house. His favourite stroll was to the harbour to see the vessels come and go, chat with the dockers between the loading and unloading of all those rich and varied cargoes, watch the engineers drain the sleech to build new quays. To all this James listened with a complacent smile, as one who played no little part in this bustling prosperous scene that so impressed his brother-in-law.

"And if I have a minute I stand at a street corner and watch the people going past. I declare, there must be as many as there are stones on Strangford shore! I like to look at a man's hands and clothes and try to tell what his daily work might be."

"And can you spot the rogues?" asked James.

"I like to look into the faces of the honest ones." James and Kate laughed.

But when Aggie had been summoned to put the child to bed, the conversation took a turn less to the liking of the host. Wandering the streets and alleys, Hugh had become aware of another township, inhabited by men and women who didn't know where next they might get food for their bellies and possessing only a clawful of dirty rags to cover that part of their bodies.

"They know right well," said Kate. "This past month we fed near a thousand of them at the Town Sovereign's soup kitchen."

"And why do they have to get their food that way?"

"Because they're shiftless," said James. "They're useless to themselves and the town. They would starve if it wasn't for the efforts of your sister and the other ladies who help at the kitchen."

Hugh, unaware of Kate's philanthropic activities, glanced at her in surprise. But he shook his head at James's explanation in a manner that brought darkness to the merchant's face. "They're not all as you say. I know carters and labourers in Bluebell Lane that work every day, six days a week, and yet their women and children have to go begging food. Can ye be surprised, and a stonebreaker earning six shillings for a week's labour?"

"They would fare better," said Kate, "if they spent less of their time and money in the dram shops."

"Plotting combination and the like against their masters," said James. He looked at his brother-in-law. "Well, haven't you heard them at it?"

"Not being of their trade they say little when I'm about."

"Do they start this talk among themselves? We believe there are fellows who go about spreading mischief."

" 'We'? Who are 'we' "?

"The masters and employers," said James impatiently. "We're putting out a reward of ten guineas for anyone who can lay evidence against these conspirators."

Hugh laughed. "That sounds to me very close to combining."

"When evil men conspire, Hugh, it's time for good men to associate."

"*Evil* men? We're on different sides o' the dike on that."

"You're on the same side as your own kin!" cried Kate.

Neither of the men paid her attention. "I would make a poor hand as an informer, James." They stared across at each other and both knew, in that inimical scrutiny, that an unbridgeable gulf had opened between them.

After a time Hugh rose. "Thank ye both," he said, "for the hospitality. Tell the wee fella I was asking after him." Kate saw him to the door. "You're welcome to come back and see us, Hugh."

"Thank ye. When the days get longer."

The days lengthened into early summer and Hugh didn't return to Talbot Place. Yet Kate felt that he was not without knowledge of herself and her son. She was less surprised than aggrieved when James told her that he had seen her brother, arm-in-arm with Aggie, in the Sunday afternoon crowd of tradespeople, servants, apprentices and idlers that jostled around the band playing outside the White Linen Hall. But she could find no good reason to chide the girl. Because she was keeping company with her brother Hugh? He was an honest lad, as good as any Gault that ever stepped in shoe-leather. So, more through resentment, than any tenderness for the young couple, she disobeyed her husband's injunction to reprimand Aggie. She had no difficulty putting a name to James's annoyance. It was understandable that a man of his growing importance should dislike the idea of his kitchen maid being courted by his brother-in-law. But he's forgotten, she thought with a snap of her mouth, the potato rigs from whence all four of us came.

*

Within the last year James's trading had grown apace, and with it his reputation and influence among the merchant fraternity. He had been diligent, but he admitted, with gratitude and humility, that the Lord had looked with favour on his efforts. "Lord, in thee have I trusted," he would murmur as he drew on his nightcap, "let me never be confounded." The tallow concern, although profitable, had never interested him, so that when an offer was made for it, he promptly accepted, having first, out of courtesy, conferred with Mr Hazlett. The price he received was little short of four thousand pounds. With this new-found capital he was now able to turn a blunder into a new and profitable undertaking. Because of a misunderstanding with the foreman of his bakery in the purchase of material, he found himself with ten unwanted casks of butter. Mr Louise Fitzgibbon offered to take them off his hands. James, ever-cautious, asked how he hoped to dispose of them, and discovered that the young merchant, having learnt his lesson in the *Irish Oak* muddle, had since built up a promising export provision trade, limited in its activities only by lack of capital. As the Lagan Trading Company they went into harness again, but this time with James firmly the senior partner.

From Fonsy he learnt that the Legg's Lane haunt and its inhabitants had been scattered after Aeneas Gordon's death. Matt McCoubrey, the giant smith, had been pressed into service against the French as a farrier; the idiot Poll had been thrown into the madhouse; Owen Fearon had been transported for horse-thieving——

"And the Doctor, Fonsy?"

"They say he's lying in some lodging-house near Smithfield Market."

As he listened to the fate that had overtaken the Doctor and his companions he felt like the sole survivor of a catastrophe. It was difficult not to feel like one whose unworthy feet had been lifted up and set on dry land. A dweller at the ford, as Pringle Hazlett put it. What had the Doctor got for his two vessels?

"They were took in Greenock for debt, cap'n."

His new clerk, a youth with a taste in neckcloths, entered the counting-house followed by Mr Hazlett and Mr Adair. It was close to midday and the luncheon-hour. James reached for his hat.

"We want a word with you, James," said Tom Adair.

"We can talk over the table."

"Now, if you please," said Adair with a glance at Fonsy and the clerk. Puzzled, James waved his employees out of the office.

"You know," began Mr Adair, "that since the death of Gilbert McIlveen, the town's been short a magistrate?"

"McIlveen died a year ago. Surely they've picked someone since to take his place?"

"Two names have been considered and both turned down. We, for our part, wouldn't accept the gentleman proposed in Lord Donegall's interest. Now we learn that his Lordship won't accept our man."

James nodded to show that he appreciated the gravity of the situation and the weight of the parties involved. "Well, it sounds a confounded nuisance. And to judge by our streets at night, the town needs its full force of magistrates and law-officers. But," and he put on his hat, "I've heard nothing that couldn't have been said over a chop. I'm hungered, gentlemen."

Mr Hazlett raised his hand. "There's more, James."

"We're here," said Mr Adair, "as spokesmen for your friends in the Chamber of Commerce." James felt his scalp begin to tingle. "Would you consider taking on the office and duties of a magistrate?"

He stared at the questioner. "Are you serious?" He looked from one to the other and saw that they were very serious. "But, God help ye, Tom, what qualities have I for such an . . . honour?"

At his use of the word the two elderly merchants smiled and relaxed. Mr Hazlett took the stool. Mr Adair perched himself on the edge of the desk. "You're a man of no party. You pay twenty guineas and more in tax in the year. You're well-read," concluded Mr Hazlett.

"You're known as a man of integrity. What value is there in that if it doesn't procure you position?" urged Mr Adair.

James turned to Mr Hazlett. His old friend smiled. "It's hard to put it different—or better, James."

"Aren't you defeating your own case by clapping a label on me—the 'merchants' magistrate'?"

"No," said Pringle Hazlett. "No one's asking you to dispense justice to suit your friends. But the fact is that there's no third party in the town, no appreciable professional class such as in Dublin. And the feeling is that the Donegall family is well enough represented in the corporation and the courts."

"Too well represented," said Adair, "between the marquis, and his kinsmen, the Chichesters and Skeffingtons. What sort of sense does a title like 'Lord of the Castle' make on Liverpool 'change? Damme, give me 'merchants' magistrate' any day. It means something——"

Mr Hazlett halted him. "We agreed, Tom, that Gault must not be laid open to the charge of partiality. Let us say no more. What's your answer, James?"

"I'm curious to know who was your first choice and in what way he was found wanting."

The elderly merchant hesitated. "I'd ask ye not to pursue

that, James. The final choice of magistracy lies with Dr Brewster, the Town Sovereign. When you meet that gentleman, the less you know of what's gone before—on either side—the better."

"There was nothing discreditable?"

"Nothing. You may rest on that."

"I'll be happy to go with you."

He had exchanged courtesies with Dr Brewster on a few occasions at the Assembly Rooms and suchlike venues. Nothing more than that. While carefully avoiding any oddness of behaviour, he was inclined to keep himself in the background when such superior personages were about. He had learnt that when men are busily and successfully pursuing money, they remain largely indifferent to each other's origins. But Dr William Brewster, Vicar of St Anne's, Town Sovereign, Chief Magistrate, had an amplitude of leisure and wealth and authority to interest himself in such matters. And it wasn't enough, James had discovered, to practise reticence about one's past. The years, like tides, threw up fragments of a man's past, to be pieced together by the curious or the malicious. Did he know of the events, the shrewd smooth-faced dignitary would certainly speculate on the immediate past history of a young Dissenter who threw over his studies at Glasgow, to arrive back in Ireland, oddly enough, about the time of the recent rebellion. With excitement and foreboding he looked forward to the meeting with the Town Sovereign.

A week later, with his two friends, he was invited to dine with Dr Brewster at the Donegall Arms. As they made their way towards the tavern, Hazlett and Adair explained to James that the Town Sovereign understood him to be a person of responsible but independent opinion, and that nothing under that head would be raised at the dinner table. With the reverend doctor were Mr Kilbee, the Town Attorney, and Mr Clulow of the Ballast Board. From Mr Kilbee he won no more than a cool nod. Adept himself in such social niceties, James took his place at table in a manner equally reserved. Mr Clulow, James decided, had the busiest mouth he had ever seen on a man. Declining food, he sat alternately biting the hem of his linen handkerchief or sucking the silver head of his cane, refreshing himself occasionally from a glass of wine. As the meal progressed his gaze rarely shifted from the young merchant's face. James had only to catch his eye to be immediately smothered in the most genial of smiles and nods. After a little, suspecting impudence behind this affability, he avoided his attention.

Dr Brewster and Mr Kilbee, James knew, had favoured the Donegall family's candidate. But he was gratified to see, that in the company of the two senior merchants, they kept their opinions to themselves. Mr Kilbee, in fact, said nothing of the magistracy, and James concluded that if the attorney had suffered a defeat, he wasn't going to cry it aloud. On one occasion Dr Brewster began, "The citizens of Belfast have much for which to thank the marquis and his family—" Mr Adair's soup spoon paused in mid-air. "But," continued the Town Sovereign, "our immediate need is to find someone competent and willing to take on these duties. You, Mr Gault, have the approval of these estimable gentlemen. That being so, I welcome your interest in applying the law in Belfast." His great full-bottomed wig shook from side to side. "And trust me, sir, this damnable unrest among working-people hasn't eased the work of the courts." Mr Adair had resumed his soup.

Nervous of being thought a catechizer by the watchful merchants across the table, the Town Sovereign's conversation, for the rest of the meal, was mostly of a general nature. Had he heard that Mr Gault had been to Glasgow University? Yes, said James, shuffling out of the query by adding that much to his regret he had read little in law, a remark that brought a silent sunburst of mirth to the face of Mr Clulow.

"Mr Gault's concern is wholly understandable," said the Town Sovereign, turning with what James suspected was a wink, on the gentleman from the Ballast Office. "But the magistrates are well-guided by the officers of the Court, eh, Mr Kilbee?"

"You may rely on that, Mr Gault," said Mr Kilbee. It was the sole remark that the attorney addressed to the aspirant during the meal. He spoke only to his neighbour at table, Pringle Hazlett, on such matters, as far as James could overhear, as the unrest among the masons and carpenters, who alleged that they and their families were starving, and the recent ruinous increases in prices of French brandy.

Their breath still redolent with the flavours and savours of the eating-house, the three merchants parted at the corner of Weighill Lane. Mr Adair's face was still flushed with wine, truculence and triumph. "Damn Kilbee and his airs. But, by God, they danced to a different jig this time!" With that he linked Pringle Hazlett's arm and turned into High Street.

Two days later Mr Clulow appeared at the Weighill Lane counting-house. He was already grinning when James opened the door. "Passing," he said, "I thought I would step by and congratulate you, Mr Gault, sir."

James joined him on the cobbles of the lane. "On what, sir?"

"On being appointed a magistrate, Mr Gault."

"You're ahead of me. I understand that I've first to be advised of the Chief Magistrate's approval. So you see, sir, your good wishes are premature."

Mr Clulow's fixed grin widened to a laugh. "Well, I can tell you, Mr Gault——"

"No, you can *not* tell me!" cried James in exasperation. "I'll have the word from the proper quarter, Mr Clulow."

Mr Clulow wagged his head deprecatingly. "You're quite right, sir. But you must understand my gratification on your . . . now, your success in the export trade, I'm aware of that," said Mr Clulow, perking up. "I see the figures that pass through the Ballast Office. For being such a short time in the business, your firm, the Lagan Trading Company, is doing remarkably well."

"I'm in partnership only . . . with Mr Louis Fitzgibbon."

"An uncommon partnership," said Mr Clulow looking at him sharply.

"In what way?"

"Between a Protestant and a Papist."

James smiled mirthlessly. "I'll give ye a bit of advice that was once given to me—never mix religion and business. You spoil two good things."

Mr Clulow dragged his toe on the cobbles. "There are those who don't take it so lightly. But you can satisfy them easily enough."

"Speak plainly."

"Make your religious loyalties plain. Join the Orange Institution."

"And this would satisfy your friends 'who don't take it so lightly' eh?"

"Sir, you would immediately gain their confidence and win their support in your interest."

"Tell me, Clulow. Is this your real reason for calling today?"

Surprised into frankness, Mr Clulow forgot to smile. "Yes."

"I would hope this is not a condition laid down by Dr Brewster?"

"No, no . . . I wouldn't go as far as that——"

"I'm pleased to hear it," said James harshly. "Your own idea, is it?"

"It's the opinion of a number of influential men in Belfast that the new magistrate should be an Orangeman."

"Well, let them find themselves one. For my part I won't parade the streets in gingerbread mummery for the sake of a seat on the bench. That's all I have to say, sir. Good day to you."

Mr Clulow's face, as he turned away, seemed strangely naked without its grin.

But later, when his annoyance had somewhat cooled, James began to have misgivings. Clulow, for all his denial, could well have been an agent for the Town Sovereign and his clique. Unaware of any ambition for public place until it had been aroused by Adair and Hazlett there was nothing now he so much desired as that vacant magistracy. It would be intolerable if he had thrown it away by a few hasty words. He valued Kate's shrewdness enough to tell her of the encounter. To herself she thought him rather a fool to have scruples about such a little thing but aloud gave her opinion that he had acted sensibly enough.

"And what call or license has this Clulow to gabble about other people's money affairs?"

He gazed at her approvingly. "Confound it, girl, I never thought to ask him that!"

James's confidence in his fortune was greatly restored by a conversation he had with Dan Ritchie in the Assembly Rooms. Mr Ritchie was not so discreet as had been his fellow-merchants. "Hassan was our man, Mr Gault."

James stared at the grain factor. "But Sam Hassan's a most reputable fellow."

"He's all that," agreed Mr Ritchie. "But he kept on about rebellion when nobody, high or low, wanted rebellion. God help him, Sam says more'n his prayers."

So James was confirmed in his prudence. Let those who want to play politics do so. But his head didn't rest easy on his pillow, until, with all due formality, he was sworn in as a magistrate of the town of Belfast.

XIX

"Look," said Mrs Masterson drawing aside the curtain of the window that overlooked the garden. Mrs Hazlett saw a patchwork of vegetable beds, tumbled heaps of soil, where potatoes, cabbages and turnips had been harvested. An elderly man, his backside raised to the ladies, was setting out young plants. "Late cabbages, I'm told," said Mrs Masterson with distaste. "She knows as much about these things as any peasant."

"I understand she's a farmer's daughter," said Mrs Hazlett about to drop the curtain. Her friend seized her by the arm. "And now, dear Harriet, *look*!" With a quivering finger Mrs Masterson pointed to a distant corner of the garden. Mrs Hazlett saw a tangled boskery of cotoneaster, tulip tree, veronica and rhododendron, heeled in and leaning crazily away, as if in flight from the encroaching vegetables.

Mrs Masterson seated herself. "My noble shrubs," and went on to mumble tearfully something about the recent horrid revolution in France.

"You're a great fool at times, Lizzie," said Mrs Hazlett. "You know very well that the vegetables are being grown by Mrs Gault for the public soup kitchen."

"The Committee has enough money to buy the stuff," said Mrs Masterson, eyeing her friend damply and ill-humouredly.

"At a thousand meals a week, for how long? And now we want a second kitchen at the markets where the need is great. Mr and Mrs Gault have been generous in their financial help. I understand that the money they might have spent on coteries and card-playing they give to the Fund."

"She's to have another child," Mrs Masterson glanced at the window and brightened up. "That'll put a halt to her depredations."

Mrs Hazlett sat up with renewed interest. "I'm concerned to hear that." The withdrawal, even temporarily, of the energetic Mrs Gault, would mean that more time would have to be given by each of the other ladies to the bothersome details of people who smelled. "I hope her lying-in won't be prolonged. Perhaps, Elizabeth," she continued with some malice, "*you* could give more than a morning in the week?"

"That I can't," cried Mrs Masterson. "And let me tell you, Harriet, that Mr Lucas is of the opinion that you're feeding able-bodied malingerers. Even Kate Gault, with all her head for ciphers and country places, was rueing that she had given food to a family of weavers from outside the town."

Mrs Hazlett sighed and let the refusal pass. She had little feeling for Belfast and its growing self-importance. She found tiresome all this business of district meal tickets, so carefully organised by people like Kate Gault. If a well-to-do merchant and his family from the other end of Ireland had presented themselves, she would have, in her languid charity, set them out soup and bread and no questions asked.

At about the same time, in the White Cross Inn, James, in the company of Mr Kelly, a fellow-magistrate, sat on the fringe of a group engaged in discussing much the same matter. Mr Kelly brought the news that some four hundred cotton weavers had assembled in a field two miles along the road to Lisburn.

"It's a murderous conspiracy," declared one of his audience, a cotton manufacturer. "They mean to attack them that won't knuckle down to their demands on money and hours."

"Throw the militia at 'em," said Mr Spifford Lamont. "Drive 'em back to their looms."

James, loath as he was to be drawn into the discussion, turned to the cotton manufacturer. "Have you proof of what you say, Mr McAllister?"

"Damme, sir, what else could they mean? They're not there for a picnic!"

"No, Mr McAllister," said Mr Kelly, "what they're about is to post their agents into Belfast to ask support among the bricklayers, carpenters, masons, bakers and carters."

As these occupations touched closely more than half the merchants present there was sudden dismay around the table. "Call it what ye like," cried Mr McAllister, "it's a conspiracy!"

"It's certainly a strike, which is against the law. I've no doubt we could find the work of combinators at the root of it. What's your opinion, Gault?"

"I can't see four hundred men being gaoled. I would let nature, that is to say hunger, disperse them."

"The dogs are slipping into the town and vittling themselves at the free kitchen. I'm told Mrs Gault takes a hand in the running of that charity?"

"You are right on both counts, Mr McAllister," said James curtly. "But only those with Committee tickets are fed now."

"If the masters joined to turn these fellows away when they showed up for work, it would bring them to their senses. Good gracious, heaven and earth, ye can get them by the waggon-load from the Mourne Mountains and like places."

Mr Sam Hassan, having been excluded from the jurisdiction of the town, considered himself free to express opinions objectionable to his fellow-merchants. "What are ye about, gentlemen? Is Lamont's suggestion anything short of combining? Yet, with two magistrates in the company, I've heard no rebuke."

"Nor will you, Mr Hassan," said Mr Kelly sharply. "If trade is to be safeguarded then employers might have to stand together. They—" the magistrate paused, looked around, and saw agreement on every face, "—*we* are for the good of the community as a whole. Without our capital, energy and gumption, *no* man eats——"

"I understand your hesitation, Mr Magistrate," the wine-merchant interrupted with brusque malice, "but Lamont's proposition is against the law, and well you know it."

"A combination of masters would be tolerated because it's not politically dangerous," said Mr Kelly with a note of finality.

James, irritated that the company should be so easily goaded by Hassan's jibes, intervened. "Tell me, Sam, how many men are in your employment?"

"Eh?" The wine-merchant stared at his interrogator in no friendly fashion. "Eight, if ye want to know, and I agree such wages with them that'll assure the delivery of your brandy and Geneva without fail!"

"Dammit, I'm relieved to hear that," said Mr McAllister. "But such an agreement without the knowledge of others in your trade is combining by a master and his men. B'jaze, Sam Hassan, you're breaking the law yourself!"

As Hassan protested amid the laughter of the others, James slipped away. He was disturbed by Kelly's reference to the town's bakers. Instead of returning to Weighill Lane he crossed Hercules Street to Winetavern Street and his bakery. To his apprehensive eye, Brady his foreman, and the six journeymen and apprentices, seemed busy enough at their ovens and kneading-tables. He had taken Brady over from Pringle Hazlett and had great confidence in him. He inquired if any strangers had been to the bakery.

"A young fella called yesterday to see the ovenman McBride. He made no secret of his real errand. He was a combinator looking support."

"I hope he got short shrift."

"I chased him."

"Are they sympathetic—McBride and the others?"

Brady glanced into the dark shop and shrugged. "Who

knows, sir. The danger would be if the town bakers come out."

James plucked his lip, his eyes on the flour-daubed figures, kneading, pounding, lifting, stacking. Even if he ran for a time at a loss, he could afford to keep his bakery working against all threats. An oven door was thrown open filling the shop with the odour of new-baked bread. His irresolution vanished. He turned to Brady who had been watching him closely.

"If I can guess what you're thinking, Mr Gault, I would advise ye against it."

"To raise their wages?" said James with an irritable laugh. "Who could protest at that, Brady?"

"Your fellow master-bakers would take it ill. *Particularly* as you're a magistrate."

He struck his cane on the ground in peevish frustration. "It's to save my business. Could I not, in some small way . . . ?" and he nodded at the bakers.

"If there was a grievance I would tell ye. But your hours are as short and your wages as high as any in the district. If I was you, Mr Gault, I wouldn't cross my bridges till I came to them."

Over dinner that evening he told Kate of his forebodings about the workers in his bakery. In a confusing world where men threw over their livelihood in order, as they maintained, to safeguard it, she had little to offer but indignation and ridicule. Then she said, "There's another eager to leave our employ. Aggie came to tell me that she wants to be free to marry our Hugh."

To James, in his present mood, it was a matter of little importance. "Could he keep her?"

"And of what concern is that and me with my second child coming?"

Here was one problem to which there was a ready answer. "You're quite right, my love. Tell her she hasn't permission to leave us until the baby's born and you have quite recovered."

*

Fonsy led her, old, ragged and stooped to the counting-house window. "Stand there, mother, till I get Mr Gault." James, his curiosity roused, had risen from his stool when the door opened and Fonsy announced that an "owld *cailleach*" sought him.

James looked through the window with distaste at the dirty cunning face turned up to him. "What does she want, Fonsy?"

"She says she's from the Doctor, cap'n."

"What doctor?"

"*The* Doctor. Your man from Legg's Lane—only he's not there no more."

"What the devil can he want with me?" he said glowering at this unlikely messenger.

"He's dying. He sent for ye."

The merchant sat down, cradling his head in his hands. He looked up. "Very well. Get the address. I can hardly be expected to walk through the streets with her."

An hour later he knocked at the door of No. 9 Batt Place, off Smithfield Market. It was opened by the old woman.

"You sent for me."

"Ye took your time in coming." She jerked her thumb over her shoulder. " 'Twas *him* sent for ye. G'wan up."

He hesitated at the foot of the stairs. "Has he had other visitors?"

"None."

"Shouldn't he have a doctor?"

"Ppf! Isn't he wan himself? He knows when he's dying."

He eyed the dark stinking ascent. "A clergyman . . . ?"

"Feth," the old woman cackled, "it's not the good God he's concarned about, 'tis the Other Fella." She peered at him contemptuously. "Are ye not for going up?"

Avoiding the wall and handrail he mounted the crazy stairs. Her shrill voice followed him. "It's the door fornenst ye."

He pushed it open. Light from one crusted window showed him the bed against the wall. He crept forward, peering down at the head pillowed in its own hair, fearful to learn at what moment he had been called to re-enter this strange creature's life. The black eyes opened on him. The voice came from a great distance. "James Gault." A hand crept from under the coverlet. With an effort he took it. It closed on his, dry and chill, colder than the rings that turned on the hollowed fingers.

He dragged a stool below him. "What can I do for ye?" he whispered.

The Doctor moved his head. James could almost hear the lips crack. "There's no nostrum . . ." James bent to the mouth ". . . for a broken heart."

He became aware of the rings embedded in his clasp. The old woman must be honest, or afraid. And the Doctor, for all his horrid surroundings, was not dying of hunger. Could such a man be affected by sorrow to the point of death? He strained to hear the fluttering voice, "There's a sweet spring well outside of Killeshandra . . . a yoke on the shoulder and two lipping cans . . ."

"D'ye want a sup of water, Doctor?" The Doctor turned away his head. "A little brandy?" James looked round for the old woman. "Dammit, there should be somebody with you, and you in this state. Does no one know, other than that old hag?"

The eyes opened again, half ice, half fire. The fleshy nose drooped in a smile. "When beggars die, Gault, there are no comets seen." The grip tightened on his hand. "Innocent . . . Aeneas Gordon . . . not guilty, m'lord Gault."

"I know . . . I knew him to be innocent." He leaned forward, speaking earnestly. "You're near your end, can I send for a clergyman?"

There was a long silence. Behind him James heard the pad of the old woman's feet. The head lifted an inch from the soiled pillow. "What you call death is ceasing to die . . . what you call birth is beginning to die. Your bones are the part of you that death abandons and remits to the grave." The dying man fell back slackly.

James leaned over him. "And your soul to heaven, I hope."

He thought he saw a smile on the submerged face. But the dilated eyes, fixed and burning, stared at some point beyond his knowing. He remembered a boyhood night when a moth had blundered into his room and struck his sleeping face. Scared out of his wits he grasped the bedside bible and beat it down on the insect as it lay spreadeagled on his pillow. Then he lay watching the gemlike light of the moth's eye diminish, dwindle and die. So it was now with the man whose hand he clasped. Slowly the glittering stare dimmed, sank, and went out in the darkness of the face. The woman was breathing huskily at his elbow. "The sowl's away. God be kind to him," and she crossed herself. James loosed his hand from the dead fingers with an amen. The woman took a fly-speckled mirror from the wall and held it to the mouth.

She turned to James. "Gimme a couple o' pennies, your honour."

Deftly she drew her hands over the dead face and the eyelids lay sealed under the coins.

"You know about these things?"

"I keep a roof over me head knowing about these things."

"Will you do what's required?"

"He'll need a clean shift."

He took money from his pocket. "Get a fine linen one."

At the door he paused. "Would you like his rings?"

She rounded on him. "May God blind the man that takes them off the dead fingers!"

James called Fonsy into the counting-house. "Our friend's gone." He counted six guineas into the little man's palm. "Attend to the funeral. Order a casket—all that's required."

On the third morning Fonsy came into the yard. "Our friend's sealed and delivered as per instructions, cap'n."

James looked at the sky. "Were there any to follow the coffin?"

"A streel o' owld wans from Legg's Lane, mourning and

girning." He held out a guinea. "I thought ye would want me to put a dram into each when all was over."

"You did right. Where was the internment?"

"Shankill burying-ground. For five shillings and a quart o' whiskey the gravedigger opened a hole for me in the paupers' corner."

James frowned.

"But he had a good coffin, cap'n. Sound but not showy. Three guineas was the price asked by a young fella new to the trade—" He proffered the coin again.

"Keep it, Fonsy."

"—by the name o' Hugh Purdie. Why, thank ye, cap'n." And Fonsy went off polishing the coin on his cuff while James stared after him.

XX

KATE HAD HAD no nursemaid for Robert Hazlett Gault. In a household where there were already two active women, she thought it foolish, for the sake of a social nicety, to employ a third to look after a child. But as she grew towards her second confinement the idea was often in her mind. Shrewdly she set it aside for the time being. Another servant would be understood by Aggie as a sign that she was free. The girl had agreed willingly that her duty was to stay until the child was born. But it was evident to Kate that the centre of her existence now lay outside the Gault household. To her mistress she confided that Hugh's skill with wood and tools had led him into the trade of coffin-making. His custom was largely among the poor and outcast in the squares and alleys around Bluebell Lane. It was laborious and not very profitable and the established coffin-makers of the town were inclined not to meddle with him. But there was no reason, dreamt Aggie, why he shouldn't have men working for him some day, all busy burying the rich. Her demands on love-making were humble, and if Hugh's talk, as they stood in the throng around the Sunday band, was largely of kerfing, plinths and muntins and he dwelt on the swelling and shrinking of corpses as they strolled along the evening Lagan towpath, yet she returned to Talbot Place light of foot and heart.

Mrs McBratney, the midwife, made her second appearance at Talbot Place. She was there little more than thirty minutes before the mistress of the house wished her out of it. Her insolence angered Kate. What had been suffered in silence by a frightened country girl on the birth of her first child was not to be borne now by Mrs James Gault. But Kate was somewhat in awe of Dr McKenna and was prepared to suffer the hectoring woman for the safe delivery of her baby.

One morning as she lay in bed she heard the midwife's voice raised in a tirade against Aggie. Kate seized a bell and shook it so violently that the tongue flew across the room. There was a fleet step on the stairs and Aggie opened the door. Seeing her with flushed face and close to tears, Kate was seized with fury.

"I heard that shouting-match. Send Mrs McBratney to me."

"Ma'am, she wants me——"

"I heard what she wants. So must the neighbourhood. I want to speak to her."

But Mrs McBratney was close behind Aggie. "Were ye calling me, Mrs Gault?"

"I was. Come in and close the door. You may go, Aggie."

Mrs McBratney picked up the brass tongue and held it out accusingly. "You've brusted your bell. What ails ye?"

"I heard you calling my servant 'girl'. You know her right name, Mrs McBratney. Use it from now out."

The midwife's face darkened. "I was only sending her home for an apron I forgot——"

"You're sending her nowhere," said the young woman on the bed.

"It's not my job to run errands," said the midwife sullenly. "If you was in your pains and Dr McKenna——"

"This time I won't tell Dr McKenna that you came unprepared for your work. Any errands that are for fetching, Robbie the gardener will fetch them."

Mrs McBratney shuffled towards the door. "I'll tell him, ma'am."

"You will not. You'll ask Aggie to tell him. And you'll ask her in a voice that can't be heard halfway across the town."

Kate lay gazing at the door as it closed softly behind the

midwife. She realised that she couldn't do without Aggie. The loss of this gentle biddable creature would cause her too much pain. She enjoyed the friendship of Harriet Hazlett and Jessica Fitzgibbon and the others. In a way the acquaintanceship of these ladies was immeasurably more important to her than the existence of her serving-girl. Yet Aggie McDowell held a secret place in her affections that no one could have dreamt of or understood. She could unbutton before Aggie, laugh, flare, share foolish secrets, discuss serious trivialities. Alone, the two young women slipped without thought into the same tongue, using the broad speech sweet to their mouths as oaten bread. And Aggie never forgot her place because she had been well-schooled. I made her, thought her mistress, she's mine. But she's trysted to your brother. She turned on her pillows. I made her, I need her more than anybody else. What of your brother? There are other lasses . . .

Kate's second child, a daughter, was born in March 1805. James, assured by Dr McKenna that all was well, returned to his busy world. Aggie was entrusted to carry the news to the grandmothers. A gig and driver had been ordered for the day so that she might visit her own family. On the evening before her trip she went into the dining-room to set the table. Her mistress was reclining in a low chair. Over her knees lay a brown lambswool shawl and a bombazine dress of the same hue. She held them up. "What do you think of these, Aggie?"

The girl fingered the clothing. "They're brave and nice."

"Then go, like a good girl, and let me see them on you."

Aggie returned. She trailed the shawl in one hand. The brown dress suited her admirably. That it lent her the air of a housekeeper did not escape her mistress.

"You look fine, Aggie. Try on the shawl."

Aggie draped it over her shoulders. Involuntarily she caressed her chin with the woolly softness.

"Mrs McCreery or her seamstress had a good eye for your size."

Startled, Aggie looked up. "Are these for me, ma'am?"

"Who else? A gift never loses by being a surprise."

The girl eyed her with a dawning shrewdness. "And me leaving?"

"You're not leaving looking fit to scare corbies," said Kate with a laugh. "And if you're set on going you'll have to help me to find a girl to take your place. And a cook. Now that Mr Gault's a magistrate we'll have to entertain more," Kate leaned back. "And if we have a cook we'll need a scullery-maid. So whoever we find, Aggie, will have to be fit to be housekeeper, for I'm going to give my time to the children."

Aggie, stunned at the news of this sudden accretion of the Gault staff, remained silent. Then at last wistfully, "Could she be a married woman?"

Kate raised herself, a smile of affection and understanding on her face. "How could she live here and look after her husband?" Then briskly, "Now off with the finery, Aggie, and clear the table. Mr Gault'll be in soon."

Kate listened with more than usual attention to Aggie's account of her visit to the country. The girl had delivered a parcel at old Mrs Gault's but she hadn't had time to call at the Purdie farm. She was sorry.

"It's no matter," said her mistress. "You found your own people well?"

"All well, thanks be. But wee Mattie had to come home from the man she hired with. He made her lift turf till she was spitting blood."

Kate shook her head in indignation. "And what of your father?"

"He's rightly," said Aggie in some surprise, thinking that she had already answered that.

"He had nothing to say?"

"Say, ma'm?"

Kate lowered her head. There had been no talk of marriage. "I was thinking that the farmer Mattie hired with might be looking his money back."

"I heard no word o' that."

"If there is, Mr Gault'll attend to it."

"Thank ye, ma'am." The girl hesitated. "I think, ma'am, that Mr Gault should go to see his mother."

"And he will, Aggie, he will," said her mistress cheerily.

But James couldn't spare a week-day away from the mart and the quays. And his Sabbaths were taken up in church business and worship. Occasionally, with an eye on the morrow, he would fetch home a fellow-merchant after evening service for a bite and a sup. So, as his visits to his mother became less frequent, his parcels to her of food, clothing and money, became more prodigal.

Hugh Purdie had been long out of his brother-in-law's mind. He was surprised therefore, when, before dinner one day, Kate questioned him on the whereabouts of her brother.

"I haven't laid eyes on him since he was last here."

"I hope he's well," she said with real concern.

"We would have heard if it was otherwise," said her husband with a lift of his eyes towards the closed door. Then he added, "His worry will be how to make his bread. There's word in the Chamber this morning that he and his like are to be barred in future from any sort of carpenting work."

Kate heard the chink of dishes on the other side of the door. She waited until Aggie came into the room, then leaned across to her husband. "What way will Hugh lose his work?"

"Eh? Well," said James with marked patience, "there's been many deaths in the town because of fever and hunger. Some of them reach the dead-house without a rag to wrap them in. The Town Corporation have asked the master joiners to tender for the work of coffining these wretched victims. They, in their turn, have had to come to an agreement with the Woodworkers Society before they can quote prices. Your brother isn't a member of that crew. He didn't serve his time to the trade."

Aggie was serving the soup. "And what," asked Kate, "if Hugh goes on with what he's doing?"

James put his finger and thumb together. "They'll squash him like a fly."

"What's he to do, then!"

"Go back to Ravara," James lifted his soup spoon. "And now, if you please, I have to go out again this evening."

Kate watched Aggie as she left the room. As the door closed, James became aware of where the exchanges had led. "Confound it," he said to his wife with an angry laugh, "you're making me into a play-actor, Mrs Gault!"

Not all of James's time, these days, was spent at Weighill Lane. In the past nine months the activities of the Lagan Trading Company had greatly increased. In that time the price of mess beef had gone up by almost a guinea a tierce, butter by ten shillings a cask. Their customers in Liverpool and Glasgow confidently forecast that if nothing untoward interrupted the war with the French, prices could well be doubled within the year. Louis Fitzgibbon and he agreed that they could no longer handle this traffic from their small counting-houses. A large well-windowed office was rented on Hanover Quay and James watched Mr Fitzgibbon embellish it (he had to admit in admirable taste) with brass, glass and mahogany. His energetic partner then suggested that they buy a small coasting brig. To be a ship-owner! The idea filled James with as much trepidation as pleasure and he begged time to give the matter more thought. There was one side of the firm's activities that he would have been happy to leave with Fitzgibbon, the entertainment of their customers. But a chance word from Jessica Fitzgibbon had fired Kate with a desire to share in these offerings of hospitality. Wasn't he the senior partner, she demanded, and wasn't he a magistrate, forbye? So James, although he could see additions to his domestic staff, agreed to arrange small evenings for visiting buyers. If the flighty Fitzgibbons whisked their charges off to the theatre, the Gaults and their guests were to be found at a coterie or a staid musical evening at the Assembly Rooms. But James had to admit, if the order books were anything to go by, that the money was well spent, and that their customers left Belfast with a good opinion of the Lagan Trading Company.

Much of his time was spent counselling with his fellows on what measures should be taken to stem the growing unrest among the town's working-people. To the other merchants he was a man of progressive, tolerant and unprejudiced habit of thought. These were not qualities likely to win him the approval of such as Mr McAllister of the Blackwater Cotton Mill, or Mr Cavana the glass-manufacturer, or Mr Watters the furniture-maker.

They were seated around a table in the Donegall Arms. Sam Hassan had just aired his opinion that as some trade combinations had won recognition in England, and even in Dublin, the merchants of Belfast had better fall into line and so blunt and confound the intrigues of the ringleaders.

"Never, never, no surrender!" cried Mr McAllister. "Flog the bastards!" Then with a malicious grin, "What way would your opinion be, Mr Gault?"

"I think Hassan's over-optimistic. Men don't change their character by joining with one and other, nor does their patience increase with their numbers. I would keep the laws against combining. But for those who think them harsh, then let them be merciful in their application."

"Well, Mr Gault," said 'Bottle' Cavana, "if any of these dogs come afore ye in court, let's see ye temper mercy with the lash."

"I hope for all our sakes, gentlemen," said James rising, "that that eventuality won't come about. I bid you good evening."

He had become accustomed to the increased stir of life at Talbot Place. Since the arrival of the cook, a decent woman called Boyle from Cavan, and a skeletal waif from the poorhouse, who was bade by the name of Tizzy, and who, according to his wife, was to be fattened up and trained as a serving-maid, James expected to see a female crossing the hall or disappearing into the darkness of the kitchen quarters. At times, when he wondered if the Gault domestic staff, including Robbie the gardener, had to be quite so numerous, he murmured to himself the words from Ecclesiastes, 'When goods increase, they are increased that eat them; and what good is there to the owners thereof, saving the beholding of them with their eyes?' But then perhaps, such persons were necessary as one rose in the world and founded a family.

Aggie had been persuaded to accept and wear the brown bombazine, and garbed thus, to oversee the duties of the cook and the little drudge. At first the cook would have none of it. Hard and ruddy as her stove rings she declared that in her day she had ruled kitchens five times as grand as this and took orders only from the mistress. But to her own astonishment, she capitulated to the modest fair-haired girl, took her into her confidence and affection, and Aggie was encouraged to perch on a kitchen stool, and round-eyed, watch her roast, seethe and braize, knead and bake, dress and garnish. As for Tizzy, who had never seen so much food on her plate in a week, nor been spoken to as if she stood upright like other creatures, she moved about in a daze of frightened unbelief.

"That girl is slow, Aggie," said her mistress eyeing her in sly reproach.

"She'll mend, ma'am, she'll mend," said Aggie primly.

One evening, on her return from her tryst with Hugh Purdie, Aggie climbed to her room and sent Tizzy to beg her mistress's pardon, pleading a headache. Kate stood with her hand on the newel-post swithering whether or not to go up. After a time she returned thoughtfully to the sitting-room. Next morning Aggie came downstairs, pale and downcast. Her mistress noted her distress and said nothing. She waited until it was again Aggie's free evening. Then, taking advantage of what she had been told by her husband, she sent for the girl.

"Aggie, Mr Gault says there's danger of riots and trouble in the town. It's no night for a woman to venture out. If you want a message carried, Robbie will take it."

The girl stood grasping the back of her mistress's chair. "There's no message, ma'am."

Kate turned questioningly.

The girl shuddered. "I've broke wi' Hugh!" she cried and the look she turned on the other woman asked not only for understanding but an acknowledgment of complicity. Then, bending over her clenched hands, she began to sob painfully.

Kate rose and took her in her arms. "There now, Aggie girl. So ye gave up Hugh, well, well . . ." Stroking the fair head she chided and comforted her as she had done many times before in the green tracks of Ravara. "What call have ye for weeping and crying? Sure ye know you're well-loved in this house. There's no reason for ye ever to leave the master and me . . ." And Kate Gault cradled the body of her servant until the sobbing subsided, the tears of loss were dried, the victory assured.

So little Aggie McDowell stayed with the Gault family, her name changed to Agnes, her loyalties committed unquestioningly, her life ordered, her meat and raiment assured, her virginity sealed. Around her waist was placed a belt from which hung the keys of the linen chest, the silver cabinet, the store-room, the wine-cellar. Nursery maids and governesses might come and go but, as the years passed, she was to remain an immutable presence in the memory of young Master Robert, of his sister Esther, and, in their turn, Thomas, Kathleen, Samuel and Louis Gault. When Mrs Masterson died, Agnes, now thinner of lip and hair, extended her authority over the many rooms and chambers in No. 7 Talbot Place, the residence of the wealthy town merchant, James Gault.

XXI

THE THUNDEROUS RAT-TAT on the outer door awakened James. Again it sounded through the house. As Kate stirred he clambered out of bed and pulled on his dressing-gown. He picked up a stout stick in the hall before he opened the door. A constable stood on the step, lantern raised. "Put on ye, Mr Gault, and come out. There's trouble at your bakery."

There was a stench of burning in the air. Many of the street lamps had been extinguished. A murmurous clamour rising from the streets mingled with the crimson-shot darkness that hung over the town. Figures melted into alleys and entries at the sight of the constable's cape and lantern. A gable in the Corn Market stood out black against the glare of fire. Turning the corner, James saw that Pilson's the victuallers, had been ransacked and set ablaze. In the mouth of Poultry Lane half-a-dozen men and women hung over the broken mouth of a rum keg. A couple of the women scooped up a last handful of liquor, then flapped away into the darkness. The men stood their ground for a moment then broke and fled after the women. A knot of militia, with a young lieutenant, stood at the corner of Hercules Street. The officer crooked his finger peremptorily and called, "Hi, there, what's your errand?" Behind him, James heard the constable explain that Mr Gault, the magistrate, had been sent for. Sent for what? He almost ran towards Winetavern Street, his eyes staring for a flame, a torrent of fire, a twisting ladder of smoke. But the street stretched before him, dark and deserted.

A great black hole gaped in the shutters. Loaves lay scattered over the cobbles and trodden into the mud. "Are ye there?" the constable shouted. Someone stirred in the darkness. Brady the foreman appeared, stepping warily, a raking-iron in his fist.

"They tried to wreck the place, sir."

"My own workpeople?"

"I had just locked up after tomorra-morn's batch had been set out, when McBride the ovenman, came back with that combinator and some others."

"We can lay *him* by the heels. What damage has been done?"

The foreman turned back through the splintered door, followed by James and the constable. "When I wouldn't let them in they broke through the front and smashed one oven-plate and scattered the bread——"

"And what did the ruffians hope to gain by that?" cried James.

"—and then by good chance this constable happened to come by and they ran."

As the constable raised his lantern the better to be appreciated, James saw that one side of his foreman's face was stiff with blood.

"In God's name, Brady, how did you come by that?"

"I took a lick from a cudgel." He ran his fingers gingerly above his ear. "It's quit bleeding."

"Where do you live?"

"In Mill Lane, close by, Mr Gault."

And James, having commended the man for his behaviour, charged the constable to see him safe home, and then to fetch a watchman for the bakery. Alone, he gazed morosely at the shattered front of his bakery. Expecting the place ablaze, there was surprisingly little consolation in finding that all he had suffered was some splintered timber, a broken oven-plate, a batch of loaves destroyed. It was the attack itself that shocked him. Hadn't he always treated his workmen with consideration and humanity? The malevolence of their answer baffled and infuriated him. He looked at the broken bread glimmering at his feet. This is what the rogues whine for, and when they get it, even by theft, trample it under their hooves. Then, as he stood before the wreckage, he experienced a strange elation of mind. One fact at least was clear as daylight. The merchants were right. Commonsense as well as self-interest pointed that his loyalty lay with them. No longer need he play the hang-dog democrat. He kicked a crust of bread from under his foot and walked away like a man who had rid himself of a burden that had become intolerable to his back.

In Hercules Street he stopped with the militia, wished them well in their night's duties, and gave the sergeant a florin to treat his men. The lieutenant, for his part, insisted that Mr Gault, the magistrate, should accept an escort to see him safely home.

Gathered at the Assembly Rooms next morning, prominent citizens were happy to learn, and to assure each other, that their town had suffered little in the previous night's disorders. Pilson's victuallery was a complete loss, a few huckster stores fired, grogshops tapped, a wine-merchant's raided. "Not yours, b'God," said 'Bottle' Cavana to Sam Hassan with a grin that did not quite conceal his chagrin, and at that moment lost a customer for his magnums and jeroboams. But Mr Cavana was happily calculating the many broken windows and lamp panes that needed replacing. Pringle Hazlett, questioned by James, was of the opinion that the Dublin Insurance Company would not compensate him for riot damage. He had further unpalatable advice for the young man.

"If your bakers show their faces, take them back."

James stared at him.

"You don't make money out of cold ovens, James."

"Not that damnable rascal, McBride!"

"Say no more about McBride," said Mr Hazlett. "He'll have fled the town. If they catch and arraign him on your information could you sit easy on the Bench that examined him?"

"I could bear it," said James grimly.

At midday the company learnt that a watchman, employed at Ekenhead's ropewalk across the river, had been killed on the previous evening, but no amount of official ingenuity had managed to implicate any of the six men held by the authorities.

"Only six o' them," said Mr McAllister gloomily, "all Protestants. And I'm told," scowling at Mr Clulow of the Ballast Board, "that one's an Orangeman. In the name o' God, what's Christianity coming to, at all, at all?"

On his way to the Court House next morning, a number of gentlemen stopped James, and charged him, as a prominent citizen, to see justice dealt to those who had stirred up civil commotion, set premises alight, endangered the commerce and prosperity of their town. They have doubts of me, he thought. He longed to tell them of his change of heart, and could not. Pedlars hawked oranges and crubeens among the crowd around the Court House. Entering by a side door he found his fellow-magistrates, Mr Corry and Mr Fox, already present. Conscious that they, at least, shared the same implacable mood, they said little to the newcomer. The three magistrates climbed the narrow wooden stairs and took their places overlooking the crowded courtroom. The uproar subsided as they appeared, fell to silence as the six accused men were led in. James, examining the papers before him, heard their stumbling tread, the rattle of the fetters that bound them. He lifted his gaze and studied them one by one. They looked well-cast for their parts, their clothing torn and dishevelled, their bodies appearing emaciated, so tightly had their wrists been dragged behind them. From their bruised and unshaven faces, fear, impudence, stupidity and truculence answered his cold shifting scrutiny. Then he felt the hair move on his skull. The sixth prisoner was Hugh Purdie.

James was the first to lower his eyes. A stifled groan escaped him. He laid down his pen. Mr Fox looked at him in curiosity. "Are you unwell, Gault?"

James rose abruptly and blundered past him, groping for

the stairs that led to the magistrates' chamber. In the moments that he was alone there, the idea entered his mind to profit by Fox's misunderstanding. He was ill, he would go home and leave Purdie to the court. Then he remembered Kate. She would have to be told of her brother's arrest and of its circumstances. He shook with rage at the thought that this crazed idiot should endanger the reputation he had so laboriously raised for himself among his fellow-townsmen. The court clerk came into the room. "My compliments to Mr Fox, Duffy, and ask him would he kindly step down for a moment."

But the silver buckles of the stout little magistrate could be seen twinkling down the dark steps. He entered followed by Mr Corry.

"Feeling poorly, eh?" cried Mr Fox, mopping his neck. "Can't blame ye, courtroom stinks like a dunghill——"

"Go home, Gault," said Mr Corry. "We'll have a word with Kilbee and settle the business in a trice."

James studied the well-meaning faces of his fellow-magistrates. He was only moderately acquainted with either of them and they would not have been his first choice as confidants.

"Nothing ails me, gentlemen. But I can't sit in the court today." He tried to compose his trembling mouth. "One of the prisoners is a relative of mine."

"Relative, eh?" Mr Fox looked at Mr Corry. "Damme, here's a poser," and they both looked at James.

With a great effort he kept from shouting *Why don't you ask me, how I, James Gault, magistrate and leading merchant, came to be allied to a fire-raiser*? Only a feeling of disloyalty to Kate restrained him from saying aloud—*by marriage, ye understand*? He lowered his head, his fists clenched on the table before him.

"Which of them, Mr Gault?" said Mr Corry, not without sympathy.

"The man at the end," responded James in a low voice. "The youngest. The farmer, Hugh Purdie."

"Farmer, eh?" cried Mr Fox brightening up. "In from

the country. His lug taken by one of these damned mischief-makers, but not a bird of that feather, at all. Eh, Corry?"

Mr Corry thought it very likely. James was about to speak when the clerk returned, and beyond him, at the top of the stairs, they saw the impatient face of Mr Kilbee, the Town Attorney.

"Go home like a good fellow," said Mr Corry, "and leave it to us." As they went out Mr Fox turned and with a broad wink laid his finger along his nose. "Leave it to us, Gault," he whispered. James sat down heavily. It's *we* who are birds of a feather. Thank God I didn't ask for leniency—or secrecy.

He would do what he could for Purdie, discreetly of course, for he must not be diminished in the public eye. Mr Fox and Mr Corry would deal lightly with his brother-in-law. It was bending justice, but his relief far outweighed his scruples on that head. He walked at an unhurried pace through the streets, called in at Weighill Lane, leafed over a few invoices, examined some stock with his clerk, proceeded homeward in the same deliberate manner.

Kate was alone in the garden room. He closed the door carefully. "I've serious news for you. Your brother was brought before the court this morning."

She turned. As always at such moments temper rather than fear showed in her face. "In the name of God, what's he done?"

"He was among those taken up after the riot."

"What'll happen to him?"

"I don't know. I left the court."

"You left the court and our Hugh there!"

"I couldn't sit on the bench, Kate, and try my own brother-in-law!"

"What'll they do to him?"

"I have made," said James with a hint of smugness, "certain arrangements."

Later, at the Assembly Rooms, sipping his coffee, he awaited the court's decision. It was Mr McAllister who brought the news. Two of the rioters were to be transported. Three of the others were to receive two hundred lashes apiece. The sixth, a farmer's boy, considered by the magistrates to have fallen into evil company on that night, was ordered a month's imprisonment in Carrickfergus gaol.

Mr McAllister expressed his disgust that no one was to be hanged. "What," he asked, "of the young constable who was beaten to death?"

"It was an elderly man," said Mr Hazlett. "He was a watchman and he died of a seizure."

"Brought on," declared Mr McAllister, "by those scoundrels!"

Mr Clulow almost rent a fine linen handkerchief in his indignation that an Orangeman should be publicly whipped. None of the brethren would lend himself to disorder and the destruction of property. Somebody should lodge an appeal. But he failed to catch James's eye.

Spifford Lamont recalled that in the days of the Rising sentences of five hundred strokes were handed out and wondered if the modest total awarded by the court was sufficient deterrent to such blaggards.

But Mr Lucas, the solicitor (having first inquired as to James's losses at the bakery and then complimented him on his fine impartiality in stepping down from the bench that morning) enlightened those present on the complexities of a judicial flogging. "You can whip a man till he dies. That's what Lamont has in mind," and he nodded towards the linen-draper who accepted the recognition with fitting modesty. "But outside a period of martial law that gives rise to complications. You can whip a man and cripple him. Then he's liable to be a charge on the town. The whipping of a man demands judgment," concluded the solicitor placing the tips of his fingers together.

And James, if somewhat repelled at the genteel brutality of the speaker, made a careful note of what he had said. Such scraps of legal lore were invaluable to the conscientious magistrate.

"I hear," said Mr Hassan, "that one of them to be sent to the Indies is a carpenter by trade. Wouldn't there be more sense in giving him his tools and setting him to repair some of the damage?"

This suggestion the merchants found so entertaining that they dispersed in what was close to good humour.

A few days later James learnt that there was more to Hugh Purdie's sentence than he was first told; and the news was not agreeable. In sending the youth to prison the magistrates had stipulated that he must quit Belfast on his release and that Mr James Gault should be surety that he did so. The merchant was not taken by surprise, therefore, when his brother-in-law appeared one morning at Weighill Lane, accompanied by a law-officer. James sent the escort outside.

"You know why you've been brought to me?"

"Yes."

"You're forbidden to live any longer in the town."

"Aye, you've taken that from me, too."

"Understand this, I had nothing to do with your sentence."

"My shelter, my livelihood, my girl, you've took all."

Puzzled, James paused to consider this charge. "Aggie? Aggie, if she had anything to do with you, broke with you of her own free will."

"You bought the lass, you and Kate," Hugh gave a gesture of hopelessness. "And now you've taken my good name——"

"And what d'ye mean by that!"

"I went round to collect my tools. My neighbours'll have nothing to do with me. They believe that I was in cahoots with the court, my sentence was so light compared to——"

James interrupted him in fury. "Why, you poor clown, d'ye complain because some villains won't trust you to carry out their devilry! *Your* good name . . ." The merchant struggled to recover his composure. "We've talked enough. You go back to Ravara tonight."

"I'm not putting my foot near that place. I'll go back to gaol, first."

"If you go back to gaol, you'll lie there till you're forgotten."

"Forgotten, even by my own sister?"

"Make up your mind that this is what you must do."

"I tell ye I won't go back to that house!"

James had expected this and was prepared for it. From a drawer he took a leather bag and a paper wrapped in oilskin. He untied the drawstring and emptied a pile of coins on to the desk.

There was a silence. "What's that?" said Hugh at last, his eyes averted from the money.

"There's twenty guineas there . . ." As he looked at the small heap of gold he thought fifteen would have sufficed. But it was the sum Kate and he had decided on. "And this," laying his finger on the document, "is your passage contracted with Captain Ferguson of the *John and Phoebe* for New Brunswick. There's sufficient there to carry you beyond St. John's. I would recommend you to take your tools." They eyed each other in silence. "D'ye want to see Kate?"

Purdie lowered his head as if pondering this. "No."

"Have you your belongings gathered?"

"*He* has them," the young man nodded to the door.

James swept the coins into the bag and drew the string. "Take it, it's not charity." Slowly Purdie's hand went to the money. He lifted it and stowed it in his pocket.

James called the turnkey in. "This man is to be taken to the tender at George Quay." He cocked a thumb at Hugh. "He knows the way. He's to stay on board until she moves out to the *John and Phoebe*, tomorrow morning. You'll see him aboard and present this ticket to her master, Captain Ferguson. Inform him, with my compliments, that as a magistrate I have a lively interest in this passenger until his arrival on the other side."

He kept his back to his brother-in-law, feeling that his words sounded as if he were making restitution. As he turned, his hand moved involuntarily in a gesture of farewell. The look on Purdie's face stilled the gesture. "I can do no more for you," he said coldly.

The young man took the wicker bag from the man's hand. "You've done enough," he said, and without a further word or look, left the counting-house, followed by his escort.

After dinner that evening Kate was restless. She rambled from dining-room to kitchen, from kitchen to parlour. She held her hands clasped before her in a manner that James had never seen before. But he kept his peace. She hurried upstairs to the children, then down again. James, settled in an easy-chair for the evening, heard her come into the parlour. For a time she stood at the window, gazing into the darkness. Although he couldn't see her, he was aware that at times she turned to look at him. He heard the flounce of her skirt. She was at his elbow. "I must see him, Jamie man!"

The quays, grey and muddy under their guttering lamps, came to his mind as he methodically closed the book on his thumb. "You can't, lass. He's gone."

"Sailed already?"

"He's aboard. It's too late."

She went back to the window, lifting her head as if she would send a message over the dark, shining roofs. "We've paid a big price, husband."

James lowered his book. "It'll be worth it, if he flourishes."

He heard her sob as she rushed swiftly past him to the door.

A strange family, he sighed, leafing over a page.